The gorgeous redh[...] me to take you to a [...] you. Do you understand?"

Mute, Roger shook his head no.

"That is sad," she said as she proceeded to force Roger's head down until his forehead touched the carpet. Panicking, Roger began struggling again, with such strength and fury . . . that Penthesilia had to use both hands and her weight to control him fully. He couldn't break free. He couldn't break free!

Finally he forced himself to think, tried to regain control of himself. But what could he do? If he tried to shout, he'd be hit. If he struggled, he'd be subdued. If he waited, he'd be killed. And he couldn't reach anything but his own "Lava Nymphs" painting under his face. . . .

The painting.

No matter how unlikely it was, he'd made another painting come to life. Achilles and Penthesilia were paintings, too, but they were real enough to kill him. Whatever he'd done by accident, Kevin Matthews had done deliberately. Maybe Roger could, too . . . strong as Achilles and Penthesilia were, they'd be nothing compared to the Lava Demon under his nose.

He ignored Red and Penny and concentrated on "Lava Nymphs." He rebuilt the volcano's interior in his mind, caught glimpses of the lean red bodies swimming within the glowing lava, looked for and found the menacing ridge of the demon's head moving forward through the lava. . . . Come to me, you ugly son of a bitch. . . .

Then the floor dropped away. Roger shrieked as he fell.

desires, kept them at bay

AARON ALLSTON

GALATEA IN 2-D

This is a work of fiction. All the characters and events portrayed in this book are fictional, and any resemblance to real people or incidents is purely coincidental.

A Baen Books Original

Baen Publishing Enterprises
P.O. Box 1403
Riverdale, NY 10471

ISBN: 0-671-72182-8

Cover art by Gary Ruddell

First printing, August 1993

Distributed by Simon & Schuster
1230 Avenue of the Americas
New York, NY 10020

Printed in the United States of America

DEDICATION

To Bonnie Binford Langley and Verna Mae
Huegele, in at the beginning but not at the end.

ACKNOWLEDGMENTS

Thanks go to Nonie Quinlan, Luray Richmond, Allen Varney, Steve Jackson, and Josepha Sherman, for sharp eyes and good judgment.

Chapter One

Highlights

Reaching for the squat bottle of ink, Roger knocked it over, and a black ink slick rolled down the drafting table toward his drawing.

Oh, it happened all the time. A glitch in his airbrush would throw a ruinous spatter of color onto a painting, or a slip with the inking pen would mar a piece of line art. Roger would watch the mistake destroy his art, then he'd pound on his drafting table and bellow outraged curses loud enough to wake the people in the apartment next door.

This piece was among the best he'd ever done. She was a woodland nymph out of Greek myth, done in black and white a few inches tall; she stared woeful and round-eyed at him from behind a thick patch of tall grass, her ears piquantly pointed, her slender body supernaturally graceful. She was perfect.

But Roger knocked the bottle over and ink poured down toward her. He didn't even grab for the bristol board; he knew he was too slow. He just squeezed his eyes shut so as not to see the nymph destroyed; then, reluctantly, he opened them again to view the damage.

The ink slick had stopped against the ruler laid across the bottom edge of the table. It covered half the piece of bristol board, the half where he'd drawn the nymph.

But the nymph wasn't under the ink.

She was walking.

Moving with the curious grace of a 1930s cartoon

character, the two-dimensional nymph walked another half-dozen steps away from the ink. On the unmarred half of the bristol board, she froze into stillness, looking straight at Roger with the same sad-eyed stare — but now she was standing upright, one hand in her flowing hair, as though she'd been drawn that way.

She wore a scrap of a dress covering only one breast, continuing down into a short skirt; the pattern on the cloth looked like oak leaves. But when he'd drawn her, high grass concealed what she wore.

A wave of exhaustion hit Roger; it felt like shock setting in. He gaped at his drawing. After only a few moments he was able to utter a feeble "Uh . . ."

It hadn't happened, naturally. Hallucinations were a lot more common than line drawings that move around. So he was hallucinating. Sure.

He squinted at his watch; years of close-in painting and sketching, too much reading, too many late-night work sessions were making him nearsighted, but he didn't need glasses. Not yet. It was 5:00 A.M., only a couple of hours after his usual bedtime. Whoops, the digital readout also said THU, not WED. He'd skipped a lot of sleep to finish his current art assignment and hadn't gone to bed even when it was done; he unwound from the assignment by working on the nymph. With no more than two hours' sleep in the last two days, it made sense that he was imagining things.

Obviously, he'd drawn it just as he saw it now, had fallen asleep and dreamt about it, had jerked awake and knocked over the bottle. That explained things.

Except . . . a tip of black-and-white grass protruded from under the ink stain.

Roger irritably brushed his brown hair out of his eyes. He didn't have time to go crazy. He had to drop off the MacMurphy Advertising art tomorrow, pick up his check, pay the worst of his past-due bills. This didn't leave much time to be institutionalized.

Tentatively, he reached out and ran his finger across

the picture of the nymph. He felt nothing except cool, flat bristol board and dry lines of ink.

Aggravated, he slumped back. "You're not going to move again, are you?" he asked. "No? Well, then, the hell with you." He snatched up the drawing, took it in both hands, prepared to tear it to shreds . . .

And didn't. There was her sad, vulnerable face staring at him, and he suddenly couldn't bring himself to rip her — her? it! — to rip it up. He tossed the bristol board back on the table.

"I'm going to bed, then. You don't go anywhere." He rose, snorted derisively at himself. A little sleep, a little cash, and he'd be all better. He pulled off his clothes and threw them into his dirty-clothes corner before flopping irritably into bed.

Cole MacMurphy, 288 pounds of advertising cynicism, shuffled quickly through Roger's drawings. The big man looked as though he'd rather dig dirt from beneath his fingernails than look at Roger's art. He glanced at the last one in the pile, a rendering of a computer desk laden with hardware, and put it facedown with the rest. "Can't use you," he said, his voice flat.

Roger's head suddenly felt light, but he kept himself under tight control. "Why is that?"

"No good."

Roger looked at the pile of illustrations. Desperation stirred in his stomach and began to creep to his throat. "They're as good as everything I showed you before. You liked those."

MacMurphy shook his head. "Didn't make myself clear. You're no good. We can't use you." He pulled a manila folder from a pile of paperwork and opened it. "You come in here two weeks ago, say your name is R.J. MacLean."

Roger's face twitched; he knew what was coming. "R.J. MacLean is a business name. Registered and everything."

"But your real name is Roger Simons. Found that out from a friend in the business. He told me all about you. You call yourself R.J. MacLean since nobody will hire Roger Simons. Right?"

A red haze obscured Roger's vision. He jumped to his feet, leaned across the desk, furious. "Look —"

"You look. We can't use Roger Simons. You're a whiner, you don't come through when you're supposed to. Nonesuch Books —"

"I did not screw Nonesuch Books! They screwed me! I delivered! They threw away those paintings!" Roger drew himself to his full height — 6'2", though his physique was lean rather than heroic — to loom over MacMurphy. "I've worked my ass off for two weeks. And now I've delivered. On deadline, Thursday at noon. So you're going to pull out your goddamned checkbook and ball-point pen, and you're —"

MacMurphy reached down beside the desk, picked up Roger's briefcase, and threw it out the open office window. The briefcase fell three stories. Roger could hear glass shatter when it hit. The sudden action shut Roger up, turning his tirade off like water from a faucet.

Then MacMurphy stood. He was Roger's height, but only a large basket of fried chicken short of 300 pounds . . . and far too much of his bulk was muscle. His voice became a low, nasty rumble. "Son, you don't come into my place and give me orders. Now, you can leave by the door. Or you can follow your briefcase. You got no time to decide."

Roger went cold. MacMurphy meant what he was saying. He was big and strong enough to back up the threat. He looked as though he wanted to. Roger glared at the other man, clenched his fist, and thought about hitting MacMurphy hard enough to break his jaw into fifteen pieces. . . . But it wouldn't happen. MacMurphy would slaughter him. The cold, sick sensation in his stomach got worse.

He didn't look away from the fat man, but he picked up his pile of illustrations and moved toward the door. He wanted to say something — God, anything — some combination of words that would crush MacMurphy, that would make the man understand just how wretchedly subhuman he was for shafting Roger this way. But every word that came to Roger's mind sounded feeble.

So he said nothing. He felt his defeat shudder across his shoulders, felt bile burning in his stomach and his throat. He walked out of the office under the eyes of a nervous secretary and several wary-looking office workers. Out to the elevator, out to the parking lot . . . The shaking and the white-hot fury didn't abate. They got worse.

His briefcase had come down on the windshield of a gleaming new BMW, smashing through the safety glass. Several people stood around the car admiring MacMurphy's handiwork. One of them, a thin man with a maroon necktie, wasn't so happy; he was screaming and thrashing, punching at the air, his tie flapping with his motions.

Roger's briefcase wasn't in or around the BMW. Someone had already grabbed it and run. The perfect cap to the perfect day. One briefcase, one drawing pad, his checkbook and a calculator — he could add these to the day's losses.

Stone-faced, his stomach churning, Roger didn't mention his part in the car owner's troubles. He turned and left.

Roger drove swerving from lane to lane, jumping through yellow lights and fresh red lights. He cursed MacMurphy and those bastards at Nonesuch Books, he swore at all the drivers on the road, he snarled at the moronic commercials on the radio, he beat the steering wheel and everything in reach.

He swore especially at the red convertible that changed lanes and cut him off. It was like an ad layout in a magazine: bright red sports car, top down; handsome yuppified driver with dark sunglasses and a victorious grin; blonde woman passenger leaning over against the driver. An American Success Story.

Roger snarled at his creaky ten-year-old Rabbit. Mr. Red Sports Car, he decided, was a 32-year-old bastard junior executive with no skills except his B.A. in Sucking Up, and was paid $65,000 a year and random blondes for not making decisions. That's life, he decided. Parasites get big money, fast cars, and loose company. The creative get the shaft.

Eventually, before he quite managed to get a speeding ticket, Roger's anger ran out of gas, leaving him weary and depressed. Another assignment shot . . . weeks of work down the drain . . . no money to throw at the bills . . . He'd had a year of this, and it wasn't getting any better. *Nothing* was getting better.

It was time to get away from everything, at least for a while. Roger checked out his wallet — it held his life's savings, a ten and two ones — and drove more carefully over to Escape Velocity Books. His favorite store . . . shelf upon shelf of science fiction, fantasy and horror paperbacks, comic books, magazines, posters, art books, everything a growing boy needs. It was his oasis from reality.

As he reached the door, he thought the interior looked a little crowded. When he entered, he decided that it was *very* crowded; but most of the customers were gathered around the end of the shop where they set up special displays. . . .

Roger craned his neck to see what was going on beyond the mass of people and caught sight of the object of all the attention. Oh, he'd only *thought* his day was complete.

There, in glory, sat Kevin Matthews, surrounded by his apostles and fans. He signed autograph after autograph, giving each admirer the little nod and smile of his blessing.

It had been years since he wore the post-modern hippie artist look. These days he kept his blond beard and mustache neatly trimmed, and his dark, expensive business suit made him look as though he were a Viking employed by some Madison Avenue firm.

And, by God, he looked up as Roger spotted him, brightened, and waved Roger over.

Roger let out a sigh and thought about walking right out again. But, no, he was already caught. He trudged through the crowd.

Kevin wasn't alone. Beside him, hidden by the crowd until Roger was right up to the table, was a woman Roger knew.

Julia Dover: face and body as model-gorgeous as ever, hair shining like a black waterfall . . . She was dressed in some glittery, short-skirted black-and-silver ensemble that cost more than Roger could guess. She gave Roger the most insincere of smiles, flashing perfect white teeth, and then turned her attention back to Kevin's fans. Kevin's adoring woman. Roger swallowed a wave of nausea and put on a false expression of good cheer.

"Big Rog!" Kevin gave Roger a welcoming grin. "What've you been up to? Haven't seen you in a while."

Roger kept his cheerful expression fixed; it was beginning to hurt his face. "Keeping ahead of the bill collectors. What's all this for?"

Kevin proudly held up a large, black hardback book; Roger belatedly noticed that most of the fans clustered around the table held copies. "My second print portfolio. *Stylings, by Kevin Matthews.* Just released and it's doing great." He handed the volume to Roger. "With my compliments."

"Thanks." Roger's stomach started to churn again. He didn't yet dare open the book. Then he caught sight of the publisher's name stamped on the spine: Nonesuch Books. He didn't even have to open it to be upset.

"So, Rog, what are you working on these days?"

Roger shrugged. "A lot of work in advertising, public relations, that sort of thing. I just dropped off a big assignment this morning."

"Good deal!" Kevin's expression turned serious. "Listen, I've tried to put your name in the ear of the publishers I deal with, but I think it's no go. After the Nonesuch Books thing . . ."

"Yeah." Roger felt his shoulders tighten. "I'm stupid, I guess; I still call them every couple of months. They've never changed their story, that I sent them nothing but a box full of cardboard. Six months' worth of work was in that crate, all insured and everything . . . but they torpedoed me. I still don't know why. That's the worst part of it. Not knowing why and not knowing what they did with my originals."

Kevin nodded. "That's life, Rog. I think you — oh, Jesus, here comes the ex."

Roger and the fans turned to follow Kevin's gaze. Just coming in the front door was a woman. . . .

Roger winced a little, both at the way Kevin had announced her arrival to his legion of fans, and at the changes time had made to Donna Matthews.

He'd seen her last a year and a half ago, about the same time Kevin had taken up with Julia and filed the divorce papers. Tall, curvaceous and in good shape, Donna hadn't been Roger's favorite physical type, but she'd looked damned good. She didn't now.

She had put on a few pounds; she strained the seams of her jeans and faded blouse. Her long brown hair, once brushed out into a glossy cascade, looked tired and limp. She was pale, her spattering of freckles more prominent. She looked like Roger felt these days, and he was surprised to find himself sympathizing with her, when he'd never really liked her.

Ignoring the crowd of fans, not even noticing Roger or Julia, she barged through the crowd. Anxious to escape whatever storm was coming, Roger slid to the side, flipped open Kevin's portfolio, and pretended to be absorbed in the first painting.

Ah, yes, here were "Achilles and Penthesilia," the Greek hero and the Amazon queen out of myth, facing each other over the plain of Troy. The two characters, like most of Kevin's subjects, looked like they'd been dipped in cooking oil and then photographed.

And then there was the slight orange tone to their skin. Kevin was still using his thick orange undercoat for all his paintings. Roger suspected that Kevin regarded it as his personal trademark and used the orange undercoat on every painting, even when it wasn't appropriate.

Kevin's voice was full of cheer: "Hi, Donna!"

"Hi, yourself." Donna's voice was low but not at all the happy, mellow contralto it had once been; it was raspy and tired. "Have you looked at a calendar lately?"

Kevin frowned and checked his watch. "It's the fifth . . . oh. I owe you a check, don't I?"

"Something like that."

Roger flipped another page and concentrated on not being noticed. Next in the portfolio was the album cover for the Concrete Zombies' latest compact disk. Five rotting corpses — one each on guitar, bass, keyboard, and drums, the last as lead singer. The setting was a graveyard, orange-tinged flesh and eyeballs were falling off the bodies, and it was all as scary as a ride on a merry-go-round.

Roger couldn't bring himself to turn another page. How this no-talent could land all the best fantasy book-cover work, publish his own portfolios, make so much money . . . He felt himself growing angry all over again, and clamped down on it.

Kevin pulled out his checkbook. "So, how's the job hunting?"

"Crummy. I seem to be poison. I can't get a job delivering papers."

Roger couldn't help looking at Donna again. The

pained tone of her voice could have been his own, and it reflected an ache, a depression he wouldn't wish on anyone.

Then the idea hit. He couldn't do much to improve his own mood, but he might be able to do something about Donna's — a *little* something . . .

He sidled over until he stood behind Kevin, opened the portfolio again, then stared right at Donna until he caught her eye. She glanced away and then back again, finally recognizing him. . . .

And he slowly, deliberately mimed a man throwing up an enormous dinner into the pages of *Stylings, by Kevin Matthews.* He flipped pages as he retched out his imaginary meal; he spent extra time and spasms over the illustrations he particularly detested.

Julia, looking off in another direction to avoid "noticing" Donna, missed it; and Roger was standing right behind Kevin. So the only ones who could see his performance were the fans — who stared incredulously at the man making fun of their hero — and Donna. Despite herself, she grinned.

Kevin wrote his check and continued to talk throughout Roger's display. "It'll work out. You just have to keep painting. Tastes change in the publishing business. Another two, three years, I'm sure you'll be back in style."

Roger carefully upended his book over Kevin's head, mimed the imaginary mass of vomit running off the pages and onto Kevin. Donna squeezed her eyes closed but her shoulders shook with suppressed laughter.

Kevin, oblivious, signed the check and tore it free. "Listen, I know I'm supposed to continue these checks only until the year is up, but I'll be happy to continue them after that. As long as it takes." He held the check toward his ex-wife and froze in mid-gesture. "Jesus, Donna, are you all right? You're as red as a beet."

Donna pried her eyes open, managed to straighten

her features. "It's nothing, Kev. Just trying to get rid of some hiccups." She took the check and tucked it away in her bodice. "Thanks a lot. Oh, be sure to say hi to Julia for me."

She glanced at Roger before she turned away; he closed the book, his expression tired but contented, and wiped his mouth. She managed to restrain herself to a mere grin on the way out.

Kevin waited until she was outside the door, then snickered and turned Julia. "Donna says hi."

"That bitch!" Julia's shrill tones made Roger's skin crawl. Her voice, as always, sounded like aluminum foil going through a paper shredder. "She knew I was here!"

"I know, honey. She's just going through some bad times, that's all." Kevin turned back to Roger. "How about you, old buddy? You look like you're having a bad time, too. Anything I can do to help?"

Roger shook his head. Funny, but after that display he *did* feel better, as though his frustration were actually dripping its way down Kevin's face and back. "Not unless you can recommend a good shrink who works for free."

"How's that?"

Roger grinned sourly. "It's nothing. I was working too late the other night and started hallucinating. Saw my drawings moving around on their own. That ever happen to you?"

Kevin lost his smile and he stared sharply at Roger. He didn't speak for a couple of awkward seconds, didn't immediately sign the next portfolio shoved before him. Finally, he managed a reply: "No, I can't think of a time. You just get some sleep. I'm sure it'll clear up."

He took a deep breath and smiled again. "Listen, I have to ignore you for a while. Autographs and all that. I'll talk to you later on."

Roger started to reply, but Kevin had already turned

his attention back to the fans. The audience was over.

Roger nodded quickly to Julia — she ignored him — and made his way to the door. There was no way he'd browse around the store if he had to listen to Kevin's fans gushing over inadequate art. He'd had enough aggravation for the day.

He half expected to find a notice of eviction or IRS audit in the mail when he got home, but he'd received only the usual past-due bill notices and junk mail.

Still, home wasn't much comfort to him. One bedroom festooned with dirty clothes, his fault; a kitchen alive with cockroaches, his landlord's and neighbors' fault; a pantry bare except for potatoes, rice, beans, and oriental noodles; a black-and-white TV not hooked up to cable; board-and-cinder-block shelves crammed with books; an ink-stained drafting table. It all looked seedy and tired.

Exhausted as he was, the day's events still ate at him; he'd never get to sleep without unwinding.

He turned to the drafting table. What would it be today? Maybe a picture of a glowing young couple in a red convertible, Godzilla looming over them, foot poised to crush them into oblivion . . .

He spotted the illustration of the nymph and decided to play with it instead.

She stood in the pose he'd seen her in last. He tried to remember drawing her that way, but couldn't. Dammit, he'd drawn her crouching behind a stand of grass, and that grass now lay under black ink on the other half of the bristol board.

He *was* crazy. But losing his mind no longer alarmed him; it was just another thing going wrong, nothing to get upset about.

He decided to paint the nymph. Perhaps, in bringing color to her, he could learn her lines and not forget how she was posed every time he looked away.

It took a minute to cut the clean half of the bristol

board away from the half saturated in black ink, and to use a straight-edged razor blade to scrape the excess ink from his drafting table. Then he brought out his tackle box filled with watercolors and got to work.

It didn't take long. Base colors on the drawing — fleshlike tan on the skin, rich sunlight-gold for the hair, dark green for the garment, sky-blue eyes. Then, with a brushful of acrylic white, he began highlighting the figure: a bit of gleam to her eyes, just a little more definition on her collarbone. He smiled; it was, to his eye, the best ink-and-watercolor he'd done in months, and he'd put color to the figure in a matter of half an hour or so. Not bad.

Lips pursed, he blew lightly on the nymph to dry the acrylic paint faster and found that his vision was blurry — overwork catching up to him. He closed his eyes and tried to remember his original mental image of the nymph. He'd captured it almost perfectly. It was good to know he could still do that. Then he opened his eyes again.

The nymph's arms were crossed across her body and her hair waved in the breeze he was creating.

Roger froze, his eyes wide. A weight settled on his chest and made it hard for him to breathe; he felt as though someone had opened a tap and drained all his energy away.

The nymph just stood there, two-dimensional, staring at him in wonder. But she didn't freeze into immobility; her hair still swirled with the air currents, and she swayed a little as she stood.

"Oh. My. God." Careful, his hand shaking, he moved the brush away from her, delicately set it down on his tackle box. The nymph watched his action as if fascinated by the slow deliberation of his movements.

Roger sat back, his gaze still fixed on the nymph. "All right. All right," he breathed. "Either I've gone completely around the bend, or . . . it's real." The enormity of what he was seeing finally hit him.

At last, he addressed the nymph: "You're real, aren't you?"

The nymph stared at him, perplexed, for a few moments. Then, slowly and unmistakably, she nodded.

Roger discovered that his heart was triphammering again. He forced his voice to remain steady. "Ah, good. Good. You're real. Of course you are. And you understand me. Uh . . . can you talk?"

The nymph cocked her head, puzzled, obviously thinking about it. Then she opened her mouth, exposing watercolor-red gums and tongue, and teeth glinting with Roger's special acrylic highlights — details Roger hadn't painted onto her. But no sound emerged.

She frowned and flexed delightfully, as though she were struggling with bonds Roger couldn't see — and then her head, her torso, her entire body emerged up from the board, rounded and three-dimensional.

In a moment, she stood before him, a moving doll three inches tall, and no trace of her remained on the bristol board beneath her bare feet.

Roger sat paralyzed. The nymph opened her mouth again and tentatively spoke: "I can. I can talk. You want me to." Her voice was faint and tinny, and Roger had to strain to hear her. Her words were English, but clipped and precise, flavored with an accent Roger didn't recognize.

Roger took a couple of deep breaths, vainly trying to slow his racing heart. *Artist Dies of Heart Attack*, he thought, *Painting Sells for Millions*. "Do, uh, do you have a name?"

The nymph thought about that for a moment and looked around in confusion. She looked back at Roger and shrugged her exquisite shoulders. "I do not know any name."

"Oh."

Roger sat back heavily, staring at his creation. She, in turn, stared around at his room, wonder on her face.

The first shock was starting to wear off, and he decided to go about this scientifically. Find out what she knows about herself, about him, about where she —

A loud knock on his door jarred him. The nymph made a faint cry of surprise or fear, and sank flat against the bristol board, freezing into stillness.

Roger sighed. Pray God that she'd move again as soon as he could get rid of whoever it was. "Nothing to worry about," he told the nymph. "Just the boys with the big butterfly nets. Come to give me a nice white jacket." He kept his eye on her as he went to the door, but she didn't move again.

He pulled the door open. Two people stood outside, a man and a woman.

The man, a tall, red-headed, thin-lipped fellow in a suit and tie, greeted Roger with a nearly friendly grin and an outstretched hand. "How do you do. You are Roger Simons? I'm Red. This is Penny. We've seen your art and are, uh . . ."

"Fans," the woman said.

"Fans of yours."

Penny, a tall brunette, wore jeans and a checkered flannel shirt, and had a red scarf tied around her neck. She wore her hair in a ponytail that reached to the base of her spine; that, and the curious slant to her eyes, gave her an exotic look. She took Roger's hand after Red released it. "We didn't know that you lived here in town until just today," she said. "Could we come in and see some of your art? We want to buy something."

Roger couldn't place their accents and was too distracted to worry about it. "Actually, I'm, uh, late for an appointment. Maybe if you could come back later —"

Red frowned. Penny looked sad and answered, "We're going out of town for a while. Could we see your art now? We would love to have a Roger Simons original."

Wait — what was he doing? Here were *paying*

customers. Though Penny was in casual dress, Red wore an expensive suit and the briefcase he held belonged in the same price range. And they were fans, too. Roger missed having fans. Especially good-looking female fans with undisguised admiration in their eyes, like Penny. The watercolor nymph would have to wait just a few minutes more; Roger's creditors demanded it.

Roger made an abrupt about-face and put on his best meet-the-people smile: "Well, in that case, come right on in. Always glad to meet someone who likes my work."

He silently cursed the wretched condition of his apartment as he led them in, and was glad that the room was lit only by the combination fluorescent/ incandescent light clamped to his drafting table. "Take a look at this one, a work in progress, while I dig out some of the paintings I have on hand."

They looked the nymph over as he pulled out one of his large portfolios and zipped it open. Oh, how he hated parting with an original. But he always took the names and addresses of his customers, against the day, please let there be such a day, when he had enough money to buy some of them back.

Red asked, "This is a Nearly Naked Nymph?"

Roger grinned as he brought over an armful of paintings. "I'm surprised you remember the Nearly Naked Nymphs. I haven't done one of those in a long time. The magazine that used to buy them, uh, made some editorial changes and didn't want any more. But, yes, that's what this one is."

"She looks alarmed, not happy or amorous like the others."

Roger set the pile of paintings on the tabletop, shrugging. "That's not how I intended to paint her. She sort of happened that way," he said, truthfully. "Here, take a look at these."

In the first painting, a man and a woman were

enjoying each other in a dark bedroom. Standing, locked
in passionate foreplay, pulling loose one another's clothes,
they were clearly only a moment or two away from
tumbling into the bed. But as she started to pull his
trousers down, she couldn't see, though the moonlight in
the painting illuminated it, that his rear end was furry and
sported an insouciant little goat's tail. Nor did she see
the horns on his forehead, revealed by his disheveled
hair. "A sort of satyr-seduces-shepherdess story," Roger
explained, "but updated to modern times. I call it 'Deceit
of My Pants.'"

Neither of them reacted to the name, but Penny
said, "I like it. Very classical. I think I must have this
one."

Red shook his head. "We haven't seen any of the
others yet."

Roger took the corners of "Deceit" and moved it
aside. The next painting showed a horrible humanlike
monster. She stood eight feet tall and had grotesque
green skin, massive muscles, lank black hair, and a
huge nose. And she was cheerful; the grin on her wide,
slavering jaws showed she was a happy creature
indeed. Her aged, wrinkled face was full of merry evil.
She held a spiked club dripping with blood in one hand
and the severed right arm of a knight-errant in the
other. She wore an oversized Santa Claus suit, minus
the fake white beard. "I did this one in college," Roger
explained, beaming. "It's called 'Carol, the Ancient
Yuletide Troll.' It's not too surprising that nobody's
wanted it for a magazine or book . . . but it's cute
anyway."

"Cute," Penny repeated, but she sounded dubious.

Roger quickly flipped to the next painting in the
stack. "Skinny-Dipping Lava Nymphs," he announced.
"This was about a year and a half ago, when I finally
worked out a technique I liked for rendering lava. We
have these Nearly Naked Nymphs adapted to life in a
volcano. And here, near the pool's edge, you see the

eyes and top of the head of some demon that's just
swum up from the bottom of the pool to see what all
the splashing is about, a monster Peeping Tom. All the
illumination comes from the lava, which was a little
tricky to paint."

Red nodded appreciatively at the cherry-red
nymphs and the deadly pool they swam in. Roger
thought he'd made a sale — two, if Penny really
wanted "Deceit of My Pants." He glanced over at
her . . . but she wasn't where she had just been, at his
left elbow.

Before he could see where she'd gotten to, he felt
her grab his right arm and twist it painfully behind
him. She slammed him down face-first on his pile of
paintings, driving the wind from his lungs.

He immediately straightened — or tried to. His
muscles wouldn't obey him. He just lay stunned,
unable to breathe.

Red spoke. "Move him. Let me use this table."

Penny jerked Roger off the table and casually
shoved him into the nearest wall. The whole apartment
boomed when he hit, and the right side of Roger's
body was jarred with pain from the impact. Paintings
spilled off the drafting table onto the floor. Roger
heard Red drop his briefcase onto the table and pop
the case's latches.

Roger recovered enough to struggle with the
woman holding his arm . . . but got nowhere. She was
so much stronger than he that it wasn't a fight.
Infuriated, his male pride bruised more than his arm,
he struggled more, not even thinking to cry out for
help. All his accumulated ideals of sexual equality were
momentarily thrown aside as he struggled to prove that
no woman could hold him against his will.

He was wrong. Penny held him. Roger had to stop
to think about what to do. He turned his head as far as
he could to see what was going on behind him.

Red pulled a canvas from his briefcase and studied

it. Roger couldn't see what was painted upon it . . . but the light caught Red just right and Roger could see strange little reflections in his face. His skin was a bit slick and shiny, with little highlights that were . . . orange. . . .

"Oh, my God," Roger said, and his words were half a moan. "You're like from — 'Achilles and Penthesilia' — but Kevin never uses models for his characters any more —"

Red/Achilles looked at him, then at Penny. "Kevin was right. Roger is too clever. Bring him over here so I can launch him."

Penthesilia effortlessly pulled Roger around and gave him a push. She kicked his feet out from under him and slammed him painfully to the carpet just in front of where "Skinny-Dipping Lava Nymphs" had landed; his nose landed on his own signature in the corner of the painting. Penny kept her grip on his arm, then used her free hand to check his pockets, taking his keys. Her voice was surprisingly gentle. "Understand that there is nothing personal to this," she whispered. "I'm sorry."

Roger regained his voice. "Look — what are you going to — I haven't done anything to you. Let go, dammit!" He sucked in a deep lungful of air to scream for help.

Penny's fist hit him just above the kidney and the sudden, excruciating pain drove all the wind from him. "If you don't do that," she suggested solemnly, "I won't have to hit you again. If you wait just a moment, this will all be over."

Red knelt and placed another painting onto the carpet beside "Lava Nymphs" and still within Roger's range of vision. The painting showed a living room, its family occupants opening the curtains over the picture window and reacting with horror to the realization that a demon-infested hell, instead of the front lawn, lay outside. It was a Kevin Matthews original, all drippy, shiny oranges and slightly wrong poses and shadows.

Red leaned low so Roger could easily see his face. Red's expression was unyielding. "I will explain," he said, "because you deserve it, because no man should die ignorant of the reason.

"You've learned to do something that Kevin says you must not do. So he has told me to kill you. I have no choice. He has altered me so I can put you into a place that will destroy you, so there will be no inconvenience of a body. Do you understand?"

Mute, Roger shook his head no.

"That is sad." Red forced Roger's head down until his forehead touched the carpet. Panicking, Roger began struggling again, with such strength and fury . . .

. . . that Penthesilia had to use both hands *and* her weight to control him fully. He couldn't break free. He couldn't break free!

Finally he forced himself to think, tried to regain control of himself. But what could he do? If he tried to shout, he'd be hit. If he struggled, he'd be subdued. If he waited, he'd be killed. And he couldn't reach anything but his own "Lava Nymphs" painting under his face. . . .

The painting.

No matter how unlikely it was, he'd made another painting, the nymph, come to life. Achilles and Penthesilia were paintings, but they were real enough to kill him.

Whatever he'd done by accident, Kevin Matthews had done deliberately. Maybe Roger could, too. Strong as Achilles and Penthesilia were, they'd be nothing compared to the Lava Demon under his nose.

How had he done it with the nymph? He'd reconstructed her in his mind, thought about her every line and color. . . .

He ignored Red and Penny and concentrated on "Lava Nymphs." He rebuilt the volcano's interior in his mind, caught glimpses of the lean red bodies swimming within the glowing lava, looked for and found the menacing ridge of the demon's head moving forward through the lava. . . . *Come to me, you ugly son of a bitch.* . . .

Then the floor dropped away. Roger shrieked as he fell.

Red and Penny stood and looked at the blank patch of carpet where Roger had been. "He's gone," she said, and there was regret in her voice. "He's in Kevin's hell. Kevin's other hell."

Red shook his head. "Something's wrong. It didn't feel like the last time I did it. He went . . . just as I was *starting* to shove him. The last time, it took more time, more effort."

"Maybe you're getting better at it."

"Maybe." His expression was unconvinced.

Chapter Two

Fighting with His Materials

Roger fell, flailing his arms, and his eyes snapped open. All he saw was a broad, burning, crackling lake of superheated lava filling the entire cavern below. There were figures swimming in this lava, his own Skinny-Dipping Lava Nymphs. He heard their merry cries as a blast of hot air roiled up from the surface of the lava pool.

All he could do was scream at the lava that would destroy him. He howled all the way down, thrashing as if he hoped he might find one solid patch of air to cling to.

Then he hit . . . but not the lava's black-orange-and-yellow surface. A long silhouette like a walkway moved under him from the side; he slammed into its yielding surface.

But it was only so yielding. The impact drove the wind from him like a sledgehammer hitting his chest. He lay stunned, unable to breathe. Gray fog washed across his vision, and a noise like a waterfall's roar echoed in his ears.

He could feel, though. He still felt the impact in his chest, the blow to his kidney, bruises from Penny's grip on his arm. He felt the lava's heat wash over him. He felt something like leather and coarse cord beneath him where he lay. And he felt motion, as though the walkway he'd fallen on were moving.

He sucked in one painful breath of hot air, then another; his ribs creaked and ached as he breathed, but his vision cleared. Then he rolled over and froze, staring up into two glowing yellow eyes each a yard in diameter.

Oh, he knew those eyes, and the face that stared down at him, illuminated by the bright lava. His Lava Demon. He'd called for it . . . but it hadn't come. He'd gone to it instead.

The face had features like a baboon's, surrounded by bright rust-red hair. Its grinding teeth were like huge, malformed chunks of veined white marble. Its eyes, empty sockets, glowed with bright yellow flame.

The torso below the baboon neck was heavily muscled like a football player's. Below Roger's vision would be the recurved goat legs; he didn't have to see them to remember how he'd painted them. Behind the demon body were the creature's black, sail-sized, leathery wings.

And Roger lay on the monster's outstretched hand. He sat on the leather pad of the palm; fingers ending in jagged curved claws like obsidian spikes curved up to cup him. Sudden fear nearly drove away the little breath Roger had left.

The Lava Demon grinned down at Roger and spoke. Its voice was like a rockslide formed into words, crackling and scraping and roaring, propelled by a wash of breath that stank like a wind from a stockyard; Roger's stomach wrenched. "Must not let this fall into my pool," it rumbled. "It would not taste as good."

Slowly, with exaggerated motion and malicious humor, the thing drew Roger toward its mouth, opening that maw wide.

Mouth or lava, be eaten or be burned — Roger, shocked beyond thinking, froze as he found himself choosing between one death and another.

"STOP!"

For a moment, he thought someone else had shouted. Then he realized it was his own voice.

. . . and the demon stopped, freezing its hand in

place all too close to its mouth. The demon's brows came down in a very human frown of puzzlement.

Roger felt a twinge of elation. A second later, the demon again moved its hand toward its mouth; Roger scrambled to his feet and shouted once more: "*Stop!*"

Again the demon froze. Again its face reflected confusion. Roger almost cheered; he knew he held some sort of power over the monstrous thing, and thought he knew why. "I painted you, I created you!" he shouted. "You have to do what I say!"

The Lava Demon scowled, and Roger finally *felt* the struggle taking place.

It was all within him, and it was like every time he'd ever fought with himself. Buy the new airbrush compressor or pay the bills . . . work on the hot assignment or blow off a day and have fun . . . He wanted the demon to stop, but another part of him wanted to kill and eat Roger. And if he came to the wrong conclusion he would die.

Roger focused himself, pushed against the demon's will as though he were trying to budge a boulder, and shouted: "Show me the way out of here. Take me there, and put me down!" Sweat from heat and exertion trickled down his face as he concentrated.

The Lava Demon's expression changed to outrage. But it grudgingly moved its hand away from its mouth and slowly turned toward its right.

Not relaxing in his mental struggle, Roger glanced over the edge. Below, maybe forty feet down, was the yellow-hot surface of the lava. The demon emerged from it at waist level, but still walked toward the side of the cavern and the glistening black stone walls there.

Roger felt the demon's hunger again. His control was slipping. He was tired; fighting with the demon's wishes was like throwing his body against a stone wall over and over. Something inside him was becoming sore and exhausted. But he pushed at the demon's desires, kept them at bay.

Thirty feet from the edge of the lava pool, the demon reluctantly extended its hand toward a dark man-height hole in the rock wall. Roger felt the demon's spiteful desire to tilt the hand over and drop the escaping prey into the lava. But a moment later the hand and its human cargo entered the hole in the rock.

It was a stone tunnel mouth, darker and a little cooler than the lava chamber. The hand held still long enough for Roger to step shakily off onto the tunnel floor, then retreated quickly into the main chamber.

Roger felt his control go. His knees buckled and he fell prone on the rough stone floor. Trembling, he almost blacked out.

Then he felt the exultation of the thing out in the lava chamber as it slipped from his control. He heard its rocky, grinding voice again: "Tired, little food? Too tired to fight? Come back now."

Too drained to stand, Roger crawled away, painfully dragging himself deeper into the darkness. He glanced back and saw the demon's hand snaking into the tunnel mouth, coming toward him —

Roger managed finally to get up on shaky feet and stumbled into darkness. The hand reached for him, closer and closer . . . and jerked to a halt a dozen feet behind him.

Roger turned to look at the groping, grasping fingers. He nearly laughed, but didn't have the energy. He sank down to the side of the tunnel and managed a faint smile. "How's it feel, ugly?" he managed, in just over a whisper. "You lost. Now beat it."

The hand and arm banged back and forth for another few moments; had he been anywhere along the arm's length, Roger would have been killed. But eventually the hand retreated and was gone.

Roger's head snapped up as he awakened. He'd fallen asleep, or passed out, and for a moment, staring into blackness, he didn't know where he was.

The glow to his left was the distant opening into the lava chamber. It hadn't been a dream. The weariness he still felt, the pain in his knees and back and chest, the oil-thick sheen of sweat all over his body, were real.

Tired as he was, he had to think logically. He took a few deep breaths, looked back toward the entrance to the lava cave, and felt the hot air flowing out of the chamber and across him. This was no dream, no sleep-deprived hallucination.

And Red and Penny trying to kill him was real. Kevin Matthews told them to, because . . . why? He frowned for a moment before the answer came. Because Roger had told him about the nymph walking around. Kevin didn't want him doing that. But Roger had gotten away and was safe, at least for the moment.

Safe . . . in one of his own paintings. The thought was crazy, but his surroundings didn't allow him to deny it. Somehow, he was *inside* "Skinny-Dipping Lava Nymphs."

No, that wasn't quite right. The Lava Demon was only suggested in "Lava Nymphs." The full view of the demon only appeared in "The Lava Demon," a different painting. He wasn't really in either painting; this was more like the setting that both paintings described.

He glanced farther into the tunnel and saw only darkness. He'd told the demon to take him to the way out, and the demon had brought him here. He was hurt, tired, thirsty, and sweating like crazy — he grimaced as he felt the stickiness of his hands; he *hated* it when his hands weren't clean. Further reflections could wait; it was time to go. Painfully, he inched his way to a standing position.

"You are awake. I am glad." It was a faint whisper, but he heard it and froze. Then he felt the movement — something stirred in his shirt pocket, then clambered from there toward his neck. . . .

His mind flashed on the scene from the safari

movies — the safari's token female on the cot, the giant
tarantula crawling up to her shoulder. But tarantulas
can't talk. *Or maybe they can, here*. His suddenly
trembling hand reached to touch whatever was climb-
ing his shirt.

And he touched smooth, warm skin, a patch of cloth,
a doll-sized human form. . . . "It's you!" he breathed,
relieved. "The nymph."

"You wouldn't wake up," she replied, aggrieved. She
reached his shoulder, then turned to sit and grabbed
his collar to steady her perch. "I was worried," she
complained.

He exhaled the last of his fear. "Well, I'm all right.
Let's go looking for someplace light, okay?"

"Okay." The slang word sounded wrong coming
from her lips.

Roger moved slowly off into the darkness, keeping
one hand on the stone wall. "How on earth did you get
here?"

"When those two people looked down at me, I could
see they were not right. I was scared, and I wanted to
be with you. When they threw you to the floor, I crept
down and clung to your garment."

"Well, they're gone now. You're safe." Roger
changed the subject. "Did you ever tell me what your
name was? Wait a minute, you said you didn't have
one. Would you like one?"

"Yes, that would be nice."

He stumbled across a large rock but caught himself;
he felt the nymph slide down his shoulder, still holding
tight to his collar, and climb back into place. He
continued forward. "Let's see, let's find something
appropriate. A diminutive name for a diminutive
nymph — Thumbelina? Tinkerbelle?"

He didn't hear anything from her, but knew when she
recoiled from the inelegant names; he felt it as he'd felt
the demon's hunger. "No, huh? Okay, how about 'created'
women from mythology. Eve? Lilith? Pandora?"

"Are these good names?" Her tone was polite, but he could feel her disinterest.

"Uh, so-so. Let's see. Who played the Bride of Frankenstein in the movie? Erma — no, Elsa. Elsa Lanchester. How about Elsa? Or Elsie?"

"I like Elsie."

"Elsie it is, then." All the while, he was making slow and steady progress forward, using his conversation to keep his mind, and hers, off their situation. "Elsie the nymph. So, if you're a nymph, do you know anything nymphlike?"

"What do you mean?"

"I don't know — like trees and forests and growing things? Satyrs, maybe?"

She was silent a long moment, and he could feel her searching among her senses and feelings. Then he felt her brighten. "Yes! I can feel trees and forest. Wind and bees and rivers flowing. I know where they are."

"You're kidding. Where?"

She went silent again, and he lost track of what she was feeling — her mind drifted away from his. But her grip on his collar never faltered.

Finally: "Straight ahead and a little down."

"Down? You don't mean up?"

"No, down. Follow the hot wind. It will lead us there. It escapes ahead of us and is happy to be free."

"Uh . . . sure."

As he walked, he grew thirstier and thirstier, until talking was a chore; Elsie grew silent as he did.

The tunnel curved and twisted, but in its round-about way took him in one direction, gradually rising. In spite of the darkness, he still managed to make fair time. And after perhaps half an hour the tunnel grew brighter, and he could abandon his hold on the wall and walk normally.

Past a final bend, he turned to face direct sunlight. It was no more than twenty yards up a gentle incline to the open air. He stumbled a little in his haste and emerged from the tunnel mouth.

He found himself on a stony hill face and had to blink and cover his eyes against the sudden sunlight; it took several moments for his eyes to adjust.

Far below, the black, rocky hillside descended into a thick screen of green, a forest of ferns and palm trees. In the distance, miles beyond the curtain of green, he could see blue ocean, his favorite color of sea blue.

Roger turned and looked up the slope. Above was the jagged, ugly crest of a volcano's cone, alive and smoking. The sun, only part of it visible behind the volcano, shone down at him a little more golden-orange than usual; the sky was a clean, beautiful sky blue, a color he'd always loved and had only occasionally been able to reproduce.

And it was cool — oh, God, was it cool. He moved rapidly to the side of the cave mouth and let the hot flow of air pass him by; the cooler air caressed him, carrying heat away. He leaned against a rough, upright slab of rock, his eyes closed, and gulped the fresh air.

"This is better," Elsie said a trifle smugly. "There are trees here, and cool air. And fresh water, I can smell it."

"Oh, God. Point the way."

Beyond the foot of the cone, past a thick screen of palms, banana trees, and underbrush, a waterfall splashed into a deep pool, kicked up spray where it hit, and rippled the surface of the crystal-clear water. Cliffs sheltered the pool on three sides, their shadow keeping the water cool.

Roger had the presence of mind to carefully set Elsie down on the stony bank. Then he leaped in, clothes and all, and the resulting splash still washed across the bank and knocked Elsie from her feet.

He drank until his stomach was distended, until he sloshed as he moved, until the worst of his thirst was gone. Then he floated on his back like a dead man in

the water, letting the outermost layer of salty sweat
wash away from his body. Finally, a little rested, he
stripped off his clothes, wrung them out and threw
them onto the stony bank, and scrubbed at his skin as
best he could.

Only then did he remember his companion.
"Nymph, uh, Elsie? Where are you?" The pool looked
desolate, empty.

"Here. You forgot about me." He barely heard her
chiding call, Elsie's voice was so faint, but he turned
and spotted her. She swam in a bathtub-sized cleft in
the stone bank, protected from the comparatively huge
waves Roger had been creating. Roger carefully swam
across to loom over her.

He was startled to see that she, too, was naked.

Perhaps he wouldn't have been as startled if she
weren't so perfect. When he'd drawn her — just
yesterday! — he'd given her the sort of female build he
most appreciated: lean but not lanky, long-legged,
high-breasted, fit and graceful. He'd made her a
beauty, too; looking down at her, he felt his heart
wrench a little, and was fascinated by his handiwork as
she splashed and frolicked in the little pool.

Too fascinated, maybe; he felt a twinge of desire he
was happy to have concealed by the pool and quickly
quelled by the coolness of the water. Abruptly, he
turned and moved back to where his sodden clothes
lay, then hauled himself back onto the bank.

He irritably wrung out his clothes and concluded
that he was one stupid son of a bitch. Not a good idea
to get turned on by — by whatever Elsie is. Three
inches tall and made of watercolor and imagination. A
painted nymph, for God's sake.

Why couldn't he have done her up full-sized?

And what if he had? She'd be a full-sized painted
nymph! He stood and started to get dressed.

She was still the closest thing there had ever been to
his "dream girl" —

Dream girl. He straightened and wasn't even aware when he dropped the bundle of his pants. Kevin Matthews' dream girl. Kevin had always loved straight, black hair, and big white teeth. . . .

If Kevin could recreate Achilles and Penthesilia, then he could also create his dream girl. He could create Julia.

Roger shook his head, trying to shake away his sudden suspicion. Julia didn't have the telltale orange highlights and oily sheen to her skin that Red and Penny did.

On the other hand, Kevin *was* capable of doing better work than "Achilles and Penthesilia." That was one of the things Roger despised about him. Kevin's work was sloppy because he wasn't exacting with himself, wasn't willing to put in the hours. He did the minimum necessary work on each assignment . . . when he was capable of more.

Roger stooped, picked up his pants, and put them on. So if Julia Dover was a painting, what did it mean?

Kevin took up with Julia about a year and a half ago. That would mean Kevin was capable of creating her, and things like her, at that time.

That's also about the time he began to get really successful. Started getting all the plum assignments they'd both been competing for. About the time he cut Donna loose, of course. About the time of . . .

Nonesuch Books.

That stopped Roger cold.

He shook his head, rejecting the thought. He'd take it as a given that Kevin Matthews, the great opportunist, would dump his wife for his dream girl. But deliberately, maliciously sabotage Roger's career? They'd gone to college together, been roommates for a time, collaborated on a lot of early work. . . .

Which meant nothing. Roger stood for a pained minute and accepted the truth: Kevin had shot down his career. Kevin, with whatever abilities he now employed, had gotten to Nonesuch Books, sabotaged that one assignment, and made sure the story reached every ear in the business. Roger didn't know how Kevin had done it, but if the man could actually create full-sized people like Red and Penny, there's no telling what he could do. And he must have torpedoed Donna, too. She said she couldn't get any work, either. Anger's red haze began to creep over his vision.

"You should let your clothes dry before putting them on."

Elsie sat on a fist-sized rock, again dressed in her leafy scrap of a garment, posed like an artist's model. "I spread mine out where there is sun and it is finally dry. You should, too. The air is moist. Your clothes will take forever to dry."

Roger forced his anger down and felt it begin to simmer at the back of his mind. He put on a smile he didn't really feel, for Elsie's sake. "Maybe so, but with you around, I need the fig-leaf."

She looked puzzled. "Never mind," he continued. "We're clean and we're not going to dehydrate in the next ten minutes. Let's try to figure out how to get out of here. Hop up." He extended his hand down, and when she leaped upon it, he transferred her to the shoulder perch.

Off he moved into the line of trees. As his shoes squished and his stomach sloshed, he was briefly able to grin at his sound effects.

Minutes later the anger was back, and Elsie could feel it. "What is wrong? You were so happy back at the pool."

Roger's lip trembled as he struggled to keep from snapping at his passenger. "Nothing. Everything," he grumbled, and swept aside the next frond blocking his path. The ground beyond was rough going, rocky and irregular; he slowly picked his way between boles of trees and through thick patches of ferns, looking in vain for a path or more inviting stretch of terrain.

"It's pretty." Elsie sounded uncomfortable.

"Yeah, well, it's a pain," he answered. "We have trees as thick as cars in a traffic jam, damned plants getting in the way every three steps, I'm starting to be as hot as hell —"

"You were cool only a little while ago," she said, and it sounded faintly like a reprimand.

"I only thought I was cool. It was just in comparison to that chimney we came out of. It feels like summertime now." Again, he flicked his sweaty hair out of his eyes and mopped the perspiration from his forehead.

Ahead, there was a flutter of wings, and a thick patch of foliage shuddered as brightly colored birds fled skyward at his approach; it looked like the eruption of a volcano packed with paint. He saw birds flying sunward — multicolored parrots, long-tailed quetzals, some strangely shaped red bird. . . .

That was no bird. He squinted at it as it climbed quickly out of sight. The size of a large eagle, it was the precise red of an excruciating sunburn. Except for wings, it bore no resemblance to a bird. It was shaped like an iguana, legs and tail and all, and propelled through the air by a broad pair of featherless, scaly wings.

Roger froze as the memory hit him, as the red lizard-thing disappeared above the screen of treetops. "I know where this is," he breathed. "Which painting, I mean."

"Where? You are frightened. Are we in a bad place?"

Roger shook his head. "I'm more startled than anything else. This is, well, Paradise. That's what I called it, anyway." He started walking again, still distracted. "A series of paintings I did in high school."

"High —"

"That's a place you go for years because the

government insists on it. Sort of like prison, except you get paroled every afternoon and then sentenced again the next morning. A place you can get an education, but mostly if you ignore the curriculum, figure out what you *want* to learn, and then set out to learn it."

Roger clamped down on himself before he climbed too far up on his public-education soapbox. "Anyway, I did my first acrylics when I was there. Pretty rotten, actually. My dad still has them, I think. They were of a South Seas island full of strange creatures, lots of color, beautiful women. . . .

"Come to think of it, there *was* a volcano on the island, and I'd intended to paint all sorts of creatures inside it. I never did. I guess the idea stuck with me. I must have returned to it with 'Skinny-Dipping Lava Nymphs' and 'The Lava Demon' — without realizing it." Maybe that's why the volcano's heat hadn't actually killed him; he'd never imagined the place as being deadly to all life. He shook his head, pushed another obstructive fern aside. "I'm sure that's where we are. Which means we're probably safe."

But what else did it mean? If he walked into the exact area one of the paintings showed, would he be visible to people outside the painting, as if it were a TV screen? What if something happened to the painting while he walked around within it?

And then there was the most troublesome question — couldn't it be that he really was crazy, locked up somewhere in a room with nice, soft walls, while dementia and Thorazine kept his perceptions here?

He angrily shoved that possibility aside. If it were true, there was nothing he could do about it.

He struggled to remember all the paintings he'd done in the series. There was "Leaping Lizards," which showed a flock of flying iguanas, each a different color. "The Frenzy" showed many dark-hued natives, men and women, dancing around a village fire and working themselves into an ecstatic state. "The Wind" showed the island lashed by typhoon weather — he'd have to watch out for hurricane season. There might have been one or two more canvases.

And, dammit, why couldn't he have painted a jungle that was easier to move through?

The answer was simple to remember. *Who cares whether it works, whether it makes any sense?* he'd always asked. *It only matters if it looks good.* His deep, menacing, nearly impenetrable jungle had looked good as he painted it. But now, slogging through the very undergrowth he'd created, he wished fervently that he'd imagined a path running through it.

"I hear noises."

That jarred him out of his reverie. He glanced down at Elsie, who was peering ahead. He cocked his head but couldn't hear anything but the wind, distant birdcalls, and the wavelike surge and fall of insect choruses — all sounds they'd been hearing for quite some time.

"What do you hear?"

"A . . . beating," she answered, absently. "Rhythm. Many feet stamping . . ."

The Frenzy. His village. It had to be. "Show me where," he told her, then struggled through the underbrush in the direction she indicated.

It was far from the longest walk he'd had, but it was the hardest; he'd never had to push his way through underbrush this thick before. Only a few minutes into it, he began to hear what Elsie had heard — distant jungle drums, no mistaking them. But hearing them and getting to them were two different things.

Every few feet, as he ran into another patch of brambles or ferns or thick-hanging vines, he cursed the vividness with which he'd imagined this island "paradise" and the fact that he didn't have a machete. He got some satisfaction out of ripping ferns and fronds to shreds, destroying them for the audacity they showed in blocking his path.

Next, he launched into a series of curses directed at the heat, Kevin Matthews, Cole MacMurphy, Nonesuch Books, his car, and his apartment. Each patch of fronds he tore to pieces became one of them, and the trail he left behind became littered with the mangled, leafy corpses of all the things that had ever caused him grief.

Then he caught sight of Elsie, staring at him with wide-eyed dismay.

That stopped him. "What's wrong?"

She was slow to answer. "You. You are so full of anger. You hate everything."

Under his aggravation, he could detect what she was feeling. It was fear, fear of him, what he might do to *her*.

"No! Elsie, listen. All that, what you were hearing, that's just imagination. I've never hurt anyone like that."

"Then why do you think about it? Is it good to think of making people into dead pieces of people?"

"Dammit, it's . . ." He counted slowly to ten before continuing. "Sometimes it's the only way to keep going. Bad things come raining down on you and you have to cope. Sometimes it helps to think about just scraping all the bad things out of your life, like cutting a rotten piece out of a banana. But it's all imagination, nothing but imagination."

"Then what am I? You made me like you made the pictures in your mind." Elsie's chin quivered.

The chill that took hold of Roger drove away the last of his anger. The nymph was genuinely in fear for her life — fear of him, fear of her creator. "Elsie," he began, gently, "that's different. You're real. No matter where you came from, you're real now. I know the difference between what's imaginary and what's real."

She still looked frightened, and glanced away from him. "I do not."

"You will," he said, thoughtfully. *But I can't show*

you the difference, not here. Everything is real here.
And that last thought bothered him. More subdued, he
resumed his course toward the jungle drums.

In the next few minutes, the jungle undergrowth
thinned and walking became easier. The drums were
close now. Soon, he could see through the trees to
their source: a cluster of mud-and-thatch huts, maybe
twenty of them.

It shocked him to see the village . . . because it was
just as he'd imagined it years ago. Huts were arranged
in a circle around an open central area, just as he'd
envisioned them. As he advanced through the trees, he
knew what he'd find in that open area: a bank of
drummers, beating on a series of drums made from
tree trunks and stretched animal hide; a large fire in
the center; a circle of spear-and-shield-armed men and
women dancing clockwise around the fire.

Oddly, Roger felt calm about confronting them.
He'd controlled the Lava Demon, and suspected he
could control the villagers long enough to escape if
things got ugly.

And that was a novelty. Never before, going into a
situation where violence might result, had he felt calm;
not once had he felt in charge of things.

He moved out of the final stand of trees and walked
among the huts. They were as he'd painted them:
wood frames with mud packed over them, grass-thatch
roofs, open windows and doorways draped with curtains of beads or flaps of leather. The drums were very
close and he could now hear the stamping of feet.

He passed the last of the huts and reached the
center of the village, reached the scene he'd painted
more than a dozen years before.

There they were, the natives, *his* natives. They were
tall and healthy; their skin was dusky; their features
were Roger's favorite blending of Caucasian, Black,
Oriental, and Polynesian traits. They danced in a
foot-stamping, spinning pattern that had been Roger's

high school idea of what native dances were all about; he smiled at the memory. They wore loincloths or grass skirts and flower leis; many carried crude stone-tipped javelins and tall, lozenge-shaped shields. Both men and women danced, tireless; they were reaching a stage of abandon, and he knew that the dangerous hysteria would come soon.

On the far side of the dance, a bank of five drummers kept the rhythm, each on a drum bigger than the one to his left, each intent on his music and the dancers before him.

"How lovely." That was Elsie. Distracted, Roger realized there was no way he could have heard her faint voice above the beating of the drums. But it didn't matter; he knew what she was saying.

Then one male dancer saw Roger. He froze, then leaped out from the circle, shaking his javelin and shield, sending up a wild cry of alarm. In moments the rest of the line jarred to a stop, and more of the dancers swarmed out to line up with him.

Roger drew in a deep breath and readied himself for the struggle.

"Don't attack him," came the voice, a young woman's voice, purring and persuasive instead of alarmed. "He's my friend."

The voice jolted Roger. He recognized it, but couldn't immediately place it. Then the speaker moved out from behind the crowd of dancers.

She was tanned nearly as dark as the natives, but wasn't one of them. Her face, brightly alert, was all American Midwest. Her hair was long and wavy, cocoa-brown, with a yellow rose tucked over one ear. She wore a short red-and-yellow floral print that did nothing to conceal her youthful, perfect figure. She was 17. Roger didn't have to guess that. He knew how old she'd been when he painted her.

"Tricia?" he breathed. "Tricia Davis?"

"Hi, Roger," she said, moved confidently to him.

"You've come, at last." She pressed against him, reached up for him — heedless of Elsie, who squeaked, slid out of harm's way, and dropped ignominiously to the dust far below — and drew his mouth down to hers.

Chapter Three

Drying Time

They were in Tricia's mud hut. Roger and Tricia knelt on woven grass mats only a foot or so apart. Elsie clambered atop a table jumbled with clay pots and other paraphernalia Roger didn't have the inclination to examine.

Roger, still in a daze, couldn't tear his gaze from the teenaged girl beside him. "Tricia . . ." he began.

She smiled dazzlingly. "Have you come to stay, Roger? You can stay here with me, you know. I always liked you."

Numbed, he shook his head. "You always *despised* me, Tricia. You were cheerleader clique all the way. You called me and my friends geeks and nerds."

"The men in the tribe are nice, but I've always, you know, had the feeling I was waiting for someone else. Someone better. When I saw you, I knew all at once what I'd been waiting for. . . ."

"You know, I saw you a couple of years ago, at our ten-year high school reunion." Roger frowned as he remembered. "You'd married right out of high school, to Rod Bower —"

"Rod! He was really good-looking. I liked him, too."

"— and then divorced him about a year later, since he had this thing about beating you black and blue. When I saw you, you were on your second husband, a thin, balding guy, really friendly, really smart, and you'd had two kids with him."

"Rod would never beat me. He was too good-looking."

"And you were nice. Nice to everyone. You'd learned some lessons, and you'd come out of it a lot smarter. Better looking, too, laugh lines and crow's-feet and all. When you smiled at people, you meant it. That made you even better to look at. I was happy for you."

Tricia looked reprovingly at him. "I've never done any of the things you're talking about. I went to high school and then I came here to live."

It was probably useless to explain, but he felt he should. "Yes, because I *painted* you here. In high school, I did a lot of paintings of this island, and one of them was called 'Dream Girl.' I took the best-looking girl in our class, that was you, and dropped her into this island setting, dressed in some Dorothy Lamour sarong. I made you look sad and filled with longing, waiting for the love of your life — that was supposed to be me, of course — and put you in this pretty creekside clearing under the night sky. . . ."

"I know that place! That's my favorite place. There's a huge, smooth white log there, and I stretch out on it to stare at the stars. . . ." She jumped to her feet and reached down for his hand. "Let's go there right now. You'll love it."

Gently and reluctantly, Roger pulled his hand from hers. "Look, Tricia. I'm not the same Roger you . . . remember. I'm not a maladjusted high-school junior who looks around for the cheerleader and says, 'There she is, that's my dream girl, and if she were my girl, nobody would laugh at me.'

"Back then, I saw your looks and energy and, I don't know, status. But now . . . now, I'm thirty years old and I've latched onto a little bit of sense, while you're the same shallow, self-centered girl you were in school." He shrugged. "I'm just not the man you've been waiting for."

"Yes, I *have* been waiting. And now I don't have to wait any longer." She knelt before him and threw her arms around him. "Make love to me, Roger. Right now." She closed her eyes, tossed her hair, brought her mouth toward his —

And jumped in alarm as one of the clay pots on her table teetered over the edge and smashed on the ground. Suddenly livid, she leaped to her feet and stomped over to the table, staring down at the shards. "My pot! My favorite pot. I worked for, I don't know, *hours* on that pot." She looked over the table, then spun to glare at Roger. "Where's that friend of yours, the little toy?"

Roger shook his head, indicating ignorance. Elsie was wisely keeping out of sight. Then it occurred to him: So, Tricia *had* seen Elsie. And she didn't think it strange that he was wandering around with a three-inch-tall nymph.

"Well, if she breaks any more pots, I'll throw her in my kiln. Now . . ." With an effort, she got her anger under control, resumed the self-satisfied smile Roger was growing to dislike. "Where were we?"

Roger held up a hand to forestall her. "We weren't anywhere, Tricia. I'm not going to go to bed with you, and I'd appreciate it if you wouldn't offer again, because you're one hell of a temptation."

"But —"

"No buts."

In spite of his refusal, she tried again to kneel in front of him. And, as with the Lava Demon, he found that he could feel her emotions, almost as though they were his own. They were in his mind but not a part of it, a hard knot of desire mixed with self-appreciation and a hunger for victory.

Roger grabbed at that group of feelings, exerted himself against them like squeezing his fist over a tennis ball, and pushed them away. It was hard work, and he felt his earlier weariness return. But Tricia stopped in mid-kneel, then stood upright, an expression of anger and confusion crossing her face.

"No buts," Roger repeated. "Tricia, I look at you and I'm depressed. I'm depressed because you're still young and perfect, and because you're still as shallow and horrible as you were in high school. The only difference is that you like me now. And it's my fault you're the way you are. Jesus Christ." He shook his head as the thought finally penetrated. "I'm starting to feel like Dr. Frankenstein. Anyway . . . I'm not going to bed with you, Tricia. Not *this* you."

She glowered down at him and stamped her foot. Roger winced at the stereotype. "All right, Roger," she snapped. "You and your little dolly can stay here tonight. I'm sure I can find *some* place to sleep." She stomped out of her hut, flinging aside the beaded curtain and then throwing it back as though she were slamming a door.

Roger leaned back against the hard-packed mud wall and closed his eyes. So tired . . . he always felt tired after an *ordinary* argument. Fooling around with the emotions of the people he'd created was even more exhausting.

After a moment, he looked around. "Elsie?"

"I'm here." She was back atop the table, perched on a thick platelike object.

"You didn't need to break her pot."

"Yes, I did. She was horrible. I wished I could have dropped something on her head. I hate being small."

Roger chuckled, then looked at Elsie a bit more closely. The expression on her face, solemn disappointment, was somehow different from any he'd seen her wear — not as childish or naive as usual. She stared back at him for a moment, then the expression was gone, replaced by a more familiar look of curiosity. She looked around her tabletop. "What are all these things?"

"Most of it is for making pottery. Tricia was into pottery in high school; it was her concept of fine art. You're sitting on a potter's wheel. You spin it, put clay in the center, and shape the clay while the wheel is spinning so it's more perfectly round. There's a big lump of clay there, and I'll bet, if you look around in the pots on the table, you'll find water and pigments and glazes, maybe brushes, that sort of thing."

She did hop up and began peering into the shorter pots. "Are you sad? You feel sad."

"Yeah. I was just wondering some things." He shifted to make himself more comfortable. "Like, is this Tricia doomed to be a teenaged bitch queen for the rest of her life? And is it my fault if she is?

"And how long was she waiting here for me — since high school? Or was it just a little while for her?

"And are all the nasty things I've drawn or painted actually taking place someplace, in their own little worlds, like this one?

"And what sort of idiot am I for turning her down?"

"Don't be sad. You told the demon what to do. You can do anything."

"Yeah. Sure."

Elsie found fruit in a large jar against the wall; Roger helped himself to a couple of bananas. Tricia's bed mat was hanging on wall pegs; Roger set it on the floor, then lay on it, thinking. Elsie stayed quiet, exploring Tricia's quarters and perching on the window to stare outside.

Tricia didn't return. Roger grinned sourly. Boy, was that ever a trick of the old high-school Tricia: throw herself at one boy, usually a football player, to make another jealous. He wondered, briefly, if any part of him *were* jealous. He didn't think so . . . but he knew that he might be kidding himself.

He closed his eyes, and then opened them again a moment later — at least, it felt like a moment. But it was full dark, the only illumination a sliver of moonlight. Gone were the pounding of jungle drums and shuffling of feet; instead, he could hear the gentle swell and fall of insect noises.

His eyes adjusted quickly. He could see Elsie stretched out on the bed mat close to his head; she was fast asleep. Tricia was still gone.

He must have slept for quite a while; he felt better, rested enough to know that he wouldn't drop off to sleep soon. So it was time to figure out how to get back home.

He'd come here through a painting; perhaps he needed to leave the same way. Doing a painting of his bedroom wouldn't be too hard; he knew every inch of it. Then he'd experiment with the painting, try to put himself into it. . . .

Wait a minute. He *didn't* know every inch of the apartment — certainly not where every book or dropped sock lay. What if he make a mistake? Would he end up in another fake painting-world instead of the real world? And if so, how would he get back home?

Exasperated, he glared into the darkness. Maybe Elsie would have an idea; she was a painting. Used to be, anyway.

Looking around for something quiet to do, he spotted the assortment of pots and goods atop Tricia's pottery table. There was the mound of fresh clay. . . .

It'd been a while, years really, since he'd fooled around with clay. He'd done some nice figurines in high school, in one of the few classes he'd shared with the real Tricia Davis. But it came back to him quickly as he worked clay into small gorillas and lizards, tables and pots, cars and planes.

The table and the pot were about the right scale for Elsie; he set them up behind her and, for grins, began working on several more pieces at the same scale. Imagine her surprise when she woke and found furnishings just right for her. Perhaps they'd be sturdy enough for her to play with. He carefully put together a delicate rocking chair, a bathtub, a little computer with its own table and hutch.

This task did take the edge off his worry. Finally he

felt relaxed again. He lay down, grinned for a minute at
the diorama — convincing in the dim light — of Elsie
and her furnishings; it didn't take much work to
imagine her full-size, surrounded by a bad arrangement of ugly gray furniture. Then he drifted off to
sleep again.

"Roger!" Elsie's shriek snapped him to wakefulness.
It was daylight, barely; a little sunlight trickled in
through the beaded curtains across the window and
door. Roger heaved himself upright and looked
around . . . at Tricia's changed hut.

The bed mat beneath him was much larger than the
one he'd fallen asleep on; it was now twelve feet wide
and took up most of the floor space in the hut.

It was surrounded by furniture . . . sort of. There
they were, the clay furnishings he'd made last night:
table and pot, rocking chair and bathtub, computer
and computer desk.

But they were full-size, scaled for normal human
beings. If they were still made of soft clay, they should
collapse under their own weight. But they stood
upright, gray and knobby and horribly crude compared
to real furniture.

Then Roger turned and saw Elsie. She stood five
and a half feet tall; delighted, she stretched and spun
around. "Roger! I'm tall!" Her voice, rich and lilting,
had the volume of any adult woman's.

"I'll . . . be . . . damned." Roger stood quickly and
immediately swayed as he was hit with a wave of
not-awake-yet dizziness.

Then he was hit with a wave of Elsie: the nymph
leaped to him and embraced him. "Did *you* do this?"

"I don't know." He blinked, owlish, at the tableau of
the oversized mat and the gigantic clay furniture. "I
think maybe I did . . . without knowing it."

Then he became aware that he was holding a full-size,
half-dressed, sweet-smelling, very affectionate young

woman. She looked at him, happiness in her eyes and smile, so exquisite that he found it hard to breathe.

Carefully, he circled her with his arms and drew her tighter to him. Her expression changed, curiosity intruding on her delight, as he leaned down to kiss her.

Awkward at first, she returned the kiss . . . but hers was the kiss of a fond sister or a trusting daughter. Roger felt a wave of irritation pass through him. Whatever she felt for him, it was not an adult's attraction, not yet. He broke the clinch, not willing to press the issue.

"Listen . . ." His voice was a little hoarse and he cleared it before continuing. "Let's rustle up some grub — that is, find something to eat — and then I'm going to play with the clay some more. See if I can deliberately make something happen. Maybe after that we can find a way home."

After further depleting Tricia's stock of fruits — Elsie heartily ate a normal woman's share — they left the hut. Roger carried a small floor mat and several pounds of clay that had once been the arms of his toy rocking chair.

The village was quiet but not asleep. A tribesman with a crooked leg built a fire in the center of the village. Roger could see several women carrying pots and baskets, mending things, crafting things; children played between the huts and, from the sound of it, in the near fringe of the jungle. The natives kept a wary eye on Roger and Elsie; Roger waved cheerfully at them.

"Sexist of me, I suppose," Roger said. "When I dreamed this place up, I imagined the men out hunting during the day, the women staying behind, gathering fruit and doing domestic things. A few years later, I think I would have made it all a little more egalitarian."

"What does that mean?"

"Just that I used to buy into old-fashioned values a little more than I do now. Men worked, women stayed home and kept house. That wasn't the law, it was just the way things worked, or so I thought back then."

Roger saw confusion cross her face. "Look, you'll figure it out . . . with time. There's no way to cram the whole Life In Modern America handbook into your head in two painless minutes. Keep asking questions . . . and I'll try to figure out if there are any answers for them."

At the edge of the trees, he found a patch of bare shady ground and got to work.

With threads pulled from the hems of his pants and shirts, and twigs and pieces of wood whittled into shape with his pocketknife, he constructed the frame, about two feet long by one foot high and wide.

It fell over when he wasn't supporting it. But when he and Elsie applied clay to the four sides, it stood strongly upright, and began to look like the village huts. Roger cut the grass mat with his pocketknife and had a ready-made thatch roof; once it was in place, he pegged it to the clay frame with sprigs of grass and spikes whittled from twigs.

What else? He cut some more pieces of grass mat to scale, then slid them into the hut as miniature bed mats. He tore strips of cloth from his shirttail, pegged one over the doorway and the rest over the small windows. Then it was done — a clay and thatch hut, perfectly suited to people twice the height Elsie used to be.

"Now what?" asked Elsie.

"I'm not sure." Roger lay on his stomach in front of the model hut, then scooted back a couple of feet for a better view. Elsie lay beside him and propped her head on her hands the way Roger did.

By blurring his eyes and holding his head at just the right angle, he found it easy to imagine the toy hut as a full-size dwelling, yards away instead of mere feet from him. So he held that pose and waited for something to happen.

"Elsie," he said, "I've been meaning to ask . . . you said you could feel things. You felt winds and bees and stuff. Can you feel anything else? Like, where you came from? The piece of bristol board I drew you on, back in my apartment?"

"Hmmm." She thought about it, then closed her eyes. She held herself still and breathed slowly and deeply for a full minute. Finally: "No."

He glanced at her. "No? Just like that?"

She opened her eyes, shrugged. "No, just like that. I can't feel any board. There are lots of men hunting out in the jungle, and many more animals who want to escape them. It will rain later today. But I can't feel any pieces of bristol board. Can you?"

"Nope."

She waited a beat. "How do you know? Did you try?"

"Nope."

She paused another moment, as if waiting for him to elaborate. "Well, *I* tried. You could try. How can you know you can't do something if you don't try?"

"God, you sound like my father." He fixed her with a glare, but she only giggled. "Oh, all right." He sighed, crossed his arms, and lowered his head upon them, eyes closed.

It took him a little while to relax into what he was doing. Psychically searching through unseen cosmos for a blank piece of bristol board sounded damned foolish, but he'd subjected Elsie to it; he might as well take his own medicine.

He could feel the rough ground he was lying on, warmth from Elsie beside him, a faint breeze stirring the bushes around him; he could smell the scents of this jungle — flowering plants, forest mulch, all smelling much nicer, he imagined, than any real jungle; he could hear insects buzzing, unseen things scrambling deeper in the trees, the crackling of the fire being started in the village.

But bristol board? He decided that a badger made of bristol board could walk right up to him and bite him where it counts, and he'd never feel it coming. On second thought, in this place, he'd better not have any such ideas; a mean-tempered badger might just appear.

Blank piece of bristol board . . . maybe that was the problem. All the work he'd put into that drawing was now lying right beside him, or was buried under a tidal flood of black ink. He no longer had a clear idea of what it looked like. Maybe one of his other works . . .

He switched his thoughts to the "Lava Demon" painting and called it up in his imagination. There it hung, fuzzy and indistinct, but much as he remembered it: the glowing eyes, the baboon face, the hideous grin, the ominous bulk of the demon.

He found himself irritated with the indistinctness of the image; ill-remembered areas of the canvas, around the edges and corners, were just fuzzy blotches of color. He concentrated on them; he tried to remember where each final brush stroke had fallen, what every square millimeter of it had looked like when he'd finished. . . .

Bit by bit, it came into focus. The lower edge focused into clean lines, showing lava until it disappeared out the bottom of the canvas. Middle left, a lava splash erupted into the air, rising nearly to the demon's shoulder. He could almost feel the canvas beneath his fingers.

Then he *could* feel it. Somehow his fingers brushed over the rough acrylic surface of the painting he knew so well. He could feel that it was buried under other canvases; he thought he caught a whiff of the musty scent of his mildewed carpet. All he had to do was take a step toward it, grab Elsie's hand and draw her with him —

"Roger! Your hut!"

He cursed as Elsie's shriek jarred him back, and he glared over at the nymph. But her attention wasn't on him; she stared ahead, wide-eyed.

His hut now stood a dozen yards away. It was twelve feet high and built as sturdy as a fortress. Patches of stained white cloth hung over the windows and doorway, fluttering in the breeze. The little hut that had been within arm's reach was gone.

His irritation was swept away by surprise and elation. He rose; Elsie was on her feet before he could extend a gallant hand to help her up.

"I ought to be freaked out," he told himself as much as Elsie. "But I think I'm getting a handle on this. We're going to take a quick look at my new hut . . . and then we're going to try to go home. You game?"

Elsie frowned over the question, but took it in context, and was relieved to understand that he wasn't asking her if she belonged to a species stalked by hunters. "I'm game." She smiled.

The hut was sturdy but crude. There were gaps where the roof met the upper edge of the wall, and the roof really needed to be lashed down more securely. The sleeping mats inside were impossibly thick and heavy, with rough, jagged edges.

Roger stood in the center of it and grinned stupidly for a while. At last he'd succeeded at something he set out to do.

"Roger?" Tricia's voice. She parted the shirttail curtain across the door and entered, looking around somberly. "Is this your new hut?" She looked no more surprised than if she'd found him wearing a new pair of pants.

"Yep."

Hope, undisguised, crept into her voice. "So you're staying?"

"Nope. I think we'll" — he put the slightest bit of emphasis on the last word "— be leaving pretty soon. But if I come back to visit, I'll stay here."

"Oh. Okay." She gave him a sad look and glanced at the full-size Elsie without apparently noticing the changes to the nymph. "Bye." Then she slid out and was gone.

Roger shook his head. This wasn't the real Tricia, even as she'd been in high school. In the unlikely event that the real Tricia had ever wanted him, she'd never have given up on him so meekly, so easily. He'd created her with no goals, no strength of her own, and she was just a wretched thing.

He looked at Elsie. "I didn't have anything in particular in mind when I created you, nothing except looks and legends about nymphs," he said, more for himself than for her.

"I don't understand."

"Don't worry about it. Let's go home."

He lay on his sleeping mat, one hand behind his head, the other holding Elsie's hand as she lay snuggled next to him.

This time it was easier to imagine his painting. The "Lava Demon" canvas popped up in his mind, almost complete, marred by only a couple of out-of-focus sections. He went to work on them, recalling their original lines, forcing them into focus.

In a couple of minutes the painting hovered before him, floating in the sea of reddish darkness behind his closed eyelids. Nervously, he reached for it. . . .

His outstretched fingers brushed the rough acrylic surface of the painting. He felt it as if it were right there; he could again smell the musty odor of his apartment. He needed to go there.

Roger felt light-headed for a moment . . . but the painting disappeared, dissolved away under his fingers.

He cursed. All that effort — and he'd failed.

Frustrated, he yanked his right hand out from under his head and banged it on the sleeping mat.

It wasn't a sleeping mat. It was carpet. He opened his eyes, but it was too dark to see.

Then the light came on. It was the artist's lamp clamped to his drafting table, a few feet directly over his face, pouring bright incandescent light into his eyes.

A man's voice, gruff and astonished. "Rog?"

Roger's stomach went cold. *"Dad?"*

Chapter Four

Hidden Details

"Where have you been?" roared the voice behind the light, like God Himself demanding an answer of Moses. "And who the hell is this?"

Roger scrambled to his feet. It took longer than he expected; as he rose, sudden exhaustion nearly made his knees give way. He forced himself upright; once his head was above the dazzling light from the desk lamp, he blinked to clear his eyes and stared down at his father.

C.J. Simons, though a bit shorter than his son, was what Roger knew he'd look like in forty years: he had the same dark eyes, the same height to cheekbones and angle to the chin. He also had a glare like Roger's and turned it on his son. "Well? I'm waiting for an answer!"

Roger felt his cheeks burn red as he remembered thirteen years ago, the bad, testy times after his mother's death. . . . Roger caught necking on the couch with a girl from his class, his father's unexpected return, his father's bellow, "I'm waiting for an answer!"

He kept his voice nearly polite. "This is my place, Dad. You want to ask questions, do it in a civil —"

"You do *not* speak to your father that way —"

"The hell I don't. Look around you. 'Under my roof, we do things my way.' Remember that? This is my roof." Roger discovered that his shoulders were hunched up; he forced them back down.

C.J. glared a moment longer, then snatched up his

slacks from the drafting table chair and began pulling
them on; he was dressed only in underwear and
undershirt. "You've gotten way too big for your
britches, mister. I — oh, my God, the girl has her tit
hanging out. Roger, tell this girl to stuff herself back in
her dress."

Elsie was still sitting on the floor, staring wide-eyed
at the arguing men. C.J. pointedly turned his back on
the two of them.

Roger sighed, extended a hand to help Elsie up, and
led her over to the closet. "We're going to find you a
T-shirt. If I have one clean." He rummaged through
the hangers, found a red extra-large printed with the
image of the starship *Enterprise*, and quickly helped
her pull it on over her other garment. It fit her like a
tent.

"Why is that man so mad?" she asked in a whisper.
She wasn't frightened the way she'd been when Roger
was angry . . . but she was curious, perhaps a little hurt.

"Because he thinks he has a right to be. He's my
father, and he thinks he's still raising me." Roger
turned back to his father, who was pulling on his own
shirt. "All right, Dad, the apartment is rated PG again."

"About time." C.J. faced them again; he was still
glaring. "Now, are you going to tell me where you
were?" Somehow, he didn't seem as menacing as he
should. He looked smaller than the last time Roger had
seen him, six months ago; his face was more hollow.

Roger moved to sit at the drafting table. C.J. Simons
was the world's greatest lie-detector, and that left
Roger with three choices: tell his father a lie without
even pretending it was the truth, tell him it was none
of his business, or . . .

"Sure. I'll tell you the truth, the whole truth, and
nothing but. But first, I'd really appreciate it if you'd
tell me what you're doing here." Roger pulled a piece
of bristol board from a pile and grabbed a set of black
markers from a coffee mug.

"Rog, are you drawing? Now?" The old man's glare became a scowl of confusion. "Son, I really begin to wonder if you're over the edge."

Roger smiled thinly but didn't answer. He chose a heavy-point marker and got to work, outlining big inverted-U eyes with soulful black pupils, floppy ears, a black blotch of a nose. "Yeah, me too, Dad. But please. Why are you here?"

"Your suicide note, Rog."

Roger jerked upright and turned to stare at C.J. The old man was serious. He settled down on Roger's mattress and looked at his son with none of the anger of a few moments ago. Now, his expression was one of loss and confusion.

"Dad, I didn't write a suicide note."

"It was written on your typewriter. The police confirmed it."

"The police — my typewriter? You mean that old Royal you had in World War II? I haven't had it out of the closet in the last ten years."

C.J. looked across the room, at the end table set up between two bookcases, and Roger looked, too. All the books that had been on the table were now scattered on the floor. His father's 50-year-old upright Royal sat in the middle of the table. All Roger could say was "Oh."

"The note said you couldn't live with it any more. . . ." The old man's voice became raspy with emotion. "With everybody hating you and your art . . . you were going to drive away and jump into a river where they'd never find you. You stapled the note to your front door and drove off. That's what the police said. . . ."

Roger turned away, unaccustomed to all the emotion in his father's face. "I didn't write that note," he said, subdued, and then the flash of anger hit him. Achilles and Penthesilia must have written it, or transcribed words written by Kevin, and left it to account for Roger's disappearance. Kevin Matthews didn't care who might be devastated by it.

Roger concentrated on the drawing before him, blocking in the roly-poly body, too-big paws, short pointed tail, the large black spots. A fast cartoon technique; he hadn't used it in several years and was pleased that he hadn't lost it. "Stapled to the door? Dad, I was always under the impression that suicides tended to leave the note in the typewriter, or put it in an envelope on the mantle, or grip it in their dying moments when the poison hits — that sort of thing."

"Roger, don't joke about this."

"It is a joke, Dad, and a really nasty one. But not mine." Roger switched to a finer point and began filling in details: curved lines near the nose and tail to show motion, teeth in the grinning, half-open mouth, toes in the paws. "Anyway, I never wrote that note.

"What I did do was draw a picture. Of her." He pointed at Elsie, who was rummaging through the knickknacks on top of Roger's dresser near the foot of his mattress. She smiled at him, then returned to her investigation of a crystal prism. "The picture came to life for a little while. Then I colored it in, and it came to life for good. That's who Elsie is, Dad. A picture I drew that came to life."

He spared his father a look. The old man's face froze in an interested "Oh? Tell me more" expression, but his eyes said something else. In his eyes, C.J. looked as haunted as though his son really had died. Roger winced. The last thing he wanted was to let his father think he was insane; best to get this over with quickly.

"Anyway, I told this to an old friend of mine, an artist — Kevin Matthews, I'm sure you remember him. He sent over a couple of guys he'd pulled out of one of *his* paintings, and they tried to kill me. They wanted to put me into one of Kevin's paintings, but I ended up in one of my own. Elsie went with me. My guess is that the guys who tried to kill me typed the note.

"So we wandered around in the painting for a while, and then got out, and we got back home just in time for you to jump us." He switched to a broad-headed marker and began blacking in the circles representing big spots on the body.

Pained, C.J. turned to Elsie. "Miss, what's your take on all this?"

"My take?" She looked over her shoulder and smiled at him. "Oh, what did I see? Roger hasn't told it very well at all. He left out the demon and the hot tunnel and the dancing men and the nasty girl and the hut that got big. Oh, and me getting tall. I used to be this big." She held out two fingers and measured off two inches, then four, and then decided she couldn't remember just how tall she'd been; she shrugged.

C.J. closed his eyes, his face settling into tired, tired lines.

Roger finished filling in the black spots and looked down at what he'd rendered: a good, cartoony Dalmatian puppy, grinning, hunched down in front, rear end high, tail wiggling like mad. Roger blew on it to dry the last of the ink . . . and then *looked* for the puppy as he'd once looked for Tricia's emotions.

He felt it almost immediately: a bundle of exuberance, happiness and energy, waiting underneath the smooth surface of the bristol board.

"Dad, I know you think I'm crazy." Roger looked back over his shoulder and gave his father a conspiratorial grin. "Which I am. Just like you're about to be. Come here a second and I'll show you something. You'll lose all desire to call the Sanity Police."

C.J. slowly rose and walked over, never quite losing the defeated expression of a father whose only son has run off to join the daffodils.

Roger touched the board again and felt beyond its smoothness, beyond the reek of the marker ink.

He tugged and the puppy came right up out of the page. It landed on all four paws, looked at Roger, wagged its tail, barked sharply, and then ran around in a circle. It was a Dalmatian puppy no more than six inches long, much more cartoony than realistic. It ran full tilt toward the edge of the table, then skidded to a halt, its expression comically frightened, and barely managed not to slide over the lip; it backed away and scampered to the safety of the center of the table.

Roger felt what he expected — the wave of tiredness that always seemed to hit when he used this whatever-it-was ability. Prepared for it, he managed not to slump; then he looked at his father. The old man was frozen, watching the puppy's every move, even when the delighted Elsie reached down to pet the cartoon animal. "Rog . . . Roger . . . *How did you do that?*"

"I've told you that already, Dad. I drew it, then I made it real. You know I used to like stage magic, mime, that sort of thing. . . ."

"Yeah?"

"So you know there's no way I could have done this like a coin from behind your ear or a scarf in my sleeve."

C.J. finally looked at Roger again, his expression all incredulity. "Son, when I was a combat photographer in the Big War and Korea, I saw some pretty strange things."

"You've told me."

"I've never seen anything like this. Never."

Roger nodded. "Me either, before the other day. Now I've seen things that are lots stranger."

"Can you do it again?"

"I'm pretty sure."

"Wait, wait, let me get my camera."

Roger waited until his father unpacked his Nikon. Then Roger took the puppy away from Elsie, who let out a disappointed "Awww." He put the cartoon canine back on the bristol board, petted the wriggling thing . . . and tried gently to press it back into the blank white surface from which it came.

It sank with a baffled little "Yip!" of surprise and Elsie jumped as C.J.'s flash went off. A moment later, the puppy was a drawing once again, but posed differently: sitting down, looking comically startled. Roger picked up the board, turned it around to show that there was nothing behind it, then grinned at his father. "Get set for another picture."

C.J. did. Roger put the drawing down and touched the puppy within. But as he tugged, he imagined the dog being twice as large as before.

The Dalmatian emerged again. And it was larger, heavier, harder to drag out of the page. It gave a little yelp of pain as Roger dragged it out by its ear — and another as C.J.'s flash attachment went off, blinding it. A moment later, its good humor restored, it stood wagging its tail on the blank sheet of bristol board . . . but this time it was a foot long, eight times as heavy as before. It barked again, deeper and louder.

Roger grinned conspiratorially at his father. "Think I ought to give Disney a call? Here, let me give you a better angle." He rose and stepped aside . . .

. . . and grayed out. His vision collapsed to a dark tunnel; he fell before he even knew he was off balance.

But he didn't hit hard. He felt Elsie's arms catch him and lower him down; her strength surprised him. A moment later, she had his head on her lap and shook him, calling his name; C.J. knelt alongside. "Boy, are you all right? Don't move. I'll call the ambulance —"

"No ambulance." Roger opened his eyes. "All of a sudden, I'm so tired I can't see straight. Fiddling with the paintings this way wears you out fast. . . ." Then he yelped as something warm and slick lapped against his cheek: the tongue of the cartoon Dalmatian. The dog was as worried as C.J. and Elsie. Roger grinned and scratched it behind the ears.

C.J. shook his head again. "You were gone some-where strange for a couple of days. Who knows what that did to you? You could've caught something, been hurt, I don't know what. You need a doctor."

With Elsie's help, Roger eased himself into a sitting position. His exhaustion was fading. "Dad, I don't want a doctor to see me. I don't want anybody to see me. If Kevin Matthews hears that I'm back —" He gave his father a sharp look. "What do you mean, a couple of days?" He looked at his watch, which told him that it was Friday afternoon.

"A couple of days." C.J. shrugged. "The police say the last anyone saw of you was at some bookstore Thursday afternoon."

"Right. So?"

"So one of your neighbors found the . . . suicide note Friday morning. The police didn't get around to calling me until Saturday afternoon and I drove straight here."

Roger looked at the watch C.J. wore. No digital piece of junk, it was a finely crafted Swiss watch that gave the time of day and the date . . . and told him that it was about 2 A.M. Sunday morning. "Too weird. Listen, Dad, I have to know. Do you believe what I told you?"

C.J. looked at him, then at the cartoon Dalmatian puppy now wiggling around in Elsie's lap where she sat on the floor. "I guess so. I believe you can make cartoon dogs, sure. But the rest . . . getting thrown into paintings, creating young girls . . . I don't know what to think."

"But are you willing to accept it as a working hypothesis?"

C.J.'s expression turned serious as he thought through his son's words. Finally he nodded, grim. "I suppose I don't have much of a choice."

"So if we assume everything I've said is true, then Kevin Matthews wants me dead. Once he knows I'm back, he'll try to get me again."

"I guess that's a necessary assumption. Son, tomorrow morning, I'm going to get my gun and I'm going to stay with you until all this is done. We'll get the police —" He grimaced and cut himself off before Roger could interrupt. "Never mind. That's stupid. 'Officer, I have a problem, guys out of paintings are trying to kill me.' They'd lock *you* up.

"Of course, you could show them what you do. Then they'd have to believe you."

Roger nodded. "They'll also want me to hang around while they make some calls. The feds would be very interested in what I can do. My guess is that they'd want to take me away and *tell* me what to do. So if they're sharp enough to protect me, the government owns me for the rest of my life — or I have to start running from them, too. And if they're not that good, Kevin kills me.

"Forget about your gun, forget about tomorrow. I'm getting out of here tonight. And you need to stay here and pretend that I'm still missing, so the cops and Kevin Matthews will think you have no idea where I am."

"Where will you go?"

Roger had to think about that for a moment. "First, I need to talk to someone. I think Kevin's been messing with her life, too. Then I get out of town for a while. Figure out what I can do . . . and how to defend myself.

"You said my car is missing? They probably stashed it somewhere. I need to borrow your car, at least for a while." He grinned. "Dad, can I have the keys to the car?"

Roger and C.J. packed. They dumped a few days' worth of clothes into a piece of soft-sided luggage, collected Roger's tackle boxes full of art supplies, and slid every painting and drawing they could find into Roger's large zippered portfolio. Roger put the piece of bristol board from the drafting table onto the floor, lured the wiggly Dalmatian cartoon onto it, and — with a feeling of regret that surprised him — pushed the puppy back into the board. Immediately after, he felt tired again, but didn't stand until the sensation passed. The drawing went into the portfolio.

C.J. handed over his keys and a small wad of bills from his wallet, folded around a couple of credit cards. "You may need this."

Roger looked at the little bundle as he took it. "I always felt bad taking money from you. Like it was because I'd screwed up. This time, I really don't. It's different."

"This time, you haven't screwed up." C.J. managed an uncertain smile. "And this time, I expect you to pay me back."

Roger smiled in return, and a moment later was surprised to find himself hugging his father, their first embrace in a dozen years.

Less than an hour later, Roger and Elsie shivered in the wind as they stood on the porch of Donna Matthews' house. At least, that's where Roger thought he was; he hadn't visited in a couple of years, and Donna might have moved. Even in the darkness, he could see where paint peeled from the house's wood siding and where weeds as tall as Elsie stood in the front yard. The house now really belonged to this neighborhood, with its sea of chain-link fences, cars up on blocks, and untended yards.

Grimacing, Roger pressed the doorbell for the fourth time and hoped that when the door opened it would be Donna on the other side and not some bleary-eyed cracker with a shotgun.

"There is a thumping inside," Elsie told him matter-of-factly. Roger hadn't heard anything but the muffled doorbell. "Someone is walking. . . ."

A light went on inside, and a moment later Roger stepped back as hands fumbled with locks on the other side of the door. The door opened a crack, and Roger could see Donna — one eye, anyway, and part of her cheek and mouth. Her expression brightened a little. "Roger? Do you know what time it is?"

He put on an apologetic expression and nodded. "I know. It's kind of an emergency. It couldn't wait."

She unchained the door and opened it. Then her expression closed down as she caught sight of Elsie. "And who is *this*?"

"Look, can we talk about it inside? I'm freezing, and this really is important. You'll think so, too, when you hear me out."

Donna paused, then muttered, "Oh, all right." She let the two of them inside.

Roger took a look around her living room. He didn't like what he saw.

The garage-sale furniture was all familiar, but Donna never used to let crumpled hamburger sacks, junk-food wrappers, and leaning stacks of unopened mail pile up this way.

Donna's paintings were still up on the walls. Hers were all watercolors, pastel in tone. In one painting, Ramses II and Nefertari embraced in the Pharaoh's chariot; in another, a pirate king and a 17th-century demoiselle locked in a romance-paperback clinch. But where Kevin's paintings had hung, there were still blank spaces, and not one of Donna's paintings was new to Roger.

And the place smelled bad. Food was decaying somewhere, and clothes badly needed to be washed. Booze of some sort had been spilled recently. Roger shook his head, trying and failing to see Kevin and Donna's neat, lively home under this mess.

Donna retied the sash of her blue robe before she faced her guests. She gave Elsie a long look before turning to Roger: "Been cruising the high schools?"

Roger scowled and felt his cheeks growing warm. "That's uncalled for. This is Elsie. Elsie, this is Donna. Donna, I really need to talk to you."

"So talk. So sit." Donna flopped down into a brown

overstuffed chair whose split seam poured beige stuffing onto the seat; she arranged the hem of her robe, then looked back at Roger. "Is this about what happened at the bookstore? I mean, that was cute, but not cute enough to drop by at three in the morning."

"Nothing like that." Roger found a place on the couch where no trash was piled. "I need to talk to you about Kevin."

"Forget it, then." Donna turned away from him. "Now what's she doing?"

The nymph was hopping up and down on one foot, her knees pressed together. Caught in the act, she looked desperately at Roger. "I need to go outside and find a bush. I think it was the cold air. . . ."

Donna rolled her eyes. "You don't need to make a big production of it. Bathroom's through there." She waved at the door to her bedroom.

Elsie looked confused. "I was not talking about a bath."

Donna frowned. "She's kidding, right?"

Roger cleared his throat, uncomfortable. "Well, not really. I don't suppose, uh, you could show her your bathroom? How to use it, I mean?"

"*You're* kidding, right?"

He shook his head. "Elsie's, well, not used to . . . things."

"Things." Donna fixed him with a look that was part aggravation and part confusion, then stood. "Sure, Roger. No problem." She flounced over to her bedroom door, pushed it open. "This way, Elsie. Roger, you're a lousy guest."

The women were gone a few minutes. Roger had a look around, seeing the dozens of half-read paperbacks in the bedroom, the nearly empty refrigerator, the broken TV set that showed only static for the minute he left it on. He settled in his seat again before Donna and Elsie emerged. Donna looked aggrieved; Elsie looked hurt every time her gaze fell on Donna.

Donna barged her way back to her own chair. "I get it, Roger. You're not just cruising high schools. You're cruising high schools for the head-injured."

"Knock it off. She's from . . . far away." He shoved some of the sofa's trash further away from him, then patted the new empty space beside him, an invitation for Elsie to sit. She did, still looking crestfallen. "Donna, you have to listen to me. This is important. The same day I saw you, Kevin tried to have me killed."

She gave him a scornful look. "Yeah. Sure. Kevin Matthews, Mafia illustrator. Roger, you're a raving paranoid."

"I also think Kevin arranged my trouble with Nonesuch Books. And maybe the same applies to you — he's probably pulled strings to keep *you* from working." He leaned forward and his tone became more conspiratorial. "Hasn't it occurred to you that as soon as he got big and successful, both of us, the two artists who were closest to him, got to watch our careers dry up?"

Donna shook her head. "Neither one of us needs to blame Kevin for that. You screwed up and got yourself blacklisted. And me . . . I don't know how to do anything *but* art, and I can't even do that anymore."

"Why?"

She ignored him.

"No, please. What did you mean?"

Donna looked away and drew a deep breath. After a long moment, she turned back to him, reluctance in her expression. "I think it's just the living alone, Roger. I lived with my parents, I lived with roommates in college, I lived with Kev . . . until last year, I'd never lived alone."

"I don't get it. Living alone keeps you from working?"

"I'm just a mess, Roger. I don't sleep well. I . . ." Her voiced trailed off for a moment and she looked past

Roger, through the wall, out to some great distance. "You know I've always been a big fan of Edgar Allan Poe."

"I remember." Roger glanced at the far wall, at her painting of Poe at a writing desk. In the painting, menacing characters flowed off the writer's quill pen, spilled off the side of the desk to the ground and ran off in all directions.

"I hear things, Roger. When I'm trying to fall asleep. All of them out of Poe." She looked down at the floor; no, beyond it. "Sometimes I hear Fortunato being bricked into the cellar, and I can hear him cry out, 'For the love of God, Montresor!' with all the despair in the world in his voice. Of course, we don't have a cellar . . . *I* don't have a cellar. I hear 'a tapping, as of someone gently rapping, rapping at my chamber door.' Well, at my back door and my window, actually, but there's never anything there. And then . . ." She took a deep breath, pulled her robe more tightly around her.

Roger felt the hair stir on the back of his neck, on his forearms. He rubbed his arms to rid himself of the feeling. Either Kevin had been at work on Donna . . . or she really was around the bend. "Go on."

She gave him a sidelong look. "Roger, if you ever tell anyone what I've told you, I'll say you're lying."

"I'm not going to tell anyone." He met her gaze and gave her his I'm-an-artist-and-I'm-studying-you stare, all evaluation and no judgment.

After a moment she looked again into the distance. "At night, I hear a heartbeat. Like *The Tell-Tale Heart*. Thumping away under my bed . . . I assume under my floorboards, like the story . . . this human heartbeat that *just won't stop*." She looked around wildly, fearfully. "I can't sleep, I can't think, I sure as hell can't work. Could you? I don't think so."

"Have you seen anyone about this?"

"What, a shrink? Who can afford one? I'm not a student anymore, I can't get any of that cheap counseling from the university health center —"

Elsie interrupted. "There *are* four hearts beating here. That is too many, isn't it?"

Roger and Donna both shut up and looked at her. Donna asked, "She's kidding, right?"

Roger shook his head. "I doubt it. Elsie, what do you mean?"

She shrugged. "I can hear four hearts beating in this room. One there," she pointed to Donna, "two on this couch," she pointed to Roger and herself, "and one beneath the couch."

Donna looked at her a moment more, then drew her legs up, tucking them under her, as fast as if Elsie had said there was a rabid rat under the couch.

Roger took a deep breath. "All right . . . show me."

His eye couldn't track Elsie's movements. One moment, she was sitting beside him on the couch, the next, she was on her knees, expression intent, one arm scrabbling around underneath that piece of furniture. Roger stood involuntarily and backed away a step.

Then Elsie rose with something in her hands.

It was a heart. A human heart, but bigger, twice the size of a normal heart, red and tough-looking as something out of a science-class illustration.

It had four limbs, short, stubby little legs ending in featureless nubs, all made of the same cardiac muscle. They flailed, vainly seeking purchase in the open air.

And it beat. The heart beat fast, frantically, loud enough for everyone to hear: *thump-THUMP, thump-THUMP, thump-THUMP, thump-THUMP* . . .

Roger felt reality slip away from him for a moment, but he clamped down on the sensation. "Good work, Elsie," he managed, his voice tight, then he turned to look at Donna. She sat stunned, looking at the thing in Elsie's hands.

"Donna. Donna, look at me!"

"Jesus H. Christ, that thing is real!" She finally

scrambled out of her chair, getting it between her and the heart.

"That's right. And it's something Kevin did. Do you understand me?"

"Something Kevin did." She nodded automatically, still looking at the heart. Then the stunned expression began to leave her eyes and she looked back at Roger. "Something Kevin did *to me*. What you were saying before. . . ."

Roger nodded. "He created this thing, he made it and put it here to make you crazy. Just like he screwed me over on Nonesuch Books. Do you believe me now?"

She didn't answer. She just looked back at the heart.

The heart swelled and deflated with each frantic heartbeat; its short, muscular limbs thrashed violently. Elsie was starting to lose her grip on it. "Just drop it," Roger said. "If it gets violent, I'll kick it through a wall."

She dropped the thing. It landed on its back, instantly rolled over to its feet, and scrambled madly into Donna's bedroom, disappearing under the bed. Donna watched it go; her expression was one of horror and disgust. "It really was under my bed, all this time. I'm *never* going to sleep there again. . . ."

Elsie's hands were clean; the heart's color obviously did not come off. Roger asked her, "Can you hear anything else? Anything from what we were just talking about?"

"No. No love-of-god-Montresors. No tapping. There *is* someone behind the house saying 'Nevermore.' He has a screechy voice. He started as soon as I grabbed the thing under the couch."

Roger looked at Donna. Her freckles stood out against the pallor of her skin. She gulped, then said, "*I'm* not going to look."

Reluctantly, Roger walked into the kitchen at the back of the house; Elsie and Donna followed. The back door was an old-fashioned type with a window; Roger threw the curtain aside and switched on the backyard light.

The yard was a jungle of waist-high grass and weeds. Above it, moving in and out of the light from the porch, was a bird — a raven, bigger than any Roger had ever seen, large enough to carry off a medium-sized dog. This close, even through the closed door, Roger could hear as it cawed, "Nevermore! Nevermore!"

Below the raven's orbit was a patch of earth that looked like a freshly dug hole, maybe six feet by three, a couple of feet deep.

Then, a few feet away, more earth began to heave. Something beneath stirred, pushed its way up through hard-packed earth.

It was a bare human arm, decayed, bone showing through the flesh. It was nearly white in the stark light from the floodlight, and it cast a shadow on the tall grass behind it. A second later, the other arm came up in a triumphant gesture. It held a guitar, an antique Fender dripping dirt clods.

Donna, wide-eyed, moved next to Roger and put her hands on the handle of a frying pan. The pan wasn't some sort of angry-housewife joke; it was a big, black, cast-iron skillet that could crack a man's skull.

"Concrete Zombies," Roger said in a whisper. "Donna, we've got to get out of here."

The Concrete Zombie guitarist stood out of its grave and looked at them, grinning like a skull.

Then the window beside the door shattered as something big hit it. A second zombie lunged in through the curtains and grabbed Roger by the wrist. A real rock'n'roll corpse it was, sickly strands of shoulder-length hair flopping around its head, tatters of black-leather pants and vest for clothes, studded wristbands on the rotting wrists. Shards of glass rained in; cold air washed through the room. Roger yelled and pulled away, but succeeded only in dragging the Concrete Zombie into the kitchen.

Backpedalling, Roger lost his balance and fell, and the Concrete Zombie landed on him. It bit at him, snapping at his face and throat, but he managed to brace both his hands against its neck, barely keeping its teeth away from his flesh.

Then Elsie straddled the zombie. She grabbed the thing around its forehead and eyes, hauled backwards; Roger shoved and the thing was dragged off him. It immediately turned to grab at the nymph, but she held onto its back, hanging on no matter which way it turned.

Roger made it to his feet fast. Through the door he could see the other members of the undead band. The guitarist was striding forward; the bassist, just free of the earth, shambled along behind; two more band members were erupting from the soil.

Roger threw himself at the zombie, shoved it and Elsie straight into the door, smashing the door's window out. Momentum carried all three of them half out the window, and Roger could feel a burning sensation along his side as broken glass ripped through his shirt.

But he got a hand under the thing's crotch and heaved up; Elsie let go as the Concrete Zombie spilled through the window onto the concrete porch. The thing landed with a gruesome splat.

"Everyone out!" Roger shouted. Elsie instantly ran past Donna and through the living room. Roger stumbled up to Donna, turned her around, and gave her a shove to get her started.

Behind, the Concrete Zombie made it to its feet, walked crashing into the back door. The shambling guitarist joined it. Another impact or two and that door would fly open . . . Roger ran after Elsie and Donna.

Elsie got the front door open, held it like a doorman for Donna to pass through. Roger wasn't quite to it when the back door crashed inward and he could hear clumsy, running footsteps.

He twisted the lock mechanism on the doorknob before pulling the door shut behind him. It was a gamble; if Kevin had made creatures as stupid as the zombies in the movies, maybe they wouldn't be able to unlock it; maybe they'd have to batter down the front door, too. Maybe it would cost them more time than it cost him.

He charged after Donna and Elsie to his father's car in the driveway. The keys were still in his pocket. Not like the movies. He yanked them out and got the door open immediately. Not like the movies.

Then something hit him in the temple and he crashed to the ground. It hurt so much he couldn't even grab at it; in those first seconds he couldn't so much as moan.

The gigantic black raven settled down beside his head, his blood on its beak, and steadied itself to peck through his eyes and into his brain.

Then it looked up and Donna's frying pan came down upon it. The blow smashed it to the ground, cracking its bones with clear, distinct snapping noises.

Donna stood over it, face twisted in anger, her tone harsh: "You son of a bitch." She brought the pan down on it again. *Crunch.* "You're going to drive me insane, are you?" *Crunch.* "Tap on my windows, tap on my doors, make me think I'm crazy?" *Crunch.* "Not tonight." *Crunch.* "Not any more." *Crunch.* "Nevermore." *Crunch.*

Elsie got a hand under Roger's elbow and helped him up. Her expression was frightened. "Roger, you're bleeding."

He put a hand to his temple, felt warm blood flowing. "Later." He fumbled the keys out of the door lock. "We have to go. . . ." He couldn't remember why.

The front door of the house boomed, and Roger realized he'd been hearing impacts there for a moment or two. It was so hard to think. He unlocked the car's left rear door so Elsie could get in, then sat heavily into the driver's seat. Everything around him seemed to be moving counterclockwise. He had to remember: shut the door . . . keys in the ignition. It was several moments before his father's venerable brown Lincoln roared into life, and he couldn't figure out why it didn't just immediately carry them all to safety.

Donna still pounded on the bloody mulch at her feet. That's when the front door came crashing open; five shambling things emerged and came stumbling toward them.

Elsie shoved Donna into the back seat and followed her, pulling the door shut as she'd seen Roger do. Roger got the car into gear — first gear. He rolled it straight into the garage door, killing the engine. The Concrete Zombies were on the car before he got it started again.

It didn't matter. Before they could smash in the windows, he got the engine going again, put it into reverse, and dragged the Concrete Zombies out to the street. Memory and reflex took over; he got the car into first gear, accelerated, ignored the stop signs, and the Concrete Zombies began dropping off.

Not one of them held on as far as fourth gear.

Chapter Five
Perspective Shot

Roger's head swelled like a balloon and then deflated with each beat of his heart. He reached up to grab it, to keep it from swelling, but he couldn't feel it change size from the outside. He could feel a bandage on his temple, though, and the realization that he was injured woke him.

He was in a motel room: twin beds, worn brown carpet, a color TV anchored to the wall by a flexible steel cable. Beside the window were a small circular table, a couple of chairs, and his suitcase. His portfolio leaned against the wall beneath the window and his tackle-boxes were on the table. Good. Whatever had happened, he still had his stuff.

The room's other bed was rumpled and there was a steady rainfall noise coming from beyond the closed bathroom door. That had to account for either Elsie or Donna.

Roger staggered up and found he was wearing only underwear, the bandage on his head, and another on his ribs. He made it to the sink in the alcove by the bathroom, saw his drawn features in the mirror, and splashed water on his face. Someone had thoughtfully put his toilet kit beside the sink; he found his aspirin bottle and swallowed a couple too many painkillers. But they didn't stop the pounding right away. He flopped back onto the bed to let the headache settle.

Then the door to the adjoining room opened and Donna walked in. Her jeans were dark and crisp, brand new; so were her blue-and-white-striped blouse and tennis shoes. She looked like a catalogue picture for casual wear . . . or would, if her expression weren't so serious. "Hi," she said.

Roger pulled the covers over his lower half, a reflex of modesty. "Hi yourself. Where the hell are we?"

"Lake Galloway."

"Where?"

She shrugged and moved into the room, leaving the adjoining door open. "Dinky little town way off the highway, about forty miles out of the city. You drove around at random for a while until we saw the vacancy sign. *You* checked us in. Don't you remember?"

He shook his head no, then winced as the movement made his head pound more.

"I'm not surprised. You got hit in the head. Really hard."

"The raven . . ." He put his hand to his bandaged temple and the memories washed over him. "Oh, man. The Concrete Zombies, your house . . ."

"My ex-house, you mean." She looked resentful.

"How did Kevin know I was there?"

"Well, your nymph and I talked about that. She thinks the raven and the zombies were already there, maybe for a long time, and that the bird woke the rest of them when she caught the heart. Kevin probably *didn't* know you were there."

"He does now, I bet. That was last night, right? I haven't been out for days, or anything?"

"Oh, no. That was just last night. It's Sunday now. As soon as we got you in here and bandaged up, you passed out. So Elsie and I stayed up talking until dawn and we passed out, too." Her expression became reflective. "Roger, the story she told . . . it's really true?"

"I don't know what she told you. But if it had Achilles and Penthesilia, and a demon in a volcano, and a South Seas island full of natives, and an angry old man with a camera, it's pretty much true."

"Jesus. I'd never have believed it."

"How about you? Where'd the clothes come from? You didn't go back to your house —"

"Nothing like that." She grinned at his sudden fright. "About noon, I got up and dug around in your bag, and found some clothes I could wear. Not much there, I can tell you. A T-shirt that was the bare minimum for decency, your thong sandals, which are about three inches too long for me — I was *not* the best-dressed woman in Lake Galloway. So I stole all your money and bought some clothes and things for Elsie and me at the five-and-ten-cent store down the block. Speaking of which, here's your change." She pulled a wad of bills and change from her pocket, dropped it on the table beside her. "Good thing about a town like Lake Galloway: everything's in walking distance.

"I also got a newspaper. Not the local weekly, the one from the city. Nothing about us in it." She shrugged. "Maybe we're not important enough to make the news."

"In that neighborhood? I doubt any of your neighbors even called the police, since we didn't leave any body parts behind or fire off mortar rounds.

"Listen, my father knows more or less what my situation is. But what happens when your folks try to get in touch with you and can't? They might file a missing-persons report. We could end up with both Kevin *and* the police after you."

Donna looked away and shook her head. "My folks and I aren't exactly on speaking terms, not for years. Don't ask. But that's not something we have to worry about."

They heard the shower being turned off; the shower curtain scraped across the rod. Donna glanced at the bathroom door. "She's a real case, you know."

Roger scowled. "How do you mean?"

"Oh, I suppose she's perfectly normal for a *nymph*,

Roger. But she doesn't know anything. Except that's not really true, either. I mean, she speaks English. The words she doesn't understand, she picks up out of context really fast. But she's so ignorant." She grinned wickedly. "I suppose you'll have to spend *lots* of time with her, teaching her what's what, how not to take candy from strangers, how to look both ways before she crosses the street —"

"Lay off, Donna."

"I've already managed her toilet training and shown her how to tie her new shoes. Sorry about that."

He shut his mouth and counted to ten before continuing. "Donna, we have to talk."

"What about?" She still wore her mocking smile.

"About Kevin. We have to assume that the Concrete Zombies told him I was at your place." He snorted. "Maybe they sang it to him."

Her expression became somber. "He'll be after us. I figured that part out already. That son of a bitch! How could he do that to me?" She drew a long, shuddering breath. "I spent the last three months thinking about sleeping pills, Roger. He wanted me to kill myself. Or to end up in an institution somewhere. I imagine he would have *gladly* paid for me to be put away. What did I ever do to him?"

Roger shrugged. "You tell me."

The bathroom door opened and Elsie emerged — but it was a very different Elsie. She was dressed in jeans, a blue T-shirt with Bruce Springsteen's face on it, and tennis shoes; her hair was still damp and she held a towel in her hands.

She wouldn't quite blend into a crowd of American teenagers. With her features, her slightly out-of-place pose and mannerisms, she looked like a delectable foreign exchange student, newly arrived. She looked nervously between Roger and Donna. "Is this right?"

Roger nodded approvingly. "Just right. You look fine."

Elsie smiled. She sat down on her bed and went to work on her hair with the towel.

Roger turned back to Donna. "A moment ago, I wasn't speaking rhetorically. What *did* you ever do to him? For that matter, what did I ever do to him?"

She looked thoughtful. "I don't know about me . . . but you were always a better artist than he was. Every time a magazine or book would come out with a piece of your color work on it, he'd buy it, study it for a day or two, try to figure out how you'd done everything in it; and he'd be gritting his teeth the whole time. He hated that. He hated the fact that he never caught up to you."

Roger considered that. "I think maybe you've named your own poison."

"How do you mean?"

"The same holds true of you. You were always better than he was. Maybe he resented you, too."

"But I was married to him!"

Roger shrugged. "So what? That might have made it even worse. Living in the same house with someone who was better than he was at his own profession. . . ."

"I don't think so. He was always very supportive. He always liked seeing new work from me."

"Yeah, very supportive. So tell me, what was Kevin best at?"

"Well, full-color work, I suppose. His line art was pretty bad —"

Roger shook his head. "No. He was best at *selling* his own work. He sold and sold and sold. No matter how many problems a piece of art had, he sold it, usually several times. That was his real gift. Right?"

"Well, yeah . . ."

"But not much of your work ever made it into print. Why didn't Kevin insist that you get a better agent?"

"Kevin *was* my agent. You know that. He . . ." She looked at Roger, frowning. "No. My style is pastel, very fine-line. There just wasn't much of a market for it. . . ."

"Or so Kevin said." Roger shrugged. "What if he was lying? What if he couldn't stand the competition, even from you?"

She looked down, studied the carpet. She was slow in responding. "I think we ought to have some soldiers."

"Come again?"

"Kevin has soldiers. Achilles and Penthesilia, and the Concrete Zombies, and Lord knows what else. He'll probably send them after us again. I think we need something like that."

Roger sighed. "Yeah, you're right. I'll get on it." He closed his eyes and leaned back. "I can't get used to the idea that there are people out there, hunting us. It's hard to think that way. I don't want to turn into a raving paranoid."

"Like I was." Donna stood. Her expression was bleak. "I have to go lie down for a while. We can talk about all this later." She returned to her room, closing the door behind her.

"When she is not angry, she is sad," Elsie said. She pulled the towel from her head; half-dry hair flopped across her eyes.

"She just has a lot on her mind."

"May I go to the lake?"

He looked at her and frowned. "What?"

"There is a lake nearby. People go there and swim and enjoy themselves. I would like to go, too."

"Uh, I don't think that would be a good idea. No."

She looked surprised. "But I have been in this little room for a long time . . . please, can I go?"

"Elsie, you're doing well, but you still can't pass yourself off as a normal American teenager. You open your mouth and people will know you're different. This could make people notice you, and then they'll notice Donna and me, and that will make it easier for Kevin to track us down."

She frowned, the first time Roger had seen her do

that. "I *want* to go to the lake. I will say very little. I will not talk about myself. I only want to walk along the shore and maybe swim."

"Do you have a swimsuit?"

"No . . . I do not need a suit for swimming. You saw me swim without one."

Roger felt his headache increase in strength; he covered his eyes with his hand. "Okay, look. You can go to the lake, you can walk around. But no swimming until we get you a swimsuit. And you have to be back before dark. Okay?"

"Okay." She hopped onto his bed, threw her arms around him in a happy embrace that sped his heartbeat . . . and made the pounding in his head still worse. "Thank you, Roger."

"Sure, sure. And look, if anything bad happens, just run away, run back here, okay? You know how to find your way back?"

"I know." She rose, grabbed a new San Francisco 49ers billed cap from a drawer, then opened the door. "Nothing bad will happen." Then she was gone.

Roger shook his head. He shouldn't have let her go . . . but shouldn't have had to make her stay, either. Things just weren't working out right. He sighed, then rose to get dressed. In spite of his condition, it was time to get back to work.

"What the hell is that?" Donna stood in the doorway to her room and stared wide-eyed at the dresser piled high with stacks of crisp new bills.

Roger sat at the table, sketching outlines on a piece of drafting film — semitransparent plastic that held paint very well. He didn't look up but did grin at her outburst. "Money."

"I know it's money. Where did it come from?" She moved to the dresser and pawed through the stacks.

Roger nodded to the piece of bristol board leaning against the wall behind the door. It was a watercolor painting showing the open doors of an armored car; inside the car were many well-stuffed burlap sacks. Another sack, this one real but empty, lay on the floor beside the dresser. "After we talked, I got to thinking about things we need if we're going to stay alive. Money was kind of high on the list. So are 'soldiers.' I'm working on one now. Anyway, I had a twenty, a ten, a five, and some ones left, and so they became models."

"You just painted money and pulled it into the real world?" She hefted a handful of twenties and another of tens. "Roger, that's counterfeiting!"

He nodded happily. "Very successful counterfeiting, too. The bills look and feel just like the real thing, they're sequentially numbered; I concentrated on all that kind of stuff when I was painting them. They're perfect."

She flipped through a stack of twenties, looking intently at the fine engraving and the differing numbers. "Okay . . . so they're good. But Roger, it's also wrong. Stealing."

Roger silently sketched in a few more lines on the figure before him, then looked at her. "Okay, sure. It's stealing. I've just ripped off the federal government for a hundred thousand bucks or so, assuming we spend this money, which I intend to."

"A *hundred thousand* —"

"Wait, wait, wait. I'm not through. Donna, with this ability, I can do a lot of neat things. Good things. I don't even know what all I can do; I haven't had enough time to think about it. But in order to do all this, I've got to stay alive. We have to persuade Kevin to leave us alone. And this is going to take things like lots of money and soldiers like Kevin has. Or we're dead. Right?"

"Well . . ." She wavered, looking at the bills in her hand.

"Make you a deal. You find out exactly how much

money there is in that pile. Keep an account of everything we spend. We'll call it," he grinned, "our 'drawing account.' When this is all over, we'll figure out some way to pay the government back . . . anonymously. Does that satisfy your sense of right and wrong?"

She thought about it, then nodded reluctantly. "I suppose so. It just seems wrong." She started to drop the twenties back onto the chest of drawers, then thought better of it and stuck one thick stack of them in her pocket.

"I guess we'll need to hide all that stuff before the maid comes in tomorrow. . . ."

She nodded. "Unless we want federal agents pounding on our door tomorrow afternoon, I think you're right. Uh, I'll buy a suitcase and we can stow it in the trunk of your car. What are you working on now?" She moved around to look over his shoulder.

"Captain Steele, the Man of Living Metal." Roughed out on the sheet of drafting film was a man of heroic build, stern eye and square jaw. His skintight costume was merely suggested at this point; no details had been sketched in. "I'm imagining him with a *lot* of power. The kind of guy who can pick up the *Nimitz*, project force fields strong enough to contain nuclear blasts, fly at light speed, that sort of thing. About a hundred times as powerful as Achilles and Penthesilia; he'd find it trivial to kick their asses."

"Is he out of a comic book?"

"No, I made him up. I was kind of worried about the preconceptions that come along with painting somebody else's character." Roger continued detailing Captain Steele's face, sketching in eyes that suggested keen intelligence. "Someone out of a comic book might be too good, or too neurotic, or something. I'd prefer to be charge of everything he can do and everything he thinks." He frowned; that had sounded more sinister than he intended.

"Sounds like something Kevin would say." Donna move to sit in the other chair. "I wonder why Kev hasn't created any superheroes to work for him."

"Maybe he has. Maybe we were too small and weak for him to waste a super-duper killer on. Or, maybe he just never thought of it."

"*That* sounds like Kevin, too. You know, that's the other thing he always hated about you."

"What's that?"

"That you had ideas all the time. He'd get an assignment for a cover, and if the publisher didn't tell him exactly what they wanted, down to the finest detail, he'd freak out. He couldn't come up with details the way you do. We'd sit around and have these brainstorming sessions that went on all night long. . . ."

"Oh, yeah, I remember that. From college. He hardly ever did art just to please himself, because he couldn't think of anything to do. I mean, he could reproduce a photograph, or paint a model sitting for him —"

"That's how I met him. I posed for him a couple of times. Back in the 'good old days.' "

"That's right. But I didn't realize the problem stuck with him."

"It got worse. Eventually he just started painting things out of mythology, or reading his fan mail and painting the things his fans wanted to see. He wasn't obliging them, exactly. He was taking ideas from them."

From outside the room, someone tried the door handle. Both of them jumped . . . and Roger decided he was the biggest idiot in the world. Why hadn't he painted a couple of firearms in the back of that armored car? If this was Achilles and Penthesilia, what was he going to do — thrash them with handfuls of money?

Then the someone on the other side of the door spoke: "Roger? I want in."

"Elsie?" Roger sagged in relief, then hurriedly opened the door.

She strode in cheerfully, her new jeans caked with sand and her T-shirt dirty. "It is dark, so I came home. I told you I could find it. I learned to play volleyball. I'm good at it, too."

Donna gave Roger a scathing look. "You let her go out?"

"Not now, Donna. Elsie, that means you . . . talked to people?"

She nodded energetically. "You were right. They asked where I came from."

He closed his eyes, shook his head sorrowfully. "And what did you tell them?"

"I told them to guess. They always guessed wrong and after a while they gave up. I bet they guess wrong tomorrow, too." She looked down at herself. "I didn't swim, so I need to go to the shower again," she announced — and marched into the bathroom without another word.

Roger, looking harassed, looked at Donna as he sat down.

"That's actually pretty smart," she admitted. "Odds are that nobody out there ever says, 'You're a painted nymph out of a picture.' And as long as she never tells . . ."

"Right, right. At least that's one crisis passed for the moment. And just so we'll be able to pass another one, I'm going back to work." He reached for his mechanical pencil and returned his attention to the drafting film.

The rest of Sunday night and all day Monday, Roger meticulously crafted his Captain Steele painting, making the superhuman hero as detailed and realistic as his materials would allow.

He also took a walk around Lake Galloway. It was a little farm town with a pretty lake and a lot of motels — the sort of place where people built summer lakeside homes or came to visit on weekends for water sports. He counted himself lucky; it was far enough out of the way that it might take Kevin some time to find them, but strangers were common and wouldn't cause undue talk. He did buy another city paper, but there was still no news of his "suicide" or Donna's disappearance.

Elsie discovered the wonders of TV. Roger steered her toward public television, and by Monday afternoon she knew her alphabet and could read simple sentences; he had to shake his head over the speed at which she learned. She also went out again for late-afternoon lakeside volleyball; Roger gritted his teeth and forced himself to let her go.

Donna kept mostly to her own room. On the occasions Roger noticed, it bothered him. Monday, after Elsie returned from beach games and headed off once again to the shower, he knocked on Donna's door.

"Come in."

He did, and found her sitting fully dressed on her bed, indifferently watching her television. "You doing all right?" he asked.

She snorted. "Oh, sure. Wouldn't you be? If I go home, my ex-husband finds me and kills me. If I stay here, I rot." She turned to glare at him. "Can you imagine how boring it is, sitting here, waiting for you to paint the son of Superman to come and save the day, and listening to you trying to screw up the courage to make a play for your little pointy-eared girlfriend?"

"Donna, that's not fair —"

"The hell it isn't. You've created your dream girl, Roger, just the way Kevin did, but you don't seem to know what you want to do about it. Your face lights up every time she comes in the room, but all you do is stumble around and sigh, and then go back to work. Right? And she doesn't even know what you have in store for her."

Roger leaned back against the doorjamb as if blown

back by the wind of her verbal attack. "Whoa, there. Let's get a couple of things straight. If you don't mind.

"I didn't create Elsie to *be* my 'dream girl.' Not the way we think Kevin did with Julia. I just drew a pretty girl and she came to life. Okay? So, I'm attracted to her. No big surprise there. Maybe something will come of it . . . but right now, to make a play for Elsie would be like . . . child abuse." He winced; that was the first time this thought had crossed his mind, but it was absolutely true. And aggravating as hell.

"As for the other thing: Donna, I didn't mean to make you into some sort of fugitive, and I'm not trying to keep you locked up here. But as long as you're here, you could be helping."

"Helping? Helping the Man with the Golden Brush? How?" She looked scornfully at him. "Roger, I just can't do what you do. I bought myself some brushes and paints — didn't know that, did you? They're in the chest of drawers. And I've tried to do what you do. All I get is a headache.

"I'm no use to you, and I'm no use to me. I was certainly no use to Kevin." She turned to stare at the television.

"No, don't tell me you can't help me. I've been working so hard on the money painting and Captain Steele that I haven't had time to think straight. I don't have time to figure out what we need if we're going to keep Kevin off our backs, or even to figure out all I can do. Maybe you can do that for me." It sounded good; he hoped it even sounded as though he'd thought about this before entering her room.

"What for? It's not like you're going to accomplish anything. Except counterfeiting."

Roger scowled. There was something so infuriating about that precise tone she used. . . . "What do you mean?"

She didn't look at him. "I mean, you didn't need Kevin to ruin your career. You could have done it all by yourself."

"My career was doing just fine until your husband —"

"It was not. Come on, Roger. Let's assume that Kevin did drop the big one on you with that Nonesuch Books deal. Where were you right before then? Nearly thirty, living alone in a rotten little apartment. You worked when you needed the money, and the rest of the time you doodled. What were you waiting for — some studio big shot to see one of your paintings on a magazine, and shout 'Eureka! This is the man I want to do all our posters from now on, for a million bucks a year!'? You have all the talent in the world, but you never had any discipline or ambition. You were going nowhere. Kevin just got you there faster."

"That's a lie." Roger felt like shouting it, but something held his voice in check — an uneasy feeling, like maybe she was right.

"Yeah, sure it is. You never got a normal job, so you'd have all your time available for your work. But then you never got an agent, so there wouldn't be anyone to *put* you to work. Compare that to Kevin, who has no real talent, but knew what he wanted to be, and hustled and hustled himself toward that goal.

"Then, of course, he found Merlin's magic wand, and so did you, and the two of you have conspired to ruin my life. Do you really wonder why I prefer *I Love Lucy* reruns to being with you?"

That stung. Roger felt his cheeks get hot. "You've done nothing but bitch for a long, long time. Maybe since before Kevin dumped you? Maybe that's actually why he dumped you? Couldn't stand the bitching all the time?" He realized what a low blow that was and winced as soon as the words left him.

She whirled on him, her expression hateful. "You bastard! *Get out.*" She grabbed the nearest thing at hand, the nightstand clock radio.

Roger threw up a hand to forestall her, said, "Wait, wait, *wait*."

Donna didn't. The radio hit Roger square in the

chest, and it hurt. He retreated in a hurry, got the door closed between them, and heard something shatter against it.

Elsie, toweling her hair dry, sat on her bed, facing him.

"How much of that did you hear?" he asked — quietly, so that Donna would not hear. There were no more crashes from the other room.

She was slow to answer. "Something about your golden brush." Her expression was a little nervous, though, and Roger didn't know what to make of that. Elsie continued, "She really doesn't like me, does she?"

Roger gave her a long look. Why would she ask that if all she'd heard was the last half of the conversation? But he moved around to her bed, sat heavily beside her, and shook his head. "She doesn't know you, Elsie. She'll get over it."

"What if she doesn't?"

"Then you two will never be friends. Just because two people are nice most of the time doesn't mean they'll be friends. Sometimes they'll hate one another."

"Like in politics."

He gave her a sharp look, then grinned. "You've been watching too much TV. Read a book instead. Yes, like in politics. If you can find any people in politics who are nice most of the time, that is." He shook his head and rose. "Back to work for me."

Both of them heard the exterior door to Donna's room open and close, and heard her walking away along the sidewalk. Roger sighed. What if she didn't come back? But running after her didn't seem like a good idea. He returned to his work and Elsie turned on the TV.

"Roger? You awake and decent?"

His eyes snapped open and he looked around. He was in bed; the motel room was dark but early-morning light crept in through the window; Elsie's bed and the bathroom were both empty — where was she? — and it was Donna talking to him from the other side of her door. He gave a just-awakened groan, sat up, and pulled on the pants he'd dropped beside his bed last night. "I am now."

Donna breezed in from her own room, looking altogether too awake; she clutched a roll of papers in her hand and took a look around. "Where's the nymph?"

"I don't know." He tried to think — had he told Elsie she could go out first thing in the morning? His thinking processes were still muddled.

He reached for yesterday's shirt, on the floor where he'd left it, but Donna imperiously kicked it out of his reach. "Oh, no, you don't," she admonished him; she moved over to the chest of drawers, pulled one of his shirts from the top drawer, and tossed it to him. "What is it with men and clothes all over the floor?"

Roger irritably pulled it on. "If God had meant to keep clothes off the floor, he would have invented lighter-than-air clothes," he griped. "Then I'd have clothes all over the ceiling. What got you up so early?"

"Work," she said, and waved her roll of papers at him. "I had some ideas, and —" Then her eye was caught by the painting on Roger's table. "Oh, you finished him!"

In the completed painting, the acrylic Captain Steele stood upright, his expression intense, jaw forward, pose bold. His costume was a silvery body stocking with black boots and floppy black over-tunic belted at the waist.

Roger nodded and stood. "He's ready to uphold Truth, Justice, and the Artistic Way. I'm going to pull him out today. This morning, since you woke me up before the crack of noon."

"Well, he's not bad-looking. Kind of classic Hollywood dark-and-square-jawed. Did you make sure he's straight?"

"What?" He blinked at her.

"Straight, Roger, is he straight?" She grinned at him.

"Uh . . . I actually didn't give any thought to his sexual preference. What would it matter?"

"Well, with my luck, he'll be straight but he'll share your tastes, meaning he'll go ga-ga after Elsie when she gets back."

Roger tilted his head and stared at her, trying to puzzle out her mood. She was sniping about Elsie as usual, but she seemed happy. "Donna, I'm not sure —"

"Relax, Roger. I'm just giving you a hard time. No sense of humor before morning caffeine?"

"No nervous system before morning caffeine." He finished buttoning his shirt and moved to stare down at Captain Steele, still distracted by Donna's question. He supposed he *could* determine the sexual preferences of the characters he brought to life, as part of the process by which he imagined them — but should he? And could he even avoid doing so, now that Donna had brought up the question?

"So, you're going to give him the Frankenstein treatment today?"

"Huh? Oh, yes." He shook his head to clear away distracting thoughts. "Might as well do it right now. I'd hoped Elsie would be here for it. Maybe I ought to look around for her. . . ."

"She'll be fine. She's a smart girl."

Roger gave her a quick look as she continued to stare at Captain Steele. Her last statement had been straightforward, with no mockery or insult in her voice . . . almost the first time it had been that way while she discussed Elsie.

He sat in his chair. "All right, then. Get ready to say hello to our first soldier. And goodbye to Achilles and Penthesilia." He brushed his fingers across the painting's acrylic surface.

It took him a moment to find the presence he was looking for: a suggestion of warmth, of energy, underneath his fingertips. It was so unlike the Dalmatian puppy he'd created . . . but Captain Steele wasn't a cartoon dog, he was a living robot with the power of an atom bomb. He *should* feel strange.

Roger settled deeper into his creative state, feeling his way further into the painting. There, he could sense crackling power and a physical presence. He stretched forward and his fingers encountered another hand, a human hand that was nonetheless hard and unyielding. The hand grasped his, firmly, but not crushing him. . . .

Roger pulled it toward him, toward the real world. But it was far heavier than the body of the Dalmatian puppy or the bag of money.

Distantly, he heard a screech like metal scraping across stone. Then he could feel the immensity of what it was he was trying to do: Captain Steele was massive, unmovable as an aircraft carrier, far heavier than a body of "living metal" should be. But Roger kept pulling. He began to feel his own power, the strength he used to pull his paintings into the real world; it was like a river of electricity coursing through him, speeding his heartbeat, making the hair on his arms and neck stand on end. He let the sensation wash through him; he tapped into that power as he hauled at Captain Steele's hand.

And then the strain was too much. Roger let go. The electricity snapped off as though a fuse burned out; the energy just yanked out of him. He jerked and fell back, his chair toppling . . . and that was the last he knew.

He heard Donna calling his name, but she sounded far away, and he didn't feel like answering yet. Much closer, someone was shaking him, annoying him.

Then Donna's voice was right in front of him. "Roger!" His eyes came open slowly and he looked at her. "Oh, Jesus, Roger, talk to me. Are you all right?"

He spoke, but his words came out more slowly than

they should. "Yeah. I think so. Just worn out, like before, only worse." He looked around. "Where's Captain Steele?"

"He didn't come out. Nothing did. You just threw yourself onto the floor. . . ." There was a high pitch of distress to her voice. She evidently noticed it, too, and modulated her tone. "You want to sit back up?"

"No, bury me here."

She hauled him up and set his chair upright; his legs were shaky and he was grateful to sit again.

Roger looked blearily down at the painting. "Nothing different. Nothing changed." Frustrated, he brought his fist down on the painting. "What's the matter, you son of a bitch? Afraid to come out into the real world?"

Donna stood and brushed off her knees. "What do you mean? He refused to come out?"

Roger sighed, then shook his head. "No. He was coming. I just couldn't pull him out. It was like . . . like trying to pull a car through a keyhole. I just couldn't do it. Captain Steele was . . ." He thought about it for a moment. "He was *too much power*, damn it. I could feel him, like he was this giant bottle of energy, and I couldn't make an opening big enough to drag him out. Then, when I couldn't take the strain any more and let him go, it wiped me out." He stared, angry, at Captain Steele's perfect features.

"You know, I think you just answered your own question."

"Which question?" He looked at her and tried to remember what he'd asked.

"Why Kevin didn't have any soldiers with godlike power to do his dirty work for him. Maybe he tried . . . just the way you did."

Roger nodded slowly, a glimmer of realization in his eyes. "And maybe he failed just the way I did. With a lightning bolt and a quick nap." He sagged. "Well, that's a couple of days' work down the drain . . . and now we know I can't come up with someone to wipe out Achilles and Penthesilia that easily."

Donna shrugged. "Then we just have to start at the bottom, the way Kevin did . . . but be better at it than he is. We can do that."

Roger looked puzzled. "That's kind of a change in tone from last night, isn't it?"

Donna looked abashed. "Roger . . . everything I said last night was the truth. No, hear me out. You *were* headed off into well-deserved obscurity, and it ticked me off to think of all that talent wasted. I'm not going to take back anything I said about that. On the other hand . . .

"The other night, at my place, you did wake up all the things Kevin had put there, but it wasn't your fault they were there. It was his. And then you got me away from them, in spite of being hurt, in spite of all the blood pouring down your neck . . . I'd have thought that Roger Simons would run off at the first sight of trouble, and you didn't."

"I wanted to."

"But you didn't. And while you've been here, you've been thinking about how to face Kevin, get him off our backs, instead of taking all that money you made and running off to South America. So . . . maybe you're not the Roger Simons you used to be. At the least, you're not the one I thought you were. So it's time for me to get to work, too."

Roger thought about it, then slowly nodded. "I'm glad to hear it." He pointed to her roll of papers. "That's the work?"

She nodded and spread out the roll of papers on top of Captain Steele. "After we talked, I went out last night and bought a lot of magazines at the mini-market. Gun magazines, hunting magazines, I'm-Such-A-Macho-Dude magazines, How-I-Killed-the-Godless-Commies magazines . . . they carry a *lot* of them here."

Roger stared down at the meticulous black-and-white illustrations. "This isn't your usual style."

"You didn't know I took drafting, did you? Unlike my ex, I know something about my trade other than how to sell my product." She pulled one drawing to the top. "This is the Browning Hi-Power. It's a semiautomatic pistol. It's not the biggest or the most powerful around — it was designed in the 1930s — but it's good and reliable. So the magazines say." She pulled up another sheet. "This is body armor, a combination of Kevlar and ceramic tiles. It'll stop a heavy bullet, and the ceramic plates will stop a lot of knives." She pulled up a third illustration. "The M16. It's the assault rifle they used in Vietnam, though this is the newer version of it."

As she pulled a fourth diagram to the top of the stack, Roger interrupted. "You've done a lot of work here. It'll take me forever to rerender this amount of detail . . . but it'll be worth it."

She shook her head. "First test: *Don't* rerender it."

"Why not? Are we just supposed to sit around and admire these?"

Donna grinned. "No. What I want you to do is color one or two of these pieces . . . and then try to drag them into the real world."

He stared down at the diagrams, perplexed. "Well, that'd be neat, sure. But what would it prove?"

"That we can collaborate, dummy. If I can do half the work, hand it over to you to finish up, and you can still pull it out of never-never land . . ."

Roger smacked himself in the head . . . not where his injury still throbbed. "Right. That'd cut our time in half. I'll get to work on these . . . and you can figure out what Test Number Two is going to be."

"Sounds good." She considered him for a long moment. "Roger?"

"Yeah?"

"I want you to teach me to do what you do. I'm not

going to just sit around and be protected for the rest of my life."

He looked at her soberly. "What if it can't be taught? I mean, if any artist could do it, wouldn't cartoonists rule the world?"

She grinned. "Have you looked at the world lately? Who says they don't?" Then she became serious again. "Maybe it isn't something I can learn. I want to try anyway."

Roger thought about it, then nodded. "Welcome to school," he said.

Less than an hour later, Roger pulled a heavy, gunmetal-blue Browning pistol, two extra clips of bullets, and two sets of Kevlar-and-ceramic body armor out of the piece of paper, leaving blank whiteness behind. Test Number One was successful; he could pull things out of collaborative paintings. But the collaboration didn't leave him any less tired; pulling the things from the painting was still exhausting.

"So it works," Donna said. "As long as you finish the painting, anyway. Later, we'll see what happens when you start a painting and *I* finish it."

But Test Number Two, pulling a vase and flowers off the cover of a paperback book bought in town, was a failure; Roger couldn't even enter the meditative state he needed to feel the objects "beneath the surface" of the art.

Test Number Three involved trying to pull something out of a reproduction of Roger's art — in this case, an old magazine cover he'd done, showing a barbarian warrior, axe in hand, standing atop a mound of slain enemies. Roger could enter his meditative state this time . . . but couldn't seem to "reach" all the way to the subject of his painting. He could faintly sense the barbarian, the axe, the bodies, all beneath his fingers . . . but so far away he just couldn't grasp them.

After he rested from that attempt, Donna put him

on Test Number Four. Roger sketched out and then inked a small black-and-white teddy bear. Then Donna brought in her own paints from her room and laid down a watercolor coat over it, making the bear a nice tan brown and its bow tie a cheerful red, adding character to its face and texture to its fur.

Once it was dry, Roger entered his meditative state without difficulty and felt around for the teddy bear. It was there, all right, but was elusive beneath his fingers; he could never quite grasp it.

He sighed, withdrew from it, rubbed his aching neck for a minute, then tried again. This time, he first concentrated on the design of the toy bear, the black-and-white lines he'd laid down. Then he forced himself to scrutinize Donna's color work, trying to learn every tint and every line she'd added.

It took a while, but gradually his fingers touched toy fur. Finally, he was able to pinch it between his fingers and pull. At the last moment, he imagined the teddy bear larger than the painting, a full foot and a half in length . . . and a moment later he opened his eyes to stare at the real thing, a tan bear with a red bow tie. With a flourish that belied the weariness he felt, he presented it to Donna.

"So, collaboration does work . . . both ways," she said, triumphant. "Oh, he's a darling. Oh, he's *weird*." She frowned, looking the teddy bear up and down. "No seams. We didn't give him any seams." She turned the toy around, seeing only continuous material. "There's not even a real transition between the fur and the paws of his hands and feet. The cloth just stops being furry and gets lighter in color; it's not a separate piece of cloth."

"I don't care," he announced, tired but victorious. "It's a teddy bear, the world's first perfect teddy bear." He heaved himself up and moved over to flop onto the bed. "Too many tests," he groaned. "I'm worn out."

Donna snickered and addressed the bear. "You hear

that, Yogi? Daddy can only go on for a little while and then he has to lie down. Typical male."

She was still playing with the bear, dancing it across the tabletop and making disparaging remarks about Roger's endurance, when Elsie returned. As usual, the nymph was caked with sand but cheerful.

Before she could quite make it to the shower, Roger asked, "Where've you been all day?"

She stopped at the bathroom door, looking defensive. "At the beach, as usual. Playing volleyball. They made a fire and made hot dogs and burned marshmallows. I swam, too, this time, because I have a suit now. I gave a woman in a store a little of your money for a suit, and she gave me the suit and money back. It was not hard."

Roger managed not to frown. "Yes, but you didn't ask me this time."

She looked confused, but not apologetic. "You were asleep when I got up. Must I ask you every time I want to go out?" Her question was a challenge; she put her head down but kept her attention on Roger's eyes, looking as though she expected Roger to take a swat at her.

Roger forced himself to ignore her tone. It was true that he wasn't her father, didn't even want to be. "No. You don't. But I wish you would. Elsie, I know you're having a lot of fun out there with your friends. But not everyone you meet is your friend, even when they seem to be. Some of them might pretend to like you when they really just want to hurt you."

He braced himself for the expected denial, the No-*my*-friends-aren't-like-that! argument.

Instead, she nodded. "Some of the men at the lake just want to pull my clothes off and have sex with me."

Roger's backbone acted on its own, snapping him upright as if it were part of a mousetrap. He gaped.

Elsie continued conversationally, "Some of them want to do it even if I don't want to. I think some of them even want to hurt me. I don't like them much."

Out of the corner of his eye, Roger could see Donna shaking with mirth — laughing at *him*. He found his voice again, though it sounded shrill to his ears. "How much do you know about, uh, sex?"

Elsie shrugged. "What I see on the cable TV; there's a lot of it there. And in the magazines and books down at the store and on the beach. There are even instruction manuals! It sounds like an awful lot of fun, but there seem to be complications. I will have to think about it." She brightened. "But I learned something about it today. Do you want to see?"

Roger gulped. "Uh, I guess so."

"If you want a man to stop taking your clothes off and he won't, you ball up your hand like this —" she made a fist, " — and hit him very hard in the testicles with it. Or use your knee. He loses all interest. He certainly can't run after you."

Roger felt his temple start pounding again. "Did *you* have to do that?"

Elsie shook her head. "I saw a woman on the beach do it. She was really mad. She did it more than once before she left. The man threw up." She shrugged, losing interest in the topic.

"I'm dirty." She walked into the bathroom and shut the door.

Roger flopped back onto his pillows, then pulled one out from behind him and threw it at Donna as she silently laughed at him. "Just shut up," he said, snarling . . . but then he couldn't keep himself from laughing, too.

He slept, awakening well after midnight; the day's tests had obviously worn him out. Elsie was already asleep in her own bed, and Donna had long since retired to her room with her new teddy bear.

Roger rose and clicked on the hanging light over the table. Elsie opened her eyes, looked around the room without turning her head, and closed them again, her slow breathing rhythm uninterrupted. Roger frowned at that; had she just awakened, or hadn't she?

With his senses, he reached out to touch her mind, as he'd done almost continuously in the Paradise paintings. It took him few moments to find her; it didn't seem to be as easy as it once was. But she was indeed asleep. He turned back to the table.

The products of his recent labors were still piled on the floor beside his table: one automatic pistol, ammunition, and two sets of body armor. He frowned at them, too. It's not that they weren't useful . . . just that they were a lot less than he'd hoped to accomplish today. They didn't make up for the loss of Captain Steele. He would have been such a good soldier. Now, it would be days before he could finish another painting and pull its contents out into the real world. . . .

Wait a minute. His gaze moved over to his still-zipped-up portfolio, and within a minute he'd taken all his old paintings from it and set them on the table. *I don't have to just create new paintings. I've got some soldiers in these.* . . . And he did.

He wouldn't be pulling out the Lava Demon any time soon, since he knew he couldn't control it for long; and he didn't know if the Lava Nymphs could survive normal temperatures. So those two paintings were out of the question.

"Carol, the Ancient Yuletide Troll" looked promising. She'd be terrifying in a fight.

There were assorted zombies and vampires, barbarian warriors, voluptuous and scantily clad females. He grimaced, regretting that so many of the females in his work were just objects of desire with no skills or magical powers evident. Why couldn't he have made more of them spear maidens, high-tech shock troops, sorceresses?

He wondered about the satyr in "Deceit of My

Pants." Perhaps the satyr would have some unusual abilities . . . rather, unusual abilities pertinent to their situation. But he flipped through all his paintings twice and couldn't locate that one. He sighed. It could've fallen out or been left anywhere: at his apartment, in the flight from Donna's house. . . . Maybe he'd find it. Then again, maybe it was lost in limbo, like all the paintings he'd done for Nonesuch Books.

That memory brought a growl from him. Those paintings would be useful right now. High-tech, single-pilot space fighters screaming their way through the atmospheres of strange planets, intelligent bearlike mammals on a planet with two suns, soldiers scrambling out of their barracks with weapons still on the walls . . . what he'd give to have them right now. He could almost see them . . .

That startled him. He *could* see them. He could call up their images in his mind with almost the same clarity he'd managed for "Lava Demon" just a couple of days before. But could he send himself to them, the way he had with "Lava Demon"?

He glanced again at Elsie, then at Donna's door. No, better not awaken them. If he failed, nothing was likely to happen to him. If he succeeded . . . he resolved to be gone only a short time.

Of all the paintings, he remembered "Trantham's Troopers" best, the view of the soldiers storming out of their barracks. He called up the big acrylic in his mind; he reviewed its composition, the exact placement of every aggressive space marine, male or female, charging toward the exit.

Then he reached out for them. . . .

His fingers never touched paint. His chair vanished from under him and he fell backwards, less than a foot, against a metal wall. The smell of the room became both metallic and sweaty. Shouts of "Trantham! Trantham!" from a dozen throats were loud enough to make him cringe. And he opened his eyes . . . to see the last of the space marines charge out the exit from their starship's bunkroom.

Roger slipped the rest of the way down to the grating that was the room's floor, then recovered himself and stood. Men and women were still running in the corridor outside the bunkroom, but he was alone here.

He managed to close his mouth. It had been so fast, and he was in his painting, just as he'd painted it . . . except that now all the marines were gone, leaving behind rumpled bunks, card games on card tables, books, tiny mechanical televisions or tape-players with pictures still moving on their miniature screens, weapons in the wall racks. . . .

On impulse, he pulled one of the firearms from a rack and looked at it. It was just as he'd painted it more than a year ago: shaped something like a modern assault rifle, but squat and ugly, made of a textured gray-black plastic with strange green highlights. It was cool to his touch. The weapon was heavy.

He slung it over his shoulder by its strap, grinning at the thought of taking a souvenir away from this futuristic environment. But now what? Go back to the motel? Where could he go from here?

No, he was inside "Trantham's Troopers." The painting still existed, and he wanted to get to where it was. He closed his eyes again, called the painting up in his mind, extended his hand toward it . . . and this time was rewarded with the feel of dried paint beneath his fingers.

A moment later, the sound of running in the hallway ceased. The air became cooler, fresher. The paint under his fingers changed again, to a cool, smooth surface. But his souvenir firearm was still with him.

He opened his eyes to find himself in dim light. He was in an office: rich, dark carpet beneath his feet, expensive hardwood desk and furniture to his left, a high-priced personal computer on the desk, no signs of paperwork anywhere. What light there was crept around the edges of the closed office door.

Roger's outstretched hand rested on a box holding numerous wide, deep, shallow shelves — a flat-file case, the sort used to hold maps and other oversized flat sheets.

He slid open the top drawer and saw his painting of the ursinoids under twin suns.

Immediately beneath it was "Trantham's Troopers."

He could feel his cheeks blazing red as he flipped through painting after painting. The top two shelves held all twelve of his paintings for Nonesuch Books. The next shelf down held two more of his paintings, older ones he'd sold at art shows in his first years as an illustrator, plus several canvases from other artists in the field.

Where the hell was this, and who had his art?

It didn't take him long to find out. On the desk was a framed photograph of Julia Dover; she sat in a provocative cheesecake-style pose.

In the desk were memos addressed to Kevin Matthews; they bore the Nonesuch Books letterhead. Every one of them addressed him as "Sir"; most asked him to authorize various expenditures or consider new book lines.

Roger swore, then froze and looked at the door, hoping that no one had heard. But no footsteps approached.

Anger washed across him again. Kevin had only to make a phone call to screw up Roger's life. It was obvious that Kevin had ordered his people at Nonesuch Books to substitute cardboard for his newly arrived paintings, then claim that the paintings never came. Simple to arrange, simple to get away with. But no one else at Nonesuch had any reason to hurt him. Only Kevin did.

Roger could burn this place to the ground and get away clean, leaving the way he came . . . but a lot of people would be inconvenienced, possibly unemployed, maybe even killed. These were people who probably didn't share Kevin's plans or nature.

He felt his anger slip away as though it were his blood leaving through a tube, and he let his head sag on the desk. It was the shortest temper tantrum of his life.

He'd finally found out why Nonesuch had screwed up his life, and he couldn't even bring himself to hurt them the way they'd hurt him.

It took him a few minutes to recover his energy. Then he collected his paintings from the flat-file case and turned his thoughts to home.

Chapter Six
Research

Roger swallowed a mouthful of hash browns, followed it with a swig of water, and continued. "Anyway, I used Captain Steele's painting to get back and had a short conversation with him."

For the fortieth time that morning, Donna glanced around the motel restaurant, making sure that no one was close enough to hear over the early-morning babble of conversation. But they were safe; Elsie, carefully picking her way through salad, yogurt and fruit, was the only other person close enough to hear.

"You really talked to him? What'd he say?"

"It was weird. He had this really great baritone voice. He didn't know where he was; it was all whiteness out to infinity. Well, infinity with a floor. He didn't know much about himself except his name and what he could do." Roger's expression became a little glum. "He was the most powerful thing in the universe — in his universe, anyway. But there was nothing there to be more powerful *than*.

"He hoped he could come out where we were, but if he couldn't, he'd just wait there until 'miscreants' showed up so he could defeat them." Roger shook his head in mock annoyance. "I don't know from what melodramatic part of my brain he got the word 'miscreants.' Anyway, I told him I'd look into it, and then I shifted back into the room."

"So, was he straight?"

Roger gave her an exasperated look, then mimed

grabbing up his hash browns and hurling them at her; Elsie giggled and Donna grinned.

"Anyway, what about that rifle you brought back?"

"I haven't had time to play with it. It may not do anything; I painted the marines carrying these rifles, not firing them, so it may be purely decorative. I'll try to find some empty land and test it. What I can't figure out is where it was on the painting. I looked over every inch of 'Trantham's Troopers,' and there isn't a gun missing from the wall racks. I guess it was from a rack not shown in the painting.

"Your turn. What's your first test for me today?"

Donna smiled. "Oh, no. I'll show you when we're back at the room. You'll love this one."

"Uh-huh. Make me wait." He turned to Elsie. "How about your plans?"

She looked startled at being singled out. "Some of my friends from volleyball are going to take me in to the city to shop and see a movie. Mike and Lisa and Jason and Heather and Dylan." She fidgeted.

Roger said, "The city. Where Kevin is."

"I'll be all right." Elsie's voice was tight; her expression, defiant, anticipated his objections. Roger found himself annoyed.

"Elsie, I'm really not sure that's such a good idea. What if you run into Kevin?"

"What if I do? He doesn't know what I look like."

"Achilles and Penthesilia do. They saw you when you were still a drawing."

"I would see them before they saw me, and I'd get away. They will be easy to pick out. I knew they were different, not right, when they came to your apartment."

Roger struggled with himself, still formulating his objections . . . but also curious about her last statement. "What do you mean, different?"

"They were wrong. I knew they were not of your kind. I did not know *what* they were, so I was afraid of them. I can't describe what I felt about them . . . but it nearly made me ill to see them.

"Since I've been here, I've seen real dogs, so I know the dog you made was wrong, too. Though it was not *as* wrong. It did not make me ill. It was cute." She smiled at the memory.

A nasty thought crossed Roger's mind and he struggled to put it into words. "Elsie . . . what about you? Have you ever felt wrong, the same way?"

She hesitated, then looked down. "Yes," she whispered. "When I . . . when I was first born, I knew that I was different from you. I felt hollow. Empty. On the island with the volcano, it wasn't so bad; everyone there was like that, and you were the one who was strange. When we came back, it got worse, especially when your father and Donna were mad at me." Roger saw Donna suppress a little wince of sympathy.

Elsie looked back at Roger. "But every day it gets better. Every time I learn something, every time someone speaks to me and recognizes me, I feel myself belong here just a little more." She bit her lower lip, considering her next words. "I will never be a human being, Roger. I am what you made me, a nymph. But every day, I am a little more real."

Roger felt his throat grow tight with her words. He didn't know what to say; all he could manage was "Have fun at your movie."

But from her smile, he knew he'd found the right words. Donna reached under the table and gave his knee an approving squeeze.

Back in the hotel room, Donna set the large drawing down in front of Roger, then pulled up a chair beside him as he pored over the illustration.

It was a technical drawing, two different views of a bank of controls like something out of NASA's Mission Control. The panel was thick with keyboards, television screens, and sturdy-looking joysticks.

Floating above the whole rig, not attached to it, was a spherical object; in the drawing's scale, it would have been about two and a half feet in diameter. Attached to the sphere were telephoto lenses, short antennae, and little irising panels.

Roger looked at the thing for a while, then said, "I give up. What the hell is it?"

"A flying monitor. It has a camera with a whole slew of different capabilities, like zoom and infrared and starlight. It has recording devices for sight and sound. I picked VHS so we can play its recordings in a standard VCR. It's got waldoes; those are little robot arms that can swing out and do things —"

"I *know* what waldoes are."

"Touchy, touchy. It has lockpicks and thermal imagers. It has bugs, eavesdropping devices, in a little bay. It even has weapons in case we need to defend it. And it's all controlled by the joysticks and computer gear on the control panel."

"Oh-ho. So we just send it wherever we want, get all the information we need by remote control, and keep our asses safe at home."

She nodded. "Roger, I know Kev's address in town. I never got in further than their living room, and with all that's happened I'm really curious about what's in the rest of their house. The more we know about him —"

"The more we can prepare for. Yeah." Then he frowned. "Donna, this thing will never work. The technology just doesn't exist for this."

"And the technology exists for Elsie? Look, except for Captain Straight, everything you've drawn has popped out into the real world and worked just fine. If this doesn't, well, it just means we go back to the drawing board." She snickered. "Literally."

He smiled, then his eyes narrowed as he took a look around the room. "Okay, here's problem number two. This control panel will never fit in here."

"You're right." She shrugged. "Which is fine by me.

A motel is not where I plan to spend the rest of my days — even if I'm a fugitive. Listen, it'll take you a while to color that thing as a painting —"

"A couple of days at least."

"Which gives me plenty of time to talk to a local realtor and get us a house. Somewhere we won't have a maid blundering in once a day, something with walls a little thicker than toilet paper . . ."

"No realtor." Roger shook his head. "What names do you want us to put on the lease? What sort of ID do we give them?" He thought about it. "Look, there are a lot of summer houses around here . . . and it's not tourist season yet. Maybe we could rent one from someone who'd be just as happy to have cash and no paper trail; he wouldn't have to pay taxes on it. We pay what he asks, give him a few months' advance rent in cash . . . and we leave nothing for Kevin to track down."

She considered that. "You've got a real sneaky side to you, Roger. But you make a good point. And I know just who to ask."

"Who's that?"

"Elsie's friends. They're locals."

"Sounds like a plan." He swivelled to look down at the drawing again. "I'll start on this. What are you up to for the rest of the day?"

"Some more reading, some drafting, some exercise . . ."

"*Exercise?* Didn't anyone ever teach you not to swear in public?"

Donna grinned. "I've been out of it for a while, and I'm way out of shape. It wouldn't hurt you any, either."

He gave a mock shudder. "No, thanks."

"I'll come in and pester you when I'm ready to start. You can join me."

"No, *thanks.*"

Late in the evening, Elsie returned, still entranced by her magical first experience with big-screen movies.

"It was — I don't know the words for it! Huge cars flew through the air and blew up, and huge people talked and made love and shot at each other with guns, and a helicopter flew into a building and *everything* blew up, but the nice people got away anyway. Dylan says nobody really got killed, but it's even harder to believe than on TV. I wish there'd been more kissing. I liked that part."

Roger grinned as he laid down color on Donna's diagram. "Well, I think you'll have plenty of opportunities to see more movies like that. And maybe some with lots more kissing and less blowing up. But there's something I need to tell you now."

"What is it?" She flopped down onto her bed, behind him.

"Donna and I had a talk, and we've decided that we need to move."

He waited a few seconds for her to reply, but she remained silent. Finally, he looked at her over his shoulder. Elsie sat on the edge of her bed, staring at him, her expression confused.

"Elsie? Did you hear me?"

She blinked, then blurted out, "I won't go."

"What do you mean, you won't go? Elsie, we need to move. So we can keep on taking action against Kevin. Do you understand?"

She shook her head, and her voice raised in pitch and volume. "You're just trying to get me away from Dylan."

"From . . . Dylan?" He scowled and turned further around to face her. A nasty suspicion popped into his mind; just how much of that kissing was actually going on down in the audience?

"From Dylan and the rest," she amended. Then her voice rose into a shout: "All my friends are here. I don't care what you say, I'm not leaving!"

"The hell you aren't," he snapped. "Elsie, until you're old enough to get along in the world with no help at all, you're going to do what I tell you. It's for your own good —" His voice strangled on the last word.

He'd once promised himself he'd never say those words, *for your own good*. God, he hated them. Hated them when his father said them, hated them when his mother said them, hated them in the mouths of teachers and relatives. Now he'd said them himself, and he hated them even more. But this time they were true!

Before he could struggle that thought into a shape he could cope with, Donna opened the door from her room. "What are you two doing?" she hissed. "You want everyone in the motel to hear you?"

Elsie vaulted over Roger's bed in a single graceful step, and surprised Donna by embracing her. "Tell me we don't have to move," the nymph pleaded, her face buried in Donna's shoulder. "Roger says we have to move away. I don't want to leave my friends. . . ."

Donna shot Roger a furious look, then reached up to stroke Elsie's hair. "Shhh," she soothed. "Didn't he tell you — didn't you tell her that we're staying in town? Elsie, we won't be leaving town, just the motel."

"I didn't have time," Roger grumbled. "The instant I said we were moving, she freaked out."

"Well, you should have told her right away."

Elsie looked up at Donna, then at Roger; he was surprised to see tears on her cheek. "We're not leaving town?"

Grudgingly, he shook his head. "You misunderstood. We're staying in Lake Galloway. We're just moving into a house here."

"Really?"

"Really."

The nymph sagged, her relief was so great, and Donna shot Roger another dirty look. "Come on into my room," Donna said. "We need to leave Roger alone now. He's working very hard, and he's obviously not thinking about what he's saying." She led Elsie into her room and shut the door behind them.

Roger just stared at the door for a minute, bewildered, trying to figure out just what had just happened. He hadn't done anything wrong, he told himself, but suddenly he was the villain.

"I will not be the bad guy in this discussion!" he told the door, but it didn't answer.

Dammit, if only he'd told her right away that they were only moving across town . . . but, no, he'd needed to deal with her rebellion first. Didn't he?

Next time, they might have to move far away to get clear of Kevin; she had to be willing to do as Roger ordered, because her life might depend on it. Right?

And what was all this about "Dylan," anyway?

He didn't have an answer for these questions. He just murmured, "I will not be the bad guy here," and turned miserably back to his painting.

The next afternoon, Roger and Donna went to the beach to meet Elsie's friends. Neither of them discussed what went on the night before. Since it was all Roger could think about, he didn't say anything at all; he just tried to enjoy the spring air.

The spot Elsie had described was one of the many "recreation stations" that surrounded Lake Galloway. Twenty feet from the muddy lakeshore were a pair of picnic tables and a permanently-mounted barbecue grill; halfway between this site and the next station was a stretch of imported sand with a volleyball net strung over it. Roger could see ice chests filled with beer and soft drinks; on the table were hot dogs and buns still in the wrappers, condiments, bags of chips, and other junk food.

A dozen teens raged away at a volleyball game, but Elsie wasn't with them; she sat at the picnic table. With a young man.

He was tall and good-looking, with open, amiable

features and sandy brown hair. He looked to be 18 or 19 and was in good shape — his half-unbuttoned shirt and cut-off shorts made that clear.

And Elsie was leaning against him as they talked.

Roger went rigid as he saw that. The sight of the two of them together, innocent as it might be, hit him like a slap. Abruptly he was furious again, and everything he saw took on a reddish hue as he glared at the two of them.

"Roger, be cool," Donna whispered. She grabbed his hand and squeezed it.

"Yeah, sure." His voice hissed with anger. "I've been waiting for her to learn. I've been waiting for her to, I don't know, grow up, so I could stop being her guardian. And this little punk bastard slides in to take advantage. . . ."

"Of her? Or of you? Listen, Roger, she's still a kid. Either this is nothing, or it's puppy love."

"For her, maybe. He's no puppy." Furious, he glared at the other man. But he did let Donna keep her grip on his hand; he somehow found it reassuring. Maybe she was right. Maybe this was nothing.

Elsie looked up and saw the two of them. She straightened a little, then scooted a few inches away from the young man and said something to him. Elsie looked at Roger, trying to gauge his expression; he tried to give her nothing to read.

Elsie's friend extended his hand as Roger and Donna arrived. Roger took it. "You must be Dylan." He was pleased to note that he'd kept all emotion out of his voice.

The young man nodded. "Hey," he said amiably, as if it were an answer to Roger's statement.

"Dylan, this is my cousin Roger, and his friend Donna," Elsie said, a touch of worry in her voice. "Roger, Donna, this is Dylan Scott. He lives here in town." Dylan shook Donna's hand, too, with another "Hey." Roger and Donna sat.

Roger couldn't look away from Dylan. The little bastard sure was good-looking, he admitted grudgingly. Elsie really could pick them for looks.

Dylan said, "Elsie says you're thinking of renting a house here." He sounded intelligent in spite of his monosyllabic greetings.

Roger nodded tightly. "For a while, anyway."

Dylan grinned. "Long enough for me to figure out where she's from, I hope. She only gives me one guess a day."

"You, uh, in trade school or something around here, Dylan?" Roger asked, then yelped as Donna's heel ground down on his foot below the table. He reached down to rub his injured extremity and glared at her.

"Those bugs'll eat you alive, won't they?" Dylan asked. "No, I'm taking a year off between high school and college. I'll be studying film at UCLA next year."

Roger opened his mouth to ask another question, but Donna interrupted him. "Roger, *dear*, I need to talk to Dylan about houses in town . . . and you *said* you wanted to get in some volleyball."

"I did?"

"You sure did."

Rather than challenge her let's-get-rid-of-Roger lie, he gave her an uneasy smile and stood. "Then I'd better get after it. You have fun." He limped off toward the game being played a few yards away.

Maybe it wouldn't be too bad. He didn't really want to sit there and talk to Dylan; blowing him up with sticks of dynamite seemed like a much better idea, but there were no explosives handy. And he'd always been good at volleyball, one of the few sports he liked.

He watched the game in progress for only a minute before one of the players dropped out and the others invited Roger in. He started off serving, one of his strong points, and in spite of being rusty, he helped set up one point and then aced on his next serve. Within minutes, he was completely absorbed in the game.

It took a while for him to get back into the rhythm of
the game; he fouled up three times at a stretch before
the moves began to come back to him. But he was tall
and found that he still had a lot of his high-school
grace; he was soon jumping for net shots and beating
most of the opposing players to them, though they
were ten years younger, ten years more durable. That
felt good. It also felt good to use days' worth of anger
and frustration to fuel his game.

After a couple of games, Elsie joined the other team;
Roger didn't realize it until he came up against her at
the net and she spiked a ball off his head for a point.
She grinned without malice and he grinned back, and
the next time they were at the net together she did it
again.

She was good at the game — better than he was. In
spite of his greater height and reach, she could outleap
him by a foot or more and her hand-eye coordination
was uncanny; if the ball came within her reach, she
fired it accurately over the net or set it up for a
teammate. She never seemed to miss. But she was all
friendly competition, and she cheered him on as loudly
as his own players did when he served two more aces
the next time he was at service. He knew not to serve
to *her*.

Roger got tired before he was willing to quit the
field. Maybe he really ought to start exercising with
Donna, to get his wind back. But he didn't get to
embarrass himself by collapsing; the deepening shadows of twilight and the smell of hot dogs and
hamburgers roasting nearby ended the game. Dylan
stood over the grill and called everyone over for food.

Roger loaded a paper plate with two burgers and
chips, then slid in beside Donna at the picnic table.
"Did you get what you needed?"

She smiled. "I think so. Did you?"

He gave her a quick look, then smiled in return. "I
suppose so. More than I care to admit." He glanced

over at the grill, where Elsie had joined Dylan and was helping to dole out cooked hamburger patties and hot dogs. "Maybe I'll be pissed off again later, but right now I'm doing all right."

Before they left, Roger met the rest of Dylan's group: Mike, the sports editor for the local high school's paper; Lisa, a yearbook photographer; and Jason and Heather, who were with the school band. Bright kids, all of them, the sort he'd belonged to when he was in high school; he really couldn't fault Elsie her taste in friends.

Except for Dylan, all of them were in high school, and this was not vacation season. Either they were skipping a lot of school or they were meeting only when school was over. And if that was the case, who was Elsie with the mornings and afternoons she said she was at the beach?

He looked at Dylan again and knew the answer, and felt a stab where his heart should be. But when he and Donna left, he was still able to rumple Elsie's hair with real affection, and didn't punish her for his own hurt feelings.

Over the next three days, Donna tracked down and spoke to several of the people Dylan had recommended to her, and by Saturday afternoon had wrapped up a deal on a lakeside home. It was a large old two-story house, no farther from Elsie's favorite beach site than the motel, but much farther from the center of town. It had its own little pier and boathouse, now empty. The owner, a businessman who now lived elsewhere, was happy to arrange a few months' rent for some under-the-table money, and was equally happy to have Dylan look in on the house from time to time to make sure the new tenants were doing it no harm. On Sunday afternoon, Roger, Donna and Elsie moved in, each into his own bedroom.

Meanwhile, Roger worked on the control-panel

painting. He also doctored sore muscles earned during the volleyball game . . . and did begin to work out with Donna. It was nothing too heavy, just calisthenics he remembered from school and a two- or three-mile walk each day.

Even so, he still had plenty of time to think about things.

First: Yes, Dylan and Elsie were boyfriend and girlfriend. Boyfriend and girlfriend — old-fashioned terms, those. But in this case Roger really preferred them to "lovers." It didn't sound quite as . . . consummated.

Second: Roger could either be Elsie's teacher — no, dammit, *father* — or he could be her lover. He couldn't be both. It would confuse her. It would confuse him. It was already confusing them. And all the while he behaved like some raving, jealous ex-boyfriend, she couldn't trust anything he had to say; he was jealous and irrational.

Third: He wasn't in love with Elsie. He loved her, yes. And it startled him to realize that he could say it, could understand it that way: *I love her. I love her, and I want the best for her, and I don't want to hurt her.* He wasn't in love with her, but was sad that he hadn't had the chance to find out if they could be lovers. Maybe, if he'd imagined her as an adult, fully integrated with his world . . . but all the maybes in the world didn't amount to a thing.

So he worked, and thought, and decided. His decision made him gloomy and he kept to himself for a couple of days.

On Monday morning, Elsie stuck her head in the doorway of the bedroom he and Donna used as their office, and announced, "We're all going in to town for another movie. I'll be back tonight."

Roger looked at her. "Elsie, this is a school day. Most of your friends are in school until afternoon. You're going in to town with just Dylan. Right?"

Caught in her lie like a deer caught in headlight beams, she froze and just looked at him. Finally, she nodded.

"You don't need to lie about it any more," he said.

"I don't?" She bit her lower lip, apprehensive. "You don't mind?"

It was his turn to pause. He knew the answer he wanted to give her, the answer he'd convinced himself was the right one, but he took a moment to compare it to what he was really feeling.

Then he told her the truth. "I don't mind. I just want you to be happy. But I really want you to be able to tell me the truth, about whatever you're doing. I want you to be able to come and talk to me. Whatever it is, I'll try not to get mad."

She came to him then and threw her arms around him, and he held her as she sniffled on him for a minute. This time, her embrace didn't make his heart jump; the aching weight that had settled in his chest wouldn't let it.

Finally she said, "Thank you, Roger. I *am* happy. You've made me happy. And I'll be happy when I come home." Then she slipped away and was gone.

Roger sat for a while, then got a drink to help ease the constriction in his throat, and went back to work.

That night, not long after Elsie returned with glowing tales of cinematic romance and heartbreak, Roger called her and Donna into the office and showed them the completed painting. "I've already felt around inside to make sure the gizmo is there," he explained, "and I've cleared one wall of furniture so we'll have room for the thing. You two ready?"

"Let 'er rip," Donna said, and Elsie nodded eagerly.

This time, it took only a moment. He shifted almost effortlessly into his meditative state, touched the painting, touched *beyond* the painting's surface, and strained. . . . There was a loud pop, and both women jumped as the console from Donna's sketch just blinked into existence along the office's bare wall.

Above it, hovering in the air and humming quietly, was the spy-eye drone. A moment after it appeared, a camera view of Roger, Donna and Elsie, from the hovering drone's point of view, flickered into clarity on both of the control panel's screens.

"Too cool," Donna announced, and made a grab for the joysticks.

"Hey!" Roger lunged for the same controls, but the usual weariness slowed him down. He sat heavily in the seat next to hers. "Artist's privilege. I want to drive first."

"Just like a man. Always has to drive. I bet if you got this thing lost, you wouldn't ask for directions." Donna kept her hands on the joysticks. "Besides, you're not the only one with artist's privileges here."

"Fine. Go right ahead." With a mock sulky expression, Roger slouched in his chair and pretended not to pay attention; Donna grinned at him. The weariness wasn't fading very fast and Roger was actually grateful that he could just lean back and relax while he recovered.

It didn't take Donna long to figure out the controls; she'd designed them. "Left for altitude, right for speed and orientation," she said, then barely twisted the right-hand stick. All three of them watched the floating globe execute a slow 360° rotation, just like a globe hanging in space. When it was pointed at the room's doorway, she nudged the joystick and the floating spy-eye lurched into motion. It glided forward, nearly silent, and then banged into the doorjamb.

"Takes a little getting used to," Donna allowed; she tugged it back, twisted the stick again to alter its direction, and put it neatly through the doorway.

It took them only an hour to become proficient with the spy-eye's controls. For the first half hour, Donna held the joysticks — the movement and weapon controls — while Roger puzzled out the other console, which managed the device's lock-pick tools, its battery of sensors and recording devices, and its waldoes.

The waldoes were special fun. He inserted his hands through circular portals in the control panel, sliding them into rubbery gloves; as he did so, the spindly, five-fingered artificial arms emerged from the spy-eye's interior and then moved in exact synchronicity with his hands. It wasn't long before he could use the waldoes to pick up a pen off a table, then write his name in an approximation of his own handwriting.

In the second half hour, Donna and Roger switched positions, each learning the other set of controls. Roger decided that he actually preferred the sensors and waldoes.

Finally, Elsie tried out on the joystick controls and learned to maneuver the flying ball. She didn't try the other panel; she just wanted to fly the new toy.

Roger flopped back in his chair and scowled at the ball. "Y'know, Donna, this opens up a whole new can of worms."

"So we go fishing."

"No, don't blow this off. Listen. Let's say we paint something that can't exist in the real world . . . like this." He pointed at the sphere. "We pull it into the real world. Then we open it and figure out how it works. Presto amazo, we've just become the inventors of antigravity, or whatever the hell that thing uses to stay up in the air."

Donna gave him a curious look. "So, we become the richest hardware engineers in the world. You're right, that sounds terrible."

He snorted. "All right, hold the sarcasm. Seriously — if it were that simple, why hasn't Kevin done it?"

She shrugged. "Maybe he has. Would we know about it? I don't have a friend in the patent office; how would I find out what patents Kevin might have taken out in the last year?"

"You're too reasonable. I'll withdraw the question."
He scooted back to the sensor controls. "What say we
send this thing outside and blow something up?"

"That's more like it!"

Elsie ran downstairs and held the screen door open
for the globe as Donna piloted it into the night air;
then the nymph ran along beneath, pacing it, as it
cruised over the three acres of lightly wooded land on
which the house was built. Roger was surprised at the
speed the nymph could manage through thick underbrush; even when the digital speedometer on the
screen reached 30 mph, Elsie had no trouble keeping
up with the globe. Roger knew that had to be some
sort of world record — for humans, anyway. When he
dipped the camera down to look at her, she waved, and
didn't look winded in the least.

Then Donna zipped the flying globe out over the
lake, where Elsie would not follow, and hit the buttons
to activate the weapon systems. Targeting brackets
appeared in the center of Donna's screen.

"Let's find us a target," she announced, and immediately did; a half-submerged rowboat, long abandoned
and forgotten, lay on a sandbar where the river
emptied into the lake.

She brought the sphere around carefully, aiming at
the large wooden target, and then depressed her
right-hand firing button. Instantly, the part of the hull
in the targeting brackets caught fire.

"Was that the laser?" Roger asked.

"Yep."

"Where's the 'Zap'? Where's the light show?"

"Real lasers don't do that. Unless there's dust or fog
or something in the way, you don't even see them."

"Well, this isn't a real laser. You could've designed
something that would go 'Zap.' I'm a little disappointed
in you, young lady."

Donna grinned, but didn't turn her attention away
from the camera screen. Again, she made sure her

target was right in the brackets. But this time she thumbed the left-hand button.

And Roger got his wish. The screen went white for a moment; when it cleared a moment later, the two of them could see that the rowboat was in flaming pieces drifting away in all directions. Red embers were still floating down out of the sky. "There's your 'Zap,' Roger," Donna said with a wicked smile.

"That was the particle beam? All right! Let's see Achilles and Penthesilia take one of those." Roger rubbed his hands together briskly, then put them on his set of controls and looked at her. "You ready for the real thing?"

"Always." She tugged back on the left-hand stick, and Roger was startled at how fast the globe gained altitude; within seconds the two of them were looking down on the nighttime lights of Lake Galloway.

Donna sent the spy-eye south toward the city, driving the stick forward until the on-screen speedometer reached 300 miles per hour; Elsie was barely back in the office before the lights of town showed on the screen. "You should have seen the boat blow up!" the nymph announced. "It was like lightning on TV."

Finding a specific street address wasn't quite as easy as they thought. Donna was able to pick out a couple of city landmarks from the air — the courthouse, one of the malls — and orient from there, but when she got near Kevin's neighborhood she had to dip the probe down almost to street level and use the camera to read the street signs. "Maybe you should ask directions," Roger suggested sweetly.

But a minute later the drone hovered thirty feet in the air in front of Kevin's house.

It was a big house: two rambling stories with a three-car garage. Out back were a large pool and a pool house. The house must have been ten or fifteen years old, but well kept up, and one wing and the pool house looked like recent additions. There were no cars in front and only a couple of lights shone in the windows.

"Park it for a minute," Roger said, and got to work on his own controls. He dialed the globe's camera through an infrared-imaging sequence, and the three of them watched as the house turned into fuzzy red, orange, and yellow blotches. Interior details became visible as ghostly shapes.

"I don't see anything that looks like a person," Donna decided. "If anyone's there, he's not moving. Shall I move in?"

"Please." Roger dialed the camera back to normal vision. Donna flew the globe over the house, then dropped it into the back yard and carefully guided it to the back door. "Back to you," she announced.

Roger took a moment to remember where everything was, then activated a new control. Yellow brackets appeared on his screen, zoomed in on the door lock. A moment later, a new arm, ending in a cluster of what looked like metal shavings, extended from the sphere and inserted itself in the lock. The arm performed a quick rotation . . . and nothing happened.

Donna frowned. "That's supposed to be a really sophisticated door-lock-picker-thing. It's not supposed to have such a hard time with a simple back door."

"Maybe it's not a simple back door." Roger frowned at the screen as the arm continued through a series of rotations and manipulations. "Kevin could have some pretty fancy locks."

"I suppose. Oh, there it goes." The probing limb concluded its activities and withdrew; a readout at the bottom of the screen read SUCCESSFUL TERMINATION.

Roger shook his head. "Jesus, Donna. Do you think we should sell this thing to the CIA? Make a million bucks?" He withdrew the lockpicking mechanism and slid his hands into the waldo gloves.

"CIA, no. Greenpeace, maybe."

Roger reached out one of the waldo hands, gracefully turned the doorknob, then gave the door a little shove. The door swung open without protest. Roger hit the control to activate the console's internal VCR, then depressed another button; there was a pop as the console's speakers came live. "Recorder on. Sound on. Ready to go."

Donna maneuvered the globe through the doorway; Roger took a moment to shut and lock the door with his waldoes; then they took a look around.

All Donna could say was, "That son of a bitch."

This was a large living area — a sprawling room that took up most of the rear half of the house. The carpets were golden and so thick they looked as comfortable as a bed. The furniture was covered in rich leather and worth a fortune. The paintings on the wall weren't by Kevin; they were Renaissance-era masters . . . originals, not prints. One wall was covered with state-of-the-art electronics, including a big-screen television and the most extensive quadraphonic stereo gear Roger had ever seen.

Donna was rigid, her face locked into an expression of injured anger. She jerked the spy-eye into motion again and began to explore the rest of the house, with Roger's waldoes opening each door as they came to it.

The kitchen was filled with new appliances. It also had a walk-in refrigerator and a walk-in pantry just as large. The dining room was actually a formal dining hall with a huge oak table, its surface richly gleaming, surrounded by matching high-backed chairs.

Then there was the other living room, the one at the front of the house. It had a small color TV, comfortable but not ostentatious furniture, a little coffee table, furnishings one might find in any middle-class home. "This is for visitors to see," Donna said. "Visitors like me. We never get beyond this room and never find out what kind of money he has. He had all this, and he kept me in that rathole and waited for me to go crazy. . . ." She squeezed the joystick controls so hard that her hands went white.

Roger stood and moved behind her; unasked, he put his arms around Donna and felt her shaking in anger and hurt. He laid his cheek alongside hers, but she didn't take her eyes from the screen. "I'm sorry," he whispered.

She sat rigid for another moment, then slumped, her hands sliding off the controls to flop into her lap. "Was I just not good enough for him? Or what?" Her voice cracked on the last word. Roger glanced at Elsie, who looked confused and helpless; it occurred to Roger that the nymph might not even know yet how to comfort someone.

Roger held Donna tighter. "Sure you were. You were better than he ever deserved. But good wasn't what he wanted. He wanted a slave, like Julia, someone to accommodate him any way he wanted, someone who wouldn't threaten him by being smarter or more talented than he was. Would you have done that for him? Or for anybody?"

She shook her head.

"So he left you, and he punished you." The injustice of that finally hit Roger. He found *himself* starting to shake with anger. How anyone could have been so cruel to someone like Donna — but he held himself in check, since she didn't need to experience his anger, too. "Donna, he's a bastard, maybe the worst I've ever met, and nothing he did to you was your fault. It was all him."

Slowly, she nodded. "You're right. It's just . . . it still hurts. I thought I'd gotten it out of my system, the way he just dumped me. But this brought it all back. . . ." She patted Roger's arms. "Thanks."

"Welcome." Reluctantly, he released her and sat down again. Her expression was still wounded, but she was back in control of herself.

On the ground floor, they explored a bank of guest bedrooms, then took the stairs to the second floor.

The master bedroom was full of black and chrome furniture, stylish and uncomfortable-looking. Kevin's walk-in closet was filled with formal dress, business suits, and designer-brand sportswear; Julia's was crowded with designer originals. Roger glanced over at Donna, but she no longer looked wounded; she was grim.

One of the second-story bedrooms was filled with exercise equipment and a jacuzzi. A massive pool table, a felt-topped card table, a wet bar and a big-screen TV filled the game room.

Another converted bedroom served as an office. Its desk and personal computer were identical to the ones Kevin had at Nonesuch books. The office had its own bathroom, and another door led to a room that did not open onto the main hall.

Roger motioned Donna toward the other door, but she shook her head. "We're not done here. Look at this." She moved the drone directly over the desk and added, "If you'd point that camera of yours straight down . . ."

He obliged, then grinned as the camera view showed the calendar-blotter atop his desk. "He doesn't put his schedule on the computer."

"Nope."

The two of them scanned the calendar, with Roger flipping pages with his waldoes. Many of the calendar entries were meaningless; others were highly interesting. *Call NSB about backlist. Alimony for Stupid — forget to sign the check?* That entry was crossed out, doubtless since Donna went into hiding. Roger spared her another glance; her expression was cold.

Call Berman. MArtCon XIII. The last entry was written across three days, Friday through Sunday, several weeks in the future.

"Who's Berman?" Roger asked.

"Arnie Berman. Kevin's publicity creep. Since Kevin hit it big, he hasn't had the time to do all his own press releases, arrange his convention schedule, that sort of thing; Berman does all that."

With the drone's equipment, Roger and Donna dutifully recorded everything they saw, then turned their attention to the other door out of the room. Roger used his waldoes to open it and flip the light switch on as the drone entered.

"A museum," Donna said, and she was nearly right. The walls of this windowless room were covered with Kevin's paintings; its tables and museum-style glass cases were filled with unusual items.

Roger's eye was drawn first to the original "Achilles and Penthesilia" painting, just as he'd seen it on the paperback cover and in Kevin's portfolio. Then he frowned — no, it wasn't identical to the print version. There were subtle differences in the faces of the two characters, in the gorgon-head design painted on Achilles' shield. That was odd; it wasn't like Kevin to alter a painting once it was already in print.

Donna panned the drone around, past a painting of a nude Julia; Kevin had lavished a lot more time on it than on most paintings and it was more professional, less awkward, than his usual work. Next was a menacing-looking gargoyle on a church ledge, just opening its glowing eyes to glare down on surprised passersby.

Then there was a French maid, a horrid stereotype: wide-open eyes full of naivete and willingness, a maid's black uniform and lacy white apron. The uniform featured a push-up bustier that piled her breasts uncomfortably high, and her fishnet hose were held up by garters that peeked out from beneath her abbreviated skirt. Donna's expression became contemptuous; she continued panning.

Next was the painting of Secret Service-style agents in suits and opaque sunglasses, then the one of the interior of Fort Knox with gold bars piled high, then the mythic Arabian warrior and veiled princess riding atop the flying carpet, then the winged feathered snakes rearing back to sink their fangs into the Aztec warrior.

Donna turned the camera's eye to the objects on the tables and in the museum cases. One was a medieval-style two-handed sword; as they watched, little blue flames licked up and down its blade, though no source for the flames was evident. On a stand-up rack was a set of chain-mail armor, far shinier and more beautiful than any real-world armor. "From his *Knight of Faerie* cover," Donna said. "Fairy mail armor. Good stuff, in the novel."

One museum case held an entire bank of crystal balls . . . but these were not like the crystal balls Roger had seen at street fairs and conventions. A different scene, with a different cast of characters, played on each, as if each crystal ball were a television set tuned to a different channel. Some of them just showed empty rooms: bedrooms, offices, conference rooms.

No, it wasn't exactly like TV; the images in the crystal balls didn't cut from camera to camera the way a TV show would. Each tracked only one person, following him wherever he went.

Roger frowned and pointed at one of the balls, which showed a vigorous middle-aged man seated at a desk, reading papers. "Uh, Donna — isn't that the President?"

She peered. "Yes, it is. That's the Oval Office. Is this some kind of joke?"

Slowly, he shook his head. "I don't think so. I think Kevin's spying on the White House."

"You're kidding, right?"

"No. Who are these other people?"

They looked at the other crystal balls, trying to make sense of the faces and images they saw, but none of the others were familiar. "I guess we don't travel in the right circles," Roger said. "Probably heads of business, other politicians, that sort of thing."

Elsie spoke for the first time since her return. "Roger, I hear something strange." She pointed at the two speakers on the control system — the speakers playing whatever the drone's sensors picked up.

Donna asked, "What does it sound like?"

"Scrapings, creakings," answered the nymph. "Very quiet."

Roger scowled. "Could be they've returned. We might want to get out of here. If — what the hell?"

He jerked upright as a loud "clank" sounded over the speakers. The camera view whipped to one side, then blurred and rocked as the drone zoomed across the room to slam into the wall. Roger and Donna both cringed, though neither could feel pain from the impact.

"Did you bump the controls?"

"I didn't touch them!" She touched them now, grabbing them and struggling to get the drone back under control. She righted it, steadied it, turned it around to look at the room again —

A living, bright-eyed gargoyle, the same monster from the painting, now alive and three-dimensional, charged the drone.

Donna yelped, then yanked on the controls, zooming the drone up and to the right just as the stony-skinned creature lunged for it. A crunching noise came over the speakers — the gargoyle hitting the wall instead of the drone. Then there was another clank as the drone hit the ceiling. But the camera view showed only wall and ceiling as Donna struggled to regain control of the flying sphere.

"Turn it around!" Roger shouted. "I can't see it!"

"I *know* that." Donna managed to spin the drone around, only to see the gargoyle leaping at the camera, its wings half-extended, its claws out. She yanked the controls to the side again, dodging the creature's leap but losing sight of it again. "I know, I know!" she shouted, to forestall another comment from Roger.

Instead of spinning on the gargoyle again, she centered the camera view on the door and shoved the drone into forward movement. The drone zipped into Kevin's office, out into the hall, down to the end of the hall by the top of the stairs; and only there did she whip it around to face the way they'd come.

The gargoyle, gnarled and menacing, the yellow in its eyes brighter than ever, emerged from the office door and turned their way.

Coolly, Donna brought the weapons systems up and centered the targeting bracket on the gargoyle's chest. It took a second; the gargoyle was more than halfway to them; then she thumbed the button to fire.

It was the particle beam; with the sound on, they could all hear the loud, satisfying "Zap!" the weapon made, and the screen washed out in white static for a moment. "Way to go, Donna!" Roger crowed, and Elsie clapped.

Then the screen cleared.

Gargoyle face and chest, only a couple of feet from the drone's camera. Its arms were outstretched, its hands were out of sight where the wide-angle lens distorted the camera view.

It held the drone. Donna tugged at the controls but the drone didn't budge.

"Donna . . ."

"The particle beam didn't work!"

"Try the laser."

She did, to little effect; the unseen beam traced a black scar across the gargoyle's face but seemingly did it no harm. The gargoyle merely opened its mouth — a mouth far wider, far toothier than any human's — and prepared to bite the drone.

Roger jammed his hands into the waldo controls and grabbed at the gargoyle with both "hands." On screen, they saw the two spindly robot arms grab at the creature's nose and jaw, holding the teeth away from the drone's skin.

"Good, Roger! Hold it still." Donna concentrated, carefully positioning the aiming bracket over the gargoyle's face. Roger did his best, straining against the waldo controls; their built-in resistance let him feel how hard it was to hold the gargoyle still. He couldn't, really, but he was distracting it.

Then Donna got the weapon bracket in place over the gargoyle's eye and hit the trigger. The left eye blackened; the gargoyle bellowed in pain. The camera view wobbled as the gargoyle dropped the drone and clutched its face; the drone fell less than a foot before its flight system caught it.

Donna yanked the controls sideways and sent the drone down the flight of stairs. "Good job, Roger. Let's get out of here. Fast."

Crashing and bellowing noises followed the drone as it flew to the bottom of the stairwell, through the living room, and to the back door.

Closed. Locked. Just the way Roger had left it. He cursed and activated the door-picking tool.

"Forget it, Roger, let's just go." Donna thumbed the particle-beam weapon and another loud blast sounded through the speakers; a second later, when the noise and screen static cleared, the door was gone, with only flaming pieces remaining at the hinges. The speakers caught the sound of an alarm ringing close by.

Donna launched the drone through the smoking doorway . . . and then the camera view shook again as something hit the flying sphere. She cursed and hauled back on the altitude control, but the drone ascended only a dozen feet in the time it would normally have taken to climb two hundred.

Roger traversed the camera around. Yes, it was the gargoyle again, only one eye glowing this time; its hands were out of sight around the edges of the camera, where it gripped the metal skin of the drone. In the camera view, they could see that the particle beam had done the creature damage; some of the stony skin on its chest was chipped away, leaving glassy gray surface behind. But the weapon just hadn't done *enough* damage.

The gargoyle was chewing. Wire, metal shavings, and bits of glass dribbled out of its mouth. It opened its mouth again, bit, and came away with another mouthful of drone innards. The speaker cut out, and Roger found that the waldoes no longer responded to his motions.

"No weapons, either." Donna looked at him, miserably, but didn't relax her hold on the altitude control; too slowly, the drone continued to climb. "Roger, I think it's got us."

He shook his head. "It only has the drone. We can lose it. I can paint another one."

"I'd rather Kevin didn't have *anything* from us. Nothing to study."

"I can give you that. What's the altitude?" He withdrew his hands from the waldo controls and hit another button on his console. A small black panel popped up on the control board beside his keyboard. Under it was a blinking red button.

"One hundred and twenty. Still going up. What's that?"

"Self-destruct."

"*Self-destruct?* I didn't put in a self-destruct mechanism!"

He grinned. "No, I did. What good is a spy without a cyanide pill?" He gestured at the blinking button. "Do you want to do the honors?"

She looked at him for another moment, then drove the button home.

There was no blast, no long shot of the drone and gargoyle swallowed by a fireball. The screen just went blank.

Donna sat back, disappointed. "It got us," she said.

"It didn't get anything. Everything the drone saw and heard, we have on tape." Remembering, he hit the button to stop the VCR, then sent the tape into rewind.

"Okay, so we just lost the drone. But we still got caught at it; we didn't put together a machine tough enough to deal with his stupid gargoyle . . . what are you so happy about?"

Try as he might, he couldn't keep from grinning. "Because this is the first time we've run into anything of Kevin's without losing or being chased off. It's also the first time we took any part of the fight to him, instead of the other way around. Donna, this was a draw. We bumped heads with Kevin, and now everybody gets to go back to his own corner. He's got a year or two of practice on us, and we just slapped him around. Next time, we'll be even better. Isn't that worth something?"

She thought about it for a moment, then offered a faint smile. "Maybe it is. But when you draw that replacement drone . . ."

"Yeah?"

"Give it a spray-paint attachment. I want to visit Julia's closet again."

Chapter Seven

Technique

Donna's disappearance and Roger's supposed suicide had never made it to the news, but the mysterious
explosion over Kevin's house was too big to keep from
the press. Roger read the next morning's city paper
with interest.

According to the paper, burglars broke into the
home of businessman Kevin Matthews at about 8:00
P.M. the previous night. Police speculated that the
intruders brought explosives into the house to blow
Matthews' safe — Roger frowned; he didn't know
Kevin *had* a safe — but something went wrong. The
explosives detonated in midair over Matthews' house,
shattering most of the facing windows on the block.
The police speculated that the explosive's timer activated prematurely, panicking the thieves into hurling
the device out a window. The burglars left hastily, using
a smaller charge to blow the house's back door off its
hinges.

The reporters weren't happy with the police analy-
sis. They asked questions: What about the next-door
neighbor who heard what sounded like cries of pain
and minor blasts *before* the big boom at the end? Why,
since Matthews reported nothing missing, did the
burglars not steal anything on the way out? Why did
the burglars blow off the back door when they could
just have opened it? Why weren't any of Mr. Matthews'
windows damaged by the explosion? But the police
weren't talking.

It was obvious to Roger that Kevin's house had bulletproof windows; otherwise the explosion would have shattered them, too. But where were the pieces of the gargoyle? Had it been blown into pieces too small to recognize? As Roger painted the new drone, he was irritated by all the unanswered questions.

This drone would be a much-improved version. Its camera rig would broadcast a 360° view of its surroundings. It had two sets of waldoes, one set for manipulation, one set with claw attachments for fighting. It had thicker armor — thick enough, Roger hoped, to hold back biting jaws for a while.

He pulled the drone into the real world a couple of hours after dark. Then he and Donna sent it flying back to town, to Kevin's house.

To Kevin's *empty* house. Every window was dark. Their infrared scan of the house showed nothing moving within. The back door was a new, unpainted slab of thick oak; its lock was much easier to pick than yesterday's.

Most of the house's interior was unchanged from yesterday. But the office and "art gallery" next to it were cleaned out. The bedroom closets were nearly empty of clothes. Roger didn't even bother looking for the safe; he knew that it, too, had to be empty.

"They've gone." Donna smiled victoriously. "We chased them off."

"That we did." But Roger's expression was less happy. "I wish we hadn't."

"How so?"

"Well, we're back where we started. Yesterday, we knew where he lived. Today, we don't. We've lost one of our advantages."

"True." Her smile went away. "Well, let's bring this thing back." They guided the second drone out of Kevin's house and sent it flying back toward their own home.

Once it was back, she asked, "What do we try next?"

He shook his head. "You're the brains of the outfit. You tell me."

"I wouldn't know where to start. Tracking him down would take someone who knows a lot more than I do." Her expression brightened. "That's it! Paint Sherlock Holmes."

"Now, that's an idea! But he's sort of stuck in the Victorian Age, isn't he? It might take him a while to bone up on modern forensics. Not to mention magic. How about James Bond?"

"No thanks. He'd just make passes at me and Elsie all the time, and then when trouble started, he'd walk away clean while the rest of us got blown up. How about Doc Savage? I know he was from the '30s, but he was way ahead of his time."

"Maybe." Roger thought about it. "A good guy, had an invention for everything, and real tough when it came to fights. I wonder if he'd be a match for Achilles and Penthesilia."

"Well, let's find out! First thing tomorrow morning, start sketching us a man of bronze."

He shook his head. "Not first thing. Walking around today, I found a stand of trees about half a mile from here. I want to test out the 'Trantham's Troopers' gun there tomorrow morning. Afternoon's soon enough to start on Doc."

"I suppose." She was silent for a moment. "You staying up? *Casablanca* comes on the tube in a little while. I could pop some popcorn. . . ."

"Any other time, I'd say yes. I always had a yen for Ingrid Bergman. But I'm bushed." He suppressed a yawn and checked his watch. "I get so tired pulling things out of paintings that I'm starting to take on farmer's hours. Barely nine o'clock and I'm ready to crash."

"Go ahead, then. I'll tell Ingrid you said hi."

Roger gave her a smile and headed off for his bedroom. Donna had become a lot more positive in the last few days. She was no less pushy, no more willing to take a back seat to anyone, but her cheerfulness had returned. Roger fell asleep wondering just what kind of idiot Kevin Matthews had been to throw her away.

For the first time in a dozen years, Roger woke at dawn. And despite his horror at that predicament, he couldn't go back to sleep. He rose, quietly dressed, and sneaked out. Elsie's door was still closed; he was up even before the nymph, quite a novelty for him.

It wouldn't do for someone to see him carrying an alien firearm, so he left the high-tech weapon in the trunk of the car as he drove the dirt road that passed near the stand of trees he'd chosen. Within minutes, he strode like a futuristic invader through the scrub trees, looking for a likely target and staying very alert for possible witnesses.

His first target was a blighted-looking post oak toward the center of the stand. From a half-dozen yards away, he braced the futuristic rifle in the fork of another tree, carefully aimed along the old-fashioned iron sights he'd drawn on the weapon, and slowly pulled the trigger, just as he'd done when he was twelve and learning to fire a .22 rifle.

There was no recoil, but a bright, jagged wave of blue light arced from the front of his weapon to hit the tree.

The dead oak exploded with a noise like a clap of thunder. Everything above the midpoint of the trunk leaped, flaming, into the air. The trunk stayed put, charred for three feet below the point of separation. Roger saw it all as if it were filmed in slow motion, his eyes widening.

Then flaming debris rained down on him. Roger involuntarily took a step back and stumbled on a root, ending up on his rear end. Flaming bits of wood rained on him for another few seconds. Finally, he looked at the remains of his target, and uttered an awed "Shit."

It took him a few minutes to stomp out all the flaming patches. While he waited to make sure that no one would come to investigate the noise, he looked the weapon over again, hoping to find out more about the way it worked. But there was no counter to tell how many more shots remained, no control to alter the size of the weapon's blast, no hatch allowing him to look into the weapon's guts. He spent a few more minutes complaining about the shortsighted weapon manufacturer before realizing, embarrassed, that he was griping about himself.

By the time he was ready to try another shot, traffic had increased over on the dirt road. Better to wait for another time and find a firing range farther away from people.

He put the weapon back into the trunk and drove back into town, but passed by his house. The experience with the weapon had rattled him; he decided to calm down over breakfast at the 24-hour pancake place.

Stuffed full of pecan waffles, much less jittery, Roger got back to the house just after eight in the morning. As his car slewed to a stop in the driveway, he could see Donna through the window; she was fully dressed, unusual for her in a light summer dress, and talking on the kitchen phone. But when he strolled into the kitchen, she was — atypically — laboring away at the stove. She looked over and smiled: "Morning, Roger. How do you want your eggs?"

"None for me, thanks. I was up early and ate out." As he said the words, he winced. He knew she hated to cook. She'd gone to all this trouble and he'd turned her down cold. She was going to be mad. . . .

But she wasn't. She just nodded and continued working at a pair of fried eggs. "Well, sit down and relax. I've been thinking, we just haven't had any time to goof off. Would you like a drink? Some wine?"

He eased himself down into one of the kitchen table chairs. "Donna, it's way too early in the morning for that. Thanks anyway. Goof off, huh? What about Doc Savage?"

She didn't answer immediately; she was absorbed in using a spatula to transfer the eggs to a plate. "We can always reschedule the appointment. Take today off."

He looked at her, confused. "The appointment?"

She tensed, tried to keep her voice light. "With Dr. Savage."

"Oh. Right." He blinked. What had her so distracted?

No. She wouldn't forget who Doc Savage was. Suspicion crawled across his spine. "Who were you talking to on the phone?"

"You know. The nymph."

"Elsie?"

"That's right."

"So where is she?"

"At a friend's." She brought her plate over and sat at Roger's left.

"At Dy—" He clamped down on his answer. "At David's?"

"That's right. At David's."

Jesus Christ. Roger's mouth felt dry. *This isn't Donna!* She wore Donna's face, all right, but with little hints of orange on her too-shiny skin. The sick feeling in Roger's stomach quadrupled in strength. He managed a big, fake smile to conceal the grimace he couldn't hold back. "Donna, I think I've changed my mind. A glass of wine would be nice."

"Sure."

As she began rummaging around inside the refrigerator, Roger reached out with his perceptions to find Elsie's mind. For a moment or two he felt nothing — then, he felt her, faint, very far away. This wasn't as easy as it used to be, and he couldn't hold on to the contact for long. Within moments, he'd lost her.

He did a fast rundown on his available resources. The Trantham gun, the Browning pistol, and the two sets of Kevlar-and-ceramic armor were in his trunk. Dammit. Closer at hand were the kitchen knives. His paintings were in his room, but it took time to pull anything out of a painting.

He moved up beside Donna and opened the cabinet where the glasses were kept. In the time it took him to pull out a pair of the landlord's wine glasses with his right hand, he managed to get his left hand on a kitchen knife. He hid it behind his back and sat again.

Donna finally moved enough things around to extricate the bottle — an inexpensive domestic white she liked. Rather, that the *real* Donna liked. She came back to the table; then, her smile fixed, she reversed her hold on the bottle's neck, brought it high into the air, and swung it down at Roger's head.

If he hadn't known, if he hadn't seen the tell-tale marks of Kevin's painting style, Roger would have been hit. But he swore and lunged away, getting the table between them. The bottle came down on the back of his chair, shattering, raining wine and broken glass all over the corner of the kitchen.

Still smiling, she kept her hold on the neck of the bottle; its jagged edges would slice skin like a blade. Roger pulled his own knife out before him. "Donna, whoever you are, don't do this. You don't have to. The real Donna wouldn't."

She lost her smile and moved around the table. He countered, keeping the table between them; he had to walk across the crunching glass and kick his chair out of his way.

"If you die, I get to *be* the real Donna," she said. "If you'd just relax, I could cut your throat or something. You're making this very difficult." She looked sad and tears appeared in her eyes. "Won't you let me cut your throat, Roger? I'd really appreciate it."

Roger's skin crawled, but he didn't answer. When the door was to his back, he turned and bolted into the living room, running toward the front door of the house. The not-Donna gave an outraged squeal and followed.

Roger had his car keys out by the time he slammed through the screen door, but he knew he could never get the trunk open before she got to him. So he ran around the car, his long legs and desperation keeping him ahead of Donna's simulacrum.

He looked over his shoulder. The false Donna was on the other side of the car, also heading toward the front of the vehicle, trying to head him off. He skidded to a stop beside the driver's door. The fake Donna stopped beside the passenger door and looked at him. "Okay, Roger, I give up," she wailed. "I can't kill you. I love you. I can be Donna for you. Just come back into the house."

Roger managed to find the car key by touch. "Sure. First, drop the bottle."

She looked down at her hand, then back at him. "Okay. But you have to drop the knife first. It scares me."

"Not a chance."

Her expression went from sad to savage in a split second . . . and she came over the car top at him, a leap that left her on the vehicle's roof in easy striking distance of him. He ducked away but still felt heat and ripping pain as the jagged glass grazed his cheek.

Overbalanced, she rolled off the car top to the ground. Before she stood, Roger got back to the trunk, got the key in, twisted it . . . then she was coming at him again, waving the glass weapon. He ran, circling the car.

Think, dammit! The fake Donna wasn't too bright. "I love you," indeed. He heard her slow down as she chased him around the car and knew, with a feeling of exultation, that she was going to do it again. . . .

Just before he reached the driver-side door, he
skidded to a halt, ducked left, and swung his fist. It was
a wild swing, but it didn't matter. She was hurtling
across the car at him again. His sudden stop threw off
her aim, and his fist swung around to crack into the
side of her face.

Pain slammed through his hand and he dropped the
knife. But the fake Donna rolled from the car top to
the hood, then to the ground, a nasty fall.

He didn't wait to see how she fared. He got to the
trunk, lifted the lid, grabbed at the Browning Hi-
Power with his hurt and shaking hand, clicked the
thumb safety off . . .

The simulacrum came at him again and he jerked
the trigger out of reflex.

The bullet hit her right shoulder and shock jerked
her to a stop. He fired again, aiming properly. This shot
slammed into the center of her chest. So did the next
two.

She just stood there for a moment, face paling.
Blood, an incorrect orange-red, came pulsing from the
four wounds. The bottle neck dropped from her
fingers.

She tried to say something, some other line Kevin
must have given her, but couldn't. She fell forward,
slapped down onto the driveway gravel, and lay still.

Roger felt his knees go weak. His hands trembled as
he clutched them together on the butt of the Browning. He stared down at her body, then wiped his mouth
with the sleeve of his shirt.

First came shock at what he'd done. He didn't know
exactly what the fake Donna was — human? A
machine made of paint? But she'd acted like a person
and he'd killed her.

Then came the fear. *What are the police going to
think when they see this?*

He looked around. He was close to town, so
someone had heard the shots. It was probably being

reported. The houses out here were set well apart, with trees in between, so it was not likely that anyone had seen him. But what was he going to do about the body, the blood?

Then he saw her body change.

Some blue flaked away from the false Donna's dress and spilled to the gravel. Slightly orange skin flaked away and joined it, then brown from her hair. Within moments her entire body collapsed into flakes of — he stooped to look at them — acrylic paint. Like a painted vampire under a painted sun, she dissolved into a few pounds of inorganic material.

Roger watched the false Donna disintegrate, and the sight of it upset him even as it let him off any possible hook for murder. Then, hesitantly, he used his toe to stir the mass of flakes so that they no longer even resembled a human outline.

Why had Kevin used acrylics? he wondered. He always used oils. But . . . acrylics dry a lot faster. This was a rush job.

If the police came — he spent a few moments collecting the four brass cartridges from the Browning. Then he shut the car trunk and reentered the house. Now, if the police came to investigate the gunshots, they'd find a mess of paint flakes but nothing to connect the shots with this house.

Gun in hand, he made a quick tour of the house. There was no sign of the real Donna or Elsie, no sign of violence. In fact, the living room was neater and cleaner than it had been since they moved in. Roger grimaced. Kevin's false Donna was a tidy housekeeper, probably the perfect "little woman" Kevin had wanted Donna to be.

He was dismayed to discover that all his paintings were gone. The house was stripped of every piece of art.

Then the phone rang.

"Hi, Roger. It's Kevin. Since the new, improved

Donna didn't give me another call, I had to guess that she didn't finish you off."

Anger gripped Roger, a rage that turned his knuckles white on the phone receiver. "Where are they?"

"Don't shout. They're here. With me. And your dad, too." Kevin sounded cheerful, pleased with himself.

"My *father*? You son of a bitch! He didn't have anything to do with it!"

"Why couldn't you leave my house out of this?" Kevin asked, mocking. "My back door didn't have anything to do with it!"

Adrenaline made Roger feel light-headed. He wanted more than anything to grab Kevin around the neck and crush the life out of him. Instead, he struggled for a reply. Should he threaten Kevin? Beg? Reason?

But Kevin spoke first. "If you want to see them again, you need to come over here."

"You'll just kill me."

"No, I won't. The Donna I left, she was just a backup plan. I really wish you'd been at home when my people showed up for you. Then you'd have been hauled off with the real Donna and your nymph. That's really what I wanted. You come on over, and I won't kill you."

"I don't believe you."

"I've never broken a promise, Roger. But I don't care if you believe me or not. I'll give you ten minutes to make up your mind. If you don't show by then, I'm going to kill all three of them. That's a promise, too. And it'll be your fault. You forced me to do it."

Roger automatically glanced at his watch — 8:17. "Where are you?"

"Figure it out, Roger. I'm through doing you favors." Kevin hung up.

Roger's mind seized up. Figure out where Kevin was and get there in ten minutes or less? Then he did figure it out, almost instantly. Kevin had Roger's paintings. To get to Kevin, all he had to do was travel through one of them.

Then fear hit him. Kevin had had more than a year to create soldiers, traps, weapons, defenses, and tactics. If Roger went, he was a dead man.

And if he didn't go . . . Donna, Elsie, and C.J. would die.

The fear settled in his stomach and began to wrench at it, but Roger started moving. From the car trunk he dragged the Kevlar armor, Trantham's Troopers gun, and extra clips for the Browning. He hauled everything back into the house and locked the house, too.

He put on the armor and added a winter coat over it. The Browning and its extra clips into the coat pockets. Then he checked the time — 8:21. Four minutes were gone. He swore and took stock of his resources.

Kevin's crew had also cleaned him out of paints, but he still had the pens in his shirt pocket and a supply of paper. He sat at his table and began drawing.

He started with a human body. What sort of fighter just wore black? Viet Cong? No — Japanese ninjas. The figure he sketched took on a martial arts pose, and Roger added a long sheath across the back, pouches full of deadly tricks and weapons at its waist. The figure was very crude, but distinctly a ninja assassin, and — he checked his watch — had only taken two minutes. He started another.

The second figure, a ninja with a bow, was finished two minutes later. He had only two minutes left, and some of that had to be spent getting to Kevin's. His heart thudding, he filled the rest of the page with bombs — cartoon bombs, black and round, fuses already lit. He stood when he had half a dozen bombs on the page.

Roger tucked the page into his coat pocket, picked up the Trantham's Troopers gun, and concentrated on one of his paintings. Seconds later, he vanished from the world.

❖   ❖   ❖

Roger Simons and Carol, the Ancient Yuletide Troll, materialized out of nothingness into the small bare room.

The room had unpainted concrete walls and a matching floor and ceiling; Roger could see a rectangular shape on one wall that had to be a door, but it had no knob. In the center of the room was a pile of paintings, all Roger's; he saw older works in the pile, including those his father owned. A little weariness, from emerging from the painting with Carol, settled on him.

Carol, gruesome in her Santa Claus outfit, hefted her club, then glanced up when the hissing started.

Roger caught the sound too and looked up. In the center of the ceiling was something like a water sprayer. But fine mist, not water, was issuing from it.

Roger held his breath. He'd seen the same spy movies Kevin had. *Gas.* He immediately aimed the Trantham's Troopers gun at the door, then thought better of it — there had to be people behind it, waiting for him. He spun and fired at the opposite wall.

Blue lightning arced from the front of the gun and a massive "Boom" shook the room. Concrete shrapnel exploded from the wall. Roger felt his already bloody cheek take a hit as if from a dart. But he'd blown an irregular hole, five feet across, in the center of the wall. The lawn outside was littered with chunks of concrete and brick.

He stepped through the hole. Beyond the lawn were trees and undergrowth, but no buildings; this had to be some sort of country house. He bolted for the trees and extended a little bit of attention back for his trollish companion. He found her mind, gave it a tug, and Carol lumbered after him.

The two of them reached the tree line, then turned. They were looking at the side of a sprawling, single-story brick house. The hole Roger had made was in a windowless stretch of the wall.

A handful of men emerged from that hole. They looked like Secret Service agents, all suits and sunglasses and clean-cut features, and Roger remembered their painting in Kevin's private study.

Then two more figures ran around the corner of the house, to Roger's left. Achilles carried a spear and a round shield, Penthesilia a bow; both of them wore the anachronistic Greek hoplite armor Kevin had painted them in. "What happened?" Penthesilia called. One of the agents pointed straight at Roger and Carol, shouted, "There they are!"

Roger cursed. He'd thought they were well hidden, considering the little time they'd had. Then he glanced at Carol. Her red-and-white Santa Claus suit stood out against the underbrush like a neon sign.

He pointed at Achilles and Penthesilia and said, "They're yours." Carol lunged out of the underbrush and charged toward the mythological figures, moving with a bizarre waddling gait. She began swinging her oversized club with an expression of glee on her ghastly features.

The agents began to scatter, pulling pistols from waist and shoulder holsters. Roger swung up the Trantham gun to cover them . . . then hesitated. With the pull of a trigger, he could wipe out half a dozen lives, even if they were artificial lives, and sudden anguish hit him. *I'm an artist. I'm not a soldier. I'm —*

One agent assumed a firing stance and shouted something straight out of Kevin Matthews' favorite cop shows: "Give it up, Simons. You don't have a chance."

Donna. Elsie. Dad. Roger pulled the trigger and swung the barrel back and forth.

The blue spray of destructive force washed across the men and the side of the house. The agents went down and backwards, charred black in places; bricks and boards erupted from the side of the house. The weapon's "boom" shattered windows further along the wall. In a split second, the fight was done, and artificial men lay twitching and screaming on the side lawn. Two of them immediately began to dissolve into paint. Roger looked at them for one long moment . . . but there just wasn't time to think about what he'd done.

He glanced left. Achilles reached Carol; Penthesilia stayed several steps back, at close firing range.

The troll swung her club. Achilles got his shield up, but the force of the blow knocked him off his feet. The sound of the impact cracked as an echo off the side of the house. Penthesilia fired an arrow deep into Carol's shoulder, and the troll's green blood spurted out over her red Santa tunic; the troll wailed in anger.

Roger wanted to watch but had to move. He sprinted right, staying within the treeline. As he moved, another half-dozen agents spilled out of the hole in the wall, but their attention was drawn to Carol and her opponents; they didn't spot him.

Roger reached the turn in the treeline and looked at the rear of the house: many windows, a small and unostentatious door. He was already starting to pant for breath; under the sun, wearing a coat over bulletproof body armor, he was sweltering.

Then he heard Carol's scream — a shriek of pain, not some bloodthirsty or happy war cry — and he knew the troll was dead. Unaccountably, he felt sad. But he had no time; Kevin's followers would be coming after him as soon as they picked up his trail.

He pulled the crumpled black-and-white page from his pocket and closed his eyes. When he opened them again, a ninja warrior, bow in hand, stood beside him, awaiting instructions.

It wasn't completely human. Its skin was pure white; its eyes under the mask were blotchy and irregular; its costume was black and indistinct. It gave Roger the creeps, and he was suddenly anxious to be well away from it. "Kill the Greeks and the guys in suits," he commanded, and the figure nodded. Roger was uneasily aware that his voice was shaky and tired. He didn't need to be this tired, this soon.

Roger left it behind and continued down the treeline facing the back of the house. When he was at the closest approach to the back door, he heard a scream and gunfire from around the corner of the building. They were catching up. . . .

He pulled out the page again, reached for the second ninja, and a moment later another ill-drawn Japanese assassin stood beside him, awaiting commands from its lord.

Roger felt himself sway and caught himself against the thin trunk of a tree. Running around, pulling two figures out of his art in quick succession, had already exhausted him. But he forced himself upright and spoke. "Guard my back. Kill the Greeks and the men in suits." This one nodded and drew its sword from its back sheath; the crude-looking *no-daichi* sword was menacing even if its blade was page-white instead of steel-silver.

Roger trotted as fast as he could manage toward the back door. Halfway across the lawn he triggered his weapon. The door exploded inward as though someone had taped a bomb to it; a second later, Roger charged through the flaming shards into a breakfast room, sweeping the gun barrel back and forth. His aim was sloppy, erratic; his hands were shaking.

The room was empty except for a table and metal chairs. Then a figure shattered through the glass door that led to the kitchen.

A metal man, nearly tall enough to scrape the ceiling, silvery skin, skeletal face and body — Roger had this quick impression as it reached for him. He brought his gun in line; the silver man's hand fell on it and squeezed as Roger pulled the trigger.

There was another boom, like thunder inside a house; the room's remaining windows shattered out. The blue lightning sliced through the silver man's waist, sending metallic fragments through the shattered door and into the kitchen. The rest of its body collapsed onto the linoleum floor, but its hand squeezed, crushing the barrel of Roger's weapon like an aluminum soda can. Then the silver man lay still.

"Shit." Dammit, he needed that weapon. He fished the Browning out of his pocket and took a look over his shoulder. The ninja was positioned inside the door, ready to defend Roger. From outside, Roger heard more shots and shrieks, and a faint bowstring "twang."

Roger stepped through the ruined door into a large, country-style kitchen. No one was there.

The next door, unlocked, opened onto a hallway. The agent walking toward him looked surprised and brought his upraised handgun down to aim. Roger squeezed his own trigger, once, twice, three times . . . and then the agent fired, too.

It felt like a horse kicked him in the gut. Roger sat down hard before he knew he was falling; the pain in his stomach bent him over and held him, blind and helpless, for long seconds. Then his vision began to clear.

The agent was down, already beginning to flake into paint. Roger gingerly felt around his own body.

The bullet had hit the Kevlar over one of the ceramic plates. Roger's stomach felt like tenderized meat, but the bullet hadn't penetrated. His legs didn't want to obey him, but he finally got up on them and continued tottering forward. He carefully pushed open the first door he came to. Empty bedroom.

The next door, up a few feet and on the other side of the hall, was an armory. There was a rack of automatic rifles on the wall, and three more agents struggled into body armor. Roger tensed, but they hadn't noticed him yet. The door was heavy; maybe it had muffled the sound of the shots.

He closed his eyes and focused on the paper in his left hand. A moment and an exertion of will later, he pulled the hand out of his pocket and held a bomb, heavy and ludicrously cannonball-shaped, its fuse already sputtering. He tossed it into the room, yanked the door shut, and trotted forward a few steps, clamping his hands over his ears.

The blast shook the wall and blew the door off its hinges. When Roger took his hands down, he heard nothing for a few moments . . . then the moaning started. He grimaced and kept going.

A moment later, he heard an irregular clanging, some distance behind him, behind the closed door to the kitchen. Metal on metal. Bronze on steel? Greek spear on Japanese *no-daichi*? He hurried.

Then that door slammed open; Roger turned and aimed. Achilles, covered with blood, a short sword in hand, charged him.

Roger pulled the trigger four times, fast. He saw rents appear in Achilles' armor where three of the bullets hit.

Then Achilles slammed into him. Roger felt a hell of a blow to his chest and everything went black.

He could only have been unconscious for the briefest of moments. But when he opened his eyes again, he was on his back, the great weight of Achilles bearing down on his bruised chest. Achilles' sword nicked his unprotected throat; the warrior's face, twisted in anger, was inches above his own. "You whoreson!" shouted the Greek, spitting in his anger. "I should kill you now. Cut out your guts and drape them on your face. Cut off your balls and let you watch the dogs eat them."

Fear turned Roger's bowels cold and loose, but some rational place in his mind told him that Achilles wouldn't do it. If he could, he would have done it already — he was that mad.

Achilles broke off his tirade, glared at Roger for a long moment, then reached over with his free hand and pulled Roger's gun from his nerveless fingers. He dragged Roger up to his feet. Three bullet holes showed in the cuirass on Achilles' chest, but no blood flowed through them.

Achilles shoved Roger into a room. Kevin's paintings were all over the walls. But Roger didn't look at them. Donna and Elsie jumped up from chairs and leaped on him, hugging him. Donna brushed at the blood on his cheek, whispered, "Roger, you're hurt." Elsie just cried. C.J. Simons stiffly stood and walked over to join them.

The two agents covering them with assault rifles didn't object to this demonstration, but Achilles gave the whole group a shove that staggered them further into the room. Roger regained his balance and ignored the Greek.

"Dad, I'm sorry —"

"Don't be sorry." His father's voice was gruff. "Matthews is sorry. He's one sorry son of a bitch."

"Donna, Elsie, are you okay? Did he hurt you?"

Donna shook her head. "He's been very polite. Like Fu Manchu." Her expression was grim, hopeless.

Elsie wailed, "I want to go home."

One of the agents pulled Roger aside and searched him while the other kept watch. The searcher stripped Roger of his coat and body armor, taking the black-and-white page and clips of ammunition, the pens from his shirt pocket. The agent left him the other contents of his pockets: the pitifully small pocketknife, a handful of change, his new key ring and wallet.

Then Achilles said, "Sit. No talking." His voice was flat and angry, and when he bothered to look at Roger he fingered the hilt of his sheathed sword. They sat.

Roger no longer had to walk or to talk; all he could do was think. And depression settled on him, weighed him down. *I screwed up. I failed. They got me, and we're all dead.* Donna tried to catch his eye but, weary and ashamed, he wouldn't look at her.

A couple of minutes later two battered and bruised agents walked in, carrying Penthesilia on a stretcher. The Amazon had an arrow in her chest; from the way she coughed, the shaft must have gone through her lung. There was a nasty black bruise across the left side of her face, and her bare right thigh was tied across with a blood-soaked bandage. Achilles looked at her, stricken, then gave Roger another gut-eating glare. The Greek knelt by the Amazon when her stretcher was set down; he took the hand of the semiconscious woman and spoke quietly to her.

Then Kevin walked in, dressed in a two-piece suit, his tie askew. He was unusually florid; he'd obviously been doing a lot of walking or running. He was dictating to another agent, " . . . cleaned up before I bring out the carpenters and masons. That troll body will have to go into the disposal painting, I guess, since it doesn't do us the courtesy of dissolving." He came to a stop in the center of the room. "Hey, Big Rog! By God, you gave me some trouble. Most of my agents down, my silver security guy . . . you did good." He was his usual cheery self; he could have been congratulating Roger on a basketball victory.

"Drop dead."

Kevin grinned. "Mind if I ask you a couple of questions?"

"Yes."

"Why didn't your troll disintegrate when she died?"

"I don't know."

"And those ninjas — were they really black-and-whites?"

Roger nodded, sullen.

"I'm amazed." Kevin shook his head, his expression admiring. "I didn't know you could make black-and-whites come alive. You've been doing this for what, a couple of weeks? And you've already figured out a thing or two I didn't know." His face twitched, and for an instant Roger could see the irritation and sheer envy underneath Kevin's expression. "Well, game's over, Rog, but you sure did give me a show. I might —"

Achilles stood, releasing Penthesilia's hand, and interrupted: "Put her back."

Kevin swung to glare at him. "*What* did you say?"

Achilles gestured at the Amazon. "She's dying. Put her back in the painting."

Kevin shrugged. "I can just pull you out a new one."

"She wouldn't be the same! She'd be the way she was before, when we were new." Achilles' voice was hoarse, unwillingly pleading.

Kevin grinned broadly. "You can start all over, win her affection again. Springtime *is* for lovers, you know."

Achilles took a step forward, and Roger saw the big Greek's hand twitch toward his sheathed sword. But all Achilles did was speak one desperate word: "Please."

Kevin hesitated, then shrugged and nodded. He moved beside Penthesilia, touched her and concentrated. Maybe twenty seconds later, he waved toward the painting of Achilles and Penthesilia on the wall . . . and the Amazon faded away to nothingness, disappearing off the stretcher as if she'd never been there, with only spots of blood left behind. "There," he told Achilles. "I'm going to leave her there for a while, as punishment. She screwed up and got clobbered. By a stupid joke troll and a *black and white*, for God's sake!"

Something was wrong — Roger stared at the "Achilles and Penthesilia" painting. "Wait a minute. If that was the painting she came out of, why was the painting still complete when she was running around in the real world?"

Kevin looked back at him, grinned. "Oho. So I still do know a couple of things you don't. Haven't you figured out that you don't have to wreck your painting when you pull something out of it?"

"No. I didn't know that."

"Yes, sir." Kevin held up three fingers, mocking the Boy Scout gesture. "Takes a little more concentration,

that's all. You can pull your little friends out and leave
the painting untouched. If you do it that way and your
character gets killed, you can pull out a new, fresh
copy. The new one won't have the memories or
experience the first one had outside of the painting . . .
unless you do a couple of other things . . . but it's a lot
better than wrecking your painting whenever you need
a servant."

"You're kidding," Roger said. If he could get Kevin
talking, maybe he could think of something, some way
to get out from under the guns of the surviving agents.

Kevin sat down in a chair a safe distance from
Roger. "Not at all. There are a lot of things I can do you
probably haven't figured out yet." This prospect
obviously cheered him. "For instance, did you know
you can look into your painting, watch anyone in the
world it represents? That's really handy when you've
put someone into the painting. Or that when you're
inside it, you can look out, take a look around the place
where the painting is?"

Roger shook his head and wished he'd known that
little fact when he was coming here. It might not have
done him much good, but he could've used more
breaks than he had.

Kevin smiled. "You — rather, I — can set paintings
up to react to external stimuli. Like someone prowling
around in my office. The painting is triggered, the
subject pops out of the painting and deals with it. Like
you must have tripped my gargoyle the other night.

"What else, oh, yeah. People you pull out of
paintings and leave out for a while tend to develop
annoying little traits that you didn't give them. I
mean, Penthesilia started developing an aversion to
my art — to *my* art, isn't that ironic? Stupid bitch.
But you can fix that. Put her back in the painting, do
a little touch-up work or alteration on her figure
while thinking about the traits you want to correct;
the next time you bring her out, she's all better. Just

the way you want her to be. It keeps loyal subjects loyal."

Much as he wanted to concentrate on a way out of their predicament, Roger was increasingly absorbed in what Kevin had to say. "And can you teach what you do to someone else? I mean, Achilles was able to put me into a painting . . ."

"That's not teaching. That's just reinterpreting. I shoved him back into his painting and touched him up while I thought about him having an extra ability — the power to push people into one of my paintings." Kevin's expression became a little more serious. "By the way, how did you get out of that painting of hell?"

Roger stayed silent. Achilles' eyes narrowed; he was obviously curious about that.

Kevin shook his head, grinned again. "You're a fast learner. You must have figured out how to send yourself into your own paintings before all those happy demons tore you to pieces. Too bad. I should've used one that's instantly lethal. Though I wouldn't do that to you today." He looked across the room at a painting of a white room occupied by four large, crude statues.

"Kevin . . . how did you learn to do this? Was it an accident, like it was with me?"

Matthews nodded. "More or less. I was in New York, doing a little touch-up work on a batch of paintings I'd sold to a publisher there. I fell asleep fixing a painting of a spaceship launch — you know, the one on 'Transit to Golightly.' I dreamed about the ship taking off . . . and then I woke up with this roaring in my ears, and a little spaceship had shot out of my painting and smashed into the ceiling!" He laughed. "Bunch of little dead guys inside, too. But with me, see, the painting wasn't affected. I didn't learn until later that you could pull the image off the painting with the character. I experimented for a while, then painted a computer super-genius who could transfer money electronically into dummy files, got rich quick, figured out ways to account for all that money on the stock market and in betting. That was a lot of fun.

"I set up a couple of holding companies and bought Nonesuch Books so that I could get my work into print without having a bunch of idiots telling me what's good, what's bad, what they think needs to be fixed. But it occurred to me that I could have some fun, too, so I had them contract you for all those paintings. Hope you don't mind." His grin was full of malice.

Roger kept his expression neutral in spite of the anger he felt. "Let me ask you something. You could've gotten to be the richest man in the world, had Julia, had everything you wanted . . . why couldn't you do something good, too? All you do is waste your time on this petty, bullshit revenge. Why screw up my career and Donna's? Why don't you create some guy who knows the cure to cancer? Work up a spacecraft with faster-than-light drive and a scientist to publish how it's done?"

Kevin just shook his head. "Roger, you still don't get it.

"First, screwing up your life . . . well, you deserved it. You spent all those years stealing assignments from me, winning all those awards I wanted. That's the way it was all through college. Roger this, Roger that. 'You might look at Roger Simons' stuff. You could learn a lot from him.' You know how tired I got of hearing that?" He no longer looked amused. "They were laughing at me, Roger. But nobody laughs at me anymore. They laugh at you. When I'm done, they're going to think Roger Simons painted velvet Elvises."

Kevin actually shook with anger; then, with an effort, he controlled himself, though he didn't smile again. "What else did you ask about? Oh, yes. Cures and spacecraft and such — most of that just wouldn't work."

"Why not?"

"Because science doesn't have anything to do with it, stupid!" Kevin stood and scowled down at Roger as though at an annoying child. "Look, have you created any devices, gadgets? Didn't you have some sort of blaster gun?"

"That's right."

"Did you open any of them, look inside?"

"Well . . . no."

"You would've found garbage, Rog. Parts that looked like high technology but didn't really work. An artist's visual impression of technology he can't understand."

"So if it's not technology, what is it?"

Kevin shrugged. "Beats the hell out of me. I just do what they used to do. I call it magic."

"Magic . . . crap, Kevin."

"A lot you know. Rog, if you created Dr. Superior, the Man Who Cured Cancer, you'd get some sort of weirdo with abilities no one else could understand, a guy who could work up an anti-cancer potion no one else could reproduce. I suppose you could paint a spaceship, too, but nobody could reproduce the technology that went into it. Roger, you and I, we're not Tom Swift. We're Merlin.

"Listen, I've poured a lot of money on researchers and scholars, told them to look for — what did they call it? — historical anomalies. Little patterns or weird events that would tell us about other people who could do the same thing. And I've found a few references that make me think there've been others like us.

"My guess . . . and it's only a guess . . . is that we're doing what a few people could do way back in the past. Magic, for real. It took very strong conceptual abilities, Rog. The ability to visualize something with crystal clarity, all its details, all its traits. And it probably took something else, too. Maybe something hereditary, I don't know. Otherwise all the good artists would be magicians, right?"

"And all the crummy ones, too, Kevin." Roger saw an expression of annoyance cross Kevin's face; he switched topics. "So, how did you find us?"

Kevin smiled grimly. "You screwed up, Rog. Don't feel too bad; I screwed up, too.

"You sent a flying ball to my house the night after your first visit. I'd left a new minion waiting, just in case you did something stupid like that. He was a little guy about six inches tall, wings like a bat's, flies at about the speed of sound. Your thingamajig shows up, takes off again, my little guy follows it all the way to your place, then comes back into town to fetch Achilles and Penthesilia to where you live.

"But that's where I screwed up. I gave the little guy barely enough brains to do his job. He didn't know how to read, how to give directions; he could just lead. So he had to lead Achilles and Penthesilia overland all the way to your place. It took hours. They were pretty pissed off when they called after jogging across all those miles of fields and highways all night. Good thing I made them tough.

"Penthesilia bagged your nymph with a sling when she came trotting out of the house just after dawn, and Achilles had no problem with Donna." Roger glanced at Elsie and Donna; neither one looked injured, but Elsie was still trembling. Roger felt another flash of anger.

Kevin continued, "But you weren't there, Rog. The nymph was out cold, and Donna wouldn't talk. Well, actually, she wouldn't shut up, but nothing she said was useful." He looked sourly at his ex-wife. "I didn't know when you'd get back: an hour later, a day. So I left an improved version of Donna I worked up a few days ago." He pointed to one wall, where the hasty acrylic of Donna hung. "I guess you wiped her out."

"I guess I did." Roger kept his voice level . . . but he hadn't thought up any way out of their predicament, and desperation was getting to him.

Kevin rose and stretched. "Time for you and your little group of friends to go to prison. You ready?"

"No." He sighed. "Kevin, I know what you've said,

but I know you plan to kill us. But you *don't have to*. Just let us go. Stop screwing around with us. You won't lose anything, you'll still have your fortune —"

"Forget it."

"Goddammit, do you hate us that much? Enough to kill people who don't deserve it?"

Kevin took a long time to answer. Then, finally, he shook his head, looking serious, even regretful. "No, Rog. Not enough to kill you. I hate you enough to screw up your life. And I did. If you'd left it there, I would have been happy to watch you live in a crappy little apartment and slowly go broke. That would've been fine.

"But you figured out how to do what I do. The magic. I can't have that. No one else can do what I do. You might come after me —"

"Let us go, and we won't."

"No one else can do what I do, period! Shut up!" Kevin flushed red. "You don't get a choice, you dumb son of a bitch. You do exactly as I say. *Exactly*. You're my slave. Shut the fuck up." He pinned one of his guards with his glare. "He says another word, shoot him. No, forget that. He says another word, blow the nymph's goddam head off." Then he turned to glare at Roger again. "You have anything to add?"

Roger reined in the cold hatred he felt. He just looked at Kevin, schooled his features into blankness, and shook his head.

"Good. You're learning."

Kevin had the four prisoners stand and link hands, then had the two agents lean into one another. Kevin touched Roger's back and grabbed an agent's shoulder. They waited twenty or thirty silent seconds — Roger couldn't check his watch — then, abruptly, they were *elsewhere*.

Roger stared up at four stone statues. They turned, awkward but quick, and stared back at him. Each was twelve feet tall, gray and crudely sculpted, with malevolent features and staring carved eyes.

The room was large, twenty yards on a side, twenty yards high. The white walls reflected the bright lights from the high ceiling; the glare was almost unbearable. Four plain metal-frame beds were the chamber's only furniture.

"Welcome home," Kevin said, smiling. Then he swayed against one of his agents and his knees sagged. "Hoo, boy. That was an exertion. Give me a second. Roger, old slave pal, you can talk again."

Roger didn't.

Kevin shook his head, then straightened up with an effort. "Rog, I promised I wouldn't kill you. I meant it; I always keep my promises. You go to prison, along with all your little friends, for the rest of your lives, but I won't kill you."

"Some consolation," Roger muttered.

"Of course, you're a dangerous man, so I had to account for that. You see your guards. They're here to make sure you can't whisk yourself off to one of your paintings. I'm pretty sure I don't have all your work yet. So these guys keep you here.

"Anytime you close your eyes for more than a few seconds, they assume that you're trying to go somewhere else. So they open your eyes again. You'll notice that their hands are big, strong, very clumsy. They might just bust your head trying to get your eyes open."

Roger stared into Kevin's smiling face and thought about that. "Wait a minute. What happens when I have to sleep?"

"Sorry, no exceptions. Just don't sleep."

"I see." He sighed as despair settled on him again. "Sleep deprivation. They say that kills you, too. Eventually."

Kevin shrugged. "But I want to be fair, so I gave the other statues the same order. None of your little friends gets any sleep, either."

"Of course not." The weight of Kevin's words just added to the exhaustion Roger felt.

Kevin looked a little embarrassed; he actually glanced down and scuffed his toe. "Listen, since you're not going to be around too long, I didn't bother to put in any food. Or water. And since there's no food or water, I didn't put in bathrooms."

Roger turned away, not answering. He just wanted Kevin to go.

"Well, bye, Rog. Donna, Julia asked me to tell you hi. Elsie, C.J., good to meet you." Kevin waved cheerfully, then said, "On guard."

The four statues walked stiff-legged to where the prisoners stood. Each positioned itself to stare into the face of one of the four.

Kevin touched his agents' shoulders. Half a minute later the three of them vanished from sight.

"Roger?" Elsie's voice was faint. She wrapped her arms around his neck. She was still trembling. "I don't want to die."

Chapter Eight

Self-Portrait

"You're going to be okay, Elsie." Roger wrapped his arms around the nymph. "We all will. Are you hurt? Did the stone hurt you?"

Her face buried in his shoulder, she nodded. "It hit the back of my head. I was asleep for a while —"

Donna interrupted, half a shriek: "*Elsie* —"

The nymph yanked her head up, and the oncoming hand of the giant stone sentinel stopped inches from her head. It didn't complete the grab. As she stared at it, wide-eyed, it lowered its arm and looked impassively down into her face.

Roger drew her a step away from the thing. It followed. The stony monster staring into Roger's face backed its own small step away, maintaining its distance. "Elsie, I think you'd better keep your eyes open. I'll bet Kevin was telling the truth about these things."

She nodded, then reluctantly relaxed her grip on him

Behind them, C.J. spoke. "Son, if you've got any ideas, I'd sure be glad to hear 'em. I've never been to the Bahamas. It just occurred to me that I'd like to go. Right now."

Roger grinned sourly. Good of his father to keep such a light tone. "No ideas, Dad. But I just got here."

Donna wandered over to one of the beds and flopped dispiritedly on it; her stone guardian clopped along with her. She forced herself not to stare at it.

"Kevin had enough time to allow for any ideas we might have," she said, her voice flat. "Roger, it's all over. He got us! We're dead!"

"Like hell." Roger scowled at her. "He's got us, all right. But he's not bright enough to have allowed for everything. He's stupid enough to throw you over for a brainless face. He's stupid enough never to try to pull a black-and-white into the real world. He's stupid, Donna. Let's not be stupid, too."

She glared back, but didn't answer. C.J. chuckled. "Never thought I'd see the day you told someone *else* to calm down. It's supposed to work the other way around. I figured you'd be pounding your fists bloody on the walls."

Roger gave his father a quick smile and thought about it. C.J. was right; Roger should be in a towering rage. But he wasn't. It wouldn't do any good.

He released Elsie, then moved to sit on another of the bunks. His sentinel walked along backwards, keeping its gaze on his face. The floor trembled as it walked.

"Okay. Idea." Roger's eyes narrowed. "We have white floor and my pocketknife. Maybe I could prick my finger and sketch something out in blood, something that could smash these stony sons of bitches. I drag it into existence, and we're home free."

Donna shook her head, looking dubious. "How do you drag it out without closing your eyes? Have you ever tried to do that?"

Roger nodded reluctantly.

"And did it ever work?"

"Nope. But maybe it's lack of practice —"

"And maybe it's impossible."

He gave her an exasperated stare. "Okay, try this. We get a Ping-Pong ball and cut it in half. I color in eyeballs and put the ball halves over my eyes. That way, I can close my eyes all I want but these statues think I have my eyes open, that I'm just some sort of bug-eyed idiot."

Donna looked at him as if he already *were* a bug-eyed idiot. "Roger, that's crazy. First, we don't have a Ping-Pong ball. Second —" Then she saw his grin. "You're kidding, right?"

"I'm kidding."

She looked at him a long moment, then gave him a faint smile. "Okay, we'll do stupid ideas, too. Maybe there'll be something smart in them."

"Good."

C.J. lay back on a bunk, his arms behind his head. "I don't know much about what you do, son, so let me take it analytically."

"Shoot, Dad."

"From what you've shown me, the thing you do follows a certain set of rules. You draw something, you close your eyes, you feel around for it, you pull it out, you get tired and fall over."

"Something like that."

"And Matthews has set things up to interrupt one crucial phase in the process: closing your eyes. These bruisers do that."

"That's right."

"And every time you've used this . . . ability of yours, it's followed that set of rules."

"That's right." Then Roger frowned. "No, that's not right."

He was silent a long moment, and C.J. spoke again: "Talk to me, Roger. Which one was different?"

"Two times. With Elsie, I didn't consciously pull her out of the painting. She moved around on her own first. But that was all inadvertent. My ability was starting up before I knew I was using it. And I was closing my eyes a lot then, too, so I suppose that doesn't count.

"The second time was when I was on the Paradise island with Elsie. Working with clay, in three dimensions. I made a little hut into a big hut. . . ."

The nymph interrupted, "You made *me* big, too."

"That's right. I'm trying to remember exactly how that went. I didn't touch these things when I was making them big; that part is different. I don't think it made me tired, either. Also, though I had my eyes closed both times, I wasn't concentrating on making them big when it happened. One time I was sleeping, and one time I was thinking about a painting. . . ."

"So the rules are different with sculpture."

Roger shrugged. "The rules might have been different because I was inside a painting-world instead of the real world."

Donna spoke: "Like we are now?"

Roger looked at her, then at the stone sentinel assigned to him. After several long moments he hopped up and moved into the center of the room, his sentinel quickly clip-clopping backwards to keep ahead of him. "Okay, everybody. Empty pockets." He hauled handfuls of junk out of his own pockets and sat cross-legged to deposit them on the floor.

Curious, the others joined him, emptied their own pockets into the pile, and knelt beside him. The four sentinels impassively arranged themselves around the group.

The collected pocket goods included two wallets, with a couple of hundred dollars in bills and many cards of various types; about three dollars in small change; two pocketknives, Roger's and C.J.'s; a large pack of cinnamon-flavored chewing gum, Elsie's; three key rings full of keys; two combs; a button; C.J.'s World War Two-era Marine Corps cigarette lighter; and several pretty rocks Elsie had collected. The others began adding jewelry and other objects: two wristwatches, Roger's and C.J.'s; Donna's delicate gold necklace; C.J.'s belt buckle; Elsie's billed cap; a few finger rings.

Roger thought for a couple of minutes, then reached over and picked up the pack of gum. He turned to Elsie. "If this works, Elsie, it's because of this gum.

Right now, I need everybody to chew this stuff up. Every piece. Even if you hate it."

C.J. complained: "My dentures —"

"You too, Dad." Roger popped three pieces of the stuff into his own mouth and got to work on the rest of the pile, pulling keys off the key rings, sorting out all the objects by size and shape.

Over the next half hour, Roger assembled a horrible little statue; it was held together with gluey lumps of chewed gum and hope.

Its legs were combs, with house keys gummed to the bottoms for feet. Its torso was C.J.'s buckle; its head was Roger's cheap digital wristwatch, minus the band.

It had four arms. The arms above the elbows were keys; the arms below the elbows were different. Two were pocketknives. One was C.J.'s cigarette lighter. One was a half-dollar.

Donna sat beside him and whispered. "What if Kevin is watching us now, the way he said he could?"

Roger shrugged, then adjusted the statue so that it balanced better. "If he's watching us and figures out that we can actually pull this off, he'll just come in and stop us. I can't do anything about that. If he's watching us and doesn't figure out what's going on, he won't even try to come in until all the shooting starts. That gives us thirty seconds, anyway. We just have to hope he won't get here in time."

When the statue was to his satisfaction, Roger returned the pocket goods that hadn't been used. He moved to one wall of the room and asked the other three to go to the opposite wall. They went, jittery with anticipation, still accompanied by their huge jailers.

Roger set the little statue about ten feet from the wall and stretched out in front of it, lying so that he could see the statue, his friends, and the three stone sentinels across the room. His own sentinel stood nearby, bent far over to keep its gaze on his face.

Roger didn't close his eyes, but he did blur his own

vision until the statue, his friends, the sentinels all seemed to be one fuzzy scene. The featureless blankness of the white floor helped. He tried to sharpen the image in his mind's eye.

He hadn't stared at his clay hut continuously after making it. He'd closed his eyes and turned his attention elsewhere. He couldn't close his eyes now, so he turned his stare on his stone guardian, gazing at its nearly featureless chest, seeing only the picture he'd just burned in his mind.

His head started to hurt. Why didn't any of them have any aspirin? But he took the headache as a sign that it was time to relax.

He forced the now crystal-clear image of his friends and the gum-statue from his mind and thought of something else: Escape Velocity Books, moving among the shelves, hearing the hiss of the shop's antiquated air conditioner . . .

Elsie shrieked and he was jerked out of his reverie.

His little statue was gone. No, it was across the room, fifteen feet tall, standing in the midst of the three stone guardians. The stone sentinels reacted to it, turning for the first time away from their prisoners, taking defensive postures as they faced the grotesque gummy thing.

"Get away from it!" Roger shouted and jumped to his feet. His own jailor charged toward the gum-statue.

Elsie darted out from between the sentinels, Donna a step behind her. C.J., though slowed by age, wasted no time getting away.

The gum-statue lifted one arm and the pocketknife blade snapped open as though it were a switchblade. It swung in a vicious arc, slamming the yards-long edge into Elsie's guardian, shearing its arm entirely off with a great spray of rocky shrapnel.

C.J.'s jailor swung a huge stony fist at the gum-thing, but the gum-thing brought up the half-dollar arm; the giant coin stopped the fist like a shield. Its other

pocketknife blade snapped out, stabbed toward
Donna's sentinel, sheared its way into its chest with
another tremendous clatter of shrapnel.

Roger met the others in the center of the room; all
four backed hastily away from the fight. "It's going to
tear them up," Roger crowed. "It's going to — oh, shit."

One stone sentinel got its hands on a pocketknife
arm and yanked. The arm came completely free; the
sentinel hurled it casually across the room. It crashed
into a side wall, then fell to crush one of the four
bunks.

"Son, it's *not* going to tear them up. Don't waste
time." C.J.'s tone was curt; his attention was on the
fight.

The gum-statue brought up its fourth arm. The top
of C.J.'s lighter, now five feet tall, snapped open. Flame
shot out to immolate Roger's sentinel as it charged.
The heat was amazing; even where Roger and his
friends stood, it threatened to singe them. All four
backed away. Molten pieces of rock dripped off Roger's
sentinel to sizzle against the white floor.

Roger grabbed the other three, forced himself to
shut his eyes, forced himself to think. Where did he
have a painting that Kevin wouldn't have found? He
thought of all the work he'd done in college, in high
school, earlier. He heard another knife-blade blow
struck, heard large chunks of stone rattle into the floor.
There was the sound of stone hitting metal, and a
metal crash that had to be C.J.'s lighter hitting the
floor. The heat suddenly diminished.

Wait a minute — the mural. His junior year in high
school, the mural he'd painted on one wall of the gym.
It was a huge, purple-and-gold scorpion against a
golden desert — the team mascot, too good a painting
for a team that never won.

He saw it now as he'd painted it, nine feet from floor
to the top of the painting, its tail up in an angry pose,
its pincer-claws open and ready to grab. . . .

C.J.'s voice was tight, urgent. "You'd better shake it, son. They're tearing your thingamajig to pieces. . . ."

There was a crash as another of the gum-statue's limbs was torn free and thrown.

Then Roger felt heat; it was like a desert at noon. The sound of the statues' battle vanished. The floor under his feet became sandy ground.

He heard a rattling and clacking, organic, menacing; he heard Elsie's shriek and C.J.'s curse. He never opened his eyes, just concentrated again, willing them all back out of the scorpion painting, into the real world. . . .

And everything went black.

Wherever they were, it was dark. The air was still and too warm. Roger opened his eyes into darkness; then he sagged, kept upright only by his grip on his friends. Weariness from the back-to-back transitions he'd made, from the blows he'd taken to his gut and cheek, suddenly caught up with him.

"Where are we?" Donna whispered. It seemed completely natural to her to whisper, and her words floated out into some large expanse of open air.

"A big room," Elsie said. "A basketball court."

"My old high-school gymnasium," Roger said. "In my home town. That's where the mural was painted. But what's it doing dark like this, in the middle of a school day?" He looked around, trying to catch sight of the bank of windows next to the ceiling. Sure enough, they were there, barely suggested by little cracks of light; they'd been boarded or painted over.

C.J. cleared his throat. "Been a while since you drove by the old school, hasn't it, Roger? It closed down five, six years ago. The building's condemned."

Roger snorted. "They should've condemned it when it was built. Elsie, can you lead us out of here? I think you see a lot better than we do." Recovering, he straightened and took his weight off the others, though he didn't feel at all energetic.

"Sure." The danger was past and the nymph's tone was light. She led them forward a few steps, sideways around a mass of collapsed wood — Roger correctly guessed that it was a stretch of pull-out bleachers, decayed and ruined — and to a metal door. By touch, by memory, Roger pressed down the metal bar on the door, shoved it open and pushed his way into the dark halls of his high school.

There was a little light out here. The four of them could see the hallway strewn with trash and papers, the classroom doors open all along the walls. Light filtered in from the classrooms, from the narrow ceiling-high windows — built that way, Roger remembered, to keep students from being able to look outside.

Walking slowly along the hall, Roger saw, heard and smelled the ghosts of memories from his time in this school. He smiled at one open classroom, where he and the other yearbook photographers wreaked havoc, almost the last time he'd touched a camera. A couple of dozen steps further on, he peered into the room where Coach MacNeal had taught math and Roger had studied Tricia Davis. Talk as he always did about how much he hated school, he was a little sad that this place and all the memories it held were destined for the wrecking ball.

Donna smiled as she watched him peer into doorways. Only a few minutes away from danger and he was like a kid again. But he was a tired kid; he walked slowly and seemed grateful when she slid under his arm.

The front doors wouldn't open to let them out; they were chained from the outside. But by prowling down side corridors Roger remembered, they found one set of metal doors that was simply locked; the doors let them out, then locked again once they swung closed. The four blinked in the sudden sunlight, looking at cars passing on the adjacent tree-lined street.

"Nice neighborhood," Donna said.

C.J. nodded. "Not as good as it used to be, but not bad. We're only about a mile from my house. Roger, you think we should head over there, hide out?"

"Huh?" Roger shook his head as if to clear it. "Sorry, Dad. I'm kind of tired. What did you say?"

Donna interrupted; Roger really did look too tired to be making decisions now. "He said, should we go to his house. And the answer is no. Kevin might have left another of his little batwinged things there . . . just in case. Sorry, C.J. We can't go home, you can't go home."

Elsie's breath caught. The nymph stared at her as if she'd said that Santa was dead. "We can't go home?"

Donna gently shook her head. "No, sweetie. Kevin will know soon enough that we got out. He said he could look into his paintings, remember? He'll start looking again. The first places he'll look will be our place at Lake Galloway and C.J.'s house here. He might have started already."

"But . . . Dylan . . ."

"Oh, right." Another complication. Donna put one arm absently around Elsie's waist and kept her grip on Roger, then started them walking toward the street. C.J. brought up the rear. "We should tell him," she said. "If he goes running around looking for you, and Kevin has people there —"

C.J. interrupted. "Yeah. This Dylan will be the next one in the big white room."

"C.J., is there a pay phone near here?"

"Yes, indeed. There's a shopping center about four blocks from here, on Live Oak."

"We'll find a pay phone there. Give Dylan a quick call. I need to talk to him before you do, Elsie."

A younger brother answered on the fifth ring and had to go outside to fetch Dylan. A minute later, the man himself took the phone: "Hey."

"Hey, yourself. This is Donna."

"Hey, what's up? I was going to have breakfast with Elsie, but she never showed. No one at your house."

Donna glanced through the old phone booth's glass at Elsie, who waited outside. The nymph practically hopped up and down in her desire to get to the phone.

"Dylan, listen to me. This is important. We're not in town right now, and we won't be back for a while."

"Your car's still here."

"Don't interrupt. Don't go over to the house, not until we let you know it's okay. We won't be there anyway." Donna kept her tone urgent, but not angry, not dictatorial. "If anyone asks about us, tell them that you barely know us. Tell all your friends to do the same. Don't talk about us where anyone can hear you. Don't let on that you know anything about us except our names. You understand?"

There was a long silence. Then, "Is Elsie all right?"

"Yes."

"Let me talk to her."

"Sure, in just a second. But I really need to know that you understand what I'm telling you. It's serious, Dylan."

"I understand. Let me talk to Elsie."

"Hold on." Donna slid the door open, stepped out, handed the receiver to Elsie. The nymph promptly barricaded herself in the booth and began talking brightly, rapidly.

Roger sat on the sidewalk, leaning back against the old phone booth. His eyes were closed but his posture said he was awake . . . barely.

C.J. didn't look nervous, but he kept a close eye on his son and the passing traffic. "Rog, Donna, this is your war. You know more about what's going on than I do. If we can't go home, what do we do now?"

Donna glanced at Roger. "Roger's wiped out and we need to get out of sight. We need to pool our money, get a cab, find a hotel room, get some paints. By tomorrow, we'll have all the money we need for a while." She sighed. "More counterfeiting. Damn it."

"Counterfeiting?"

"Never mind. After that, we can find a better place to stay, some place more hidden."

Roger nodded but kept his eyes shut. "I'm going to get some rest and then start on some quick paintings. Not just of stuff we need, but meadows, waterfalls, that sort of thing. I intend to spread them around, hide them where Kevin can't find them. They'll be escape routes, places we can jump to if we need to, so we won't have to face a giant purple scorpion every time we need to run for cover."

C.J. grinned. "I just about peed myself dry when I saw that thing."

"How far away was it, Dad? I had my eyes closed."

"About fifty feet, and closing. Too close for me."

Donna said, "You're a lot faster than Kevin is, you know."

Roger opened his eyes to look at her. "How do you mean?"

"He took, I don't know, maybe thirty seconds to get us into his prison painting, and it was right next to him. Maybe an equal amount of time to get out. You were a lot quicker getting us to the desert with the scorpion, then getting us to the school. And that painting was what, dozens of miles away? Hundreds?"

"No way to tell. We don't know where Kevin's country house is." Roger thought about it. "I'm not sure that distance has anything to do with it. Just the clarity and amount of detail you can manage when you're imagining the thing. But it's good to know I can beat him on the quick draw. Assuming that ever counts for anything."

Elsie pushed her way out of the booth, handed the receiver back to Donna. "He wants to talk to you again." Her smile was brilliant.

Behind the barricade of sliding glass door, Donna
said, "I'm back."

"Donna, I want to help. Let me come out where you
are. I couldn't get much out of what Elsie was telling
me, but it's obvious someone's after you. I need to be
with her."

Donna rolled her eyes. It would be better not to
have any contact with Lake Galloway for a while. But if
this kept Dylan and Elsie apart too long — well, she
knew Elsie. The nymph was stubborn enough to make
a break for Lake Galloway. Finally, Donna said, "Sure.
But not immediately. We'll figure something out when
we've settled down a bit."

"But —"

"But nothing. Someone will give you a call tomorrow. Probably Elsie. A *short* call. You may have to
pretend it's someone else; I'm going to tell her to use a
different name. This is serious stuff, Dylan."

"I understand. But I better get that call."

"You will. Bye." Donna hung up before Dylan had a
chance to say more.

At midafternoon, they checked into a large suite of
an old backstreet hotel; with them, they brought a new
piece of luggage containing new art supplies. Roger fell
asleep the instant he lay on his bed.

The dinner from room service was only fair, but it
allowed Donna to stay and work on a new illustration
— a large iron pot filled with bundles of twenty-dollar
bills. When she was through with that she began
drafting more guns and armor.

Roger woke up at midnight and did the color work
on the money-pot painting while the others slept. Long
before dawn, he closed his eyes, felt for objects inside
the painting . . . but this time he held his mental image
of the painting still and changeless as pulled. When he
opened his eyes, he held a stack of twenties in his
hand . . . and the painting was unchanged. He

restrained a whoop of triumph that would have awakened the others.

The next day, Donna visited the home of a man C.J. knew. She didn't tell him she was acquainted with C.J., only that she'd heard this man had some property for rent. The man obligingly drove her a couple of miles into the country and proudly showed her his land: a big ranch house, one creek good for fishing, one pond good for swimming, lots of space, lots of trees.

By midafternoon, they'd come to terms. She handed over a wad of cash, three months' advance rent, and no papers were signed.

Back at the hotel, C.J. read the morning paper, made a few phone calls, then took a cab to an address crosstown. The fellow who'd advertised in the paper was happy to let the old man poke around in the engine and then drive the vehicle around.

It was a decent car, an anonymous-looking blue Chevrolet with an engine in excellent condition. C.J. didn't dicker over the price and paid cash.

Roger painted the weapons and armor Donna had drafted the previous day. By the time the others were finished with their errands, each one had a gun and body armor waiting.

Elsie spent her day in the stores buying books, clothes, and supplies. She returned from her last trip with several bags of reference works: on weapons, animals, legendary creatures, surveillance techniques and devices, Achilles and Penthesilia and other characters out of Greek myth, heroes from fiction, heroes from comic books, heroes from TV, heroes from movies. . . . Elsie was strong, but could barely carry the bags of books into the room. Then she and Roger went for a short walk and called Dylan from a pay phone several blocks from the hotel to let him know everything was all right.

The next morning, Friday, barely forty-eight hours

after they'd been captured, the four moved into their rental property, leaving behind no paper trail, and breathed a sigh of relief.

A musical note, a faint "ding," woke Roger. He looked at his bedside clock — 2:13 A.M. He'd been in his new bed only two or three hours, and it took him a moment to remember that he should be alarmed by strange noises in the night. A little light flickered beyond his bedroom door, then went out.

He reached up to the headboard of his bed, felt around until he could grab the cold metal waiting there: a pistol, the .45 semiautomatic Donna had drawn for him. He stood, trying not to let the bed creak too much. *They can't have found us this fast — can they?* Quietly, he pulled the door open and listened.

There was no noise except nighttime insects outside; then, faintly, he heard a metallic scraping from the living room. He listened a moment longer, recognized what it was, and set the gun back in the headboard. He pulled on his new robe and padded out into the living room.

Donna sat on the couch in the dark, stirring sugar into her teacup. Her robe matched Roger's. She started when Roger materialized before her, but didn't spill anything. "Hi."

"Hi yourself." He sat down beside her. "Trouble sleeping?"

"Some. I made tea in the microwave. The caffeine doesn't keep me up as much as the tea calms me down."

"Yeah." His expression turned rueful, though Donna couldn't see it. "I hate all this hiding. Knowing they're out there, looking for us."

"Me, too." She laughed. "But it's a big relief, knowing there actually *is* someone out there. Back when I was at my house, I thought it was all in my head. That was worse."

"I guess it would be."

Donna took an experimental sip of her tea, set it down on the coffee table to cool. "I didn't thank you."

"For what?"

"For coming after us."

He shrugged, suddenly uncomfortable. Praise, except for his art, tended to make him edgy. "I had to."

"No, you didn't. That was very brave. I don't know if I could have done it."

Roger shook his head. "I was scared stiff the whole time, and they grabbed me before I even got near you. I screwed up, and I don't feel too good about the whole thing. Except we got out of there."

"That's what counts." She gave a little exasperated sigh. "Roger, every time I wondered about it, you let me know that Kevin throwing me out wasn't my fault. It had nothing to do with me, it was all him. That's sort of the situation here. You did everything right, and things went wrong, but you got us all out of there. The stuff in the middle just doesn't count."

Roger grinned at her sloppy comparison of events. "Maybe you're right."

"I am. So, anyway, thank you."

"You're welcome." He turned to look at her, found her already staring at him. One sliver of moonlight from the window fell across her, illuminating one eye, her nose, a corner of her mouth, but for once he wasn't interested in the chiaroscuro effect of the shadows and light. In her expression was a solemn openness he had never seen before.

Something passed between them, an exchange of signals, and after a moment of hesitation they leaned forward to hold one another. Her face tilted, their lips met . . . and weeks of worry and despair just evaporated from Roger as they kissed. He was conscious only of her warm body in his arms, her arms around his neck, her mouth on his, her faint moan . . . and then rising passion as the kiss lingered.

She lost her grip on his neck and pushed him back, not hard. "Roger, wait."

He leaned forward until their noses met. "Wait for what?" His breathing and voice were suddenly ragged.

"I don't know what this means. I — I don't know what you're thinking." Her voice was a plea.

"Me, either." He leaned forward for another kiss, and she didn't duck it. "Don't ask me to sit here and analyze it." He tightened his arms about her waist and stood, drawing her up with him. "All I know is that I want you. In my room, in my bed, with me."

"What if I say no?" she whispered.

He felt disappointment settle on him, dragging his soaring emotions down from where they'd flown. He hesitated over his answer. "Then it's no," he said. "Don't *say* no. Say yes."

She didn't say anything for a long, lonely moment. Then her arms tightened again around his neck. "Yes."

He drew her into his room and closed the door, then gently pulled her robe from her while she did the same for him. Her eyes, where he could see them in scattered bands of moonlight, were vulnerable, worried. He kissed her again, hoping to drive the worry from her eyes, to replace it with happiness. But she closed her eyes.

She pulled him down onto the bed, and he luxuriated in the incomparable feeling of bare skin on bare skin as his desire grew. His last rational thought was of Kevin's cruelty to the woman in his arms, and he silently promised that she would never have cause to remember Roger the same way.

Sunlight warmed his face, but it was clanging and banging from the kitchen that woke Roger. He had a brief, fuzzy memory of the false Donna in the kitchen of the other house, and his eyes snapped open . . . but Donna's face was six inches from his own on the same pillow, and memory of the last night came back to him. Her gaze was solemn.

He put a hand on her bare shoulder and stroked it. "Hi."

"Hi yourself."

Then, he didn't know what to say. No words swam to the surface of his thoughts. With nothing to say, all he wanted to do was get up, get dressed, go about the day's business. But he surprised himself by realizing how that might hurt Donna.

So he did nothing of the kind. He drew himself a little closer to her, put up his hand to stroke her hair. "Are you worried? About last night?"

She nodded. "I'm still not sure about it. About what it means."

"Me either." He hesitated a moment, thinking through his next words. "Sometimes I think that women want to know what a relationship is just as they're getting into it, and men want to get into the relationship before trying to figure out what it is."

"You're generalizing. I don't feel very general." There was no rebuke in her tone, just quiet acceptance, quiet worry.

"Okay." He regretted complicating her life, but he wouldn't have traded last night for anything. "Listen. Whatever else happens, or doesn't happen, I'm still your friend. I was your friend yesterday, I'll be your friend tomorrow. You might decide to kick me out of your bed, but you can't decide to kick me out of your life, because I won't go. You understand?"

"Uh-huh." She managed a tentative smile, and reached over to toy with the hair on his temple.

"You want a shower? I'll scrub your back."

Her smile broadened. "You've got a deal." But the concern didn't completely leave her face.

It turned out that the clasher-of-pots was C.J. He had an enormous, old-fashioned breakfast laid out by the time they emerged from the shower. The old table sagged under the weight of plates of scrambled eggs, bacon, hash browns, sausage links, toast, biscuits, gravy, and more. The others, with a more modern health consciousness than C.J., managed to keep from grimacing at the cholesterol-laden buffet; each managed to make a dent in the breakfast offering. But Roger resolved to lay in a supply of the breakfast foods he was used to: yogurt, hot cereals, and the like.

If C.J. and Elsie had heard what went on between Roger and Donna the previous night, or saw the glances and smiles the two exchanged this morning, they kept it to themselves.

After breakfast, it was back to business . . . and the business was taking the war back to Kevin Matthews. Donna and Roger worked together to generate more paintings of supplies and living allies.

Roger also tried to teach Donna more about what he did. He showed her how he slid into his meditative state and tried to coach her through the same process. She painted a piece of jewelry, an old-fashioned cameo, and tried to touch it beneath the painting's surface, but had no success.

C.J. sat with them, note pad in hand, and had them tell the entire story of their actions of the last two and a half weeks. He made them repeat it several times and asked questions with each retelling. He circled interesting references and discrepancies, and noted unanswered questions.

Elsie slipped into her volleyball clothes and running shoes, then spent the day going over every inch of the rented property, learning the lay of the land, looking for places to hide, determining how much of the house one could see from different places. Roger was proud of her for realizing that such information could be useful to them, and told her so.

Later in the afternoon, Roger drove Elsie back to town so they could make another call to Dylan — actually, a pair of calls.

Roger posed as a counselor from UCLA, though Dylan knew exactly who he was. "I don't think you should wait until summer to come to L.A.," Roger said. "You can arrange for a better place to live if you come out sooner." Dylan agreed and promised to tell his family he'd be leaving soon.

Roger didn't listen to Elsie's call, except to confirm that she was pretending to be Cindy, a high-school girlfriend. Her call didn't take too long and it was obvious that the prospect of Dylan joining them made her very happy. Halfway home, it surprised Roger that this didn't upset him any longer.

Donna was at work on the diagram of a parabolic microphone when C.J. called everyone into the living room. He flipped between pages in his notebook as he spoke. "Okay. I think you kids have done very, very well, all things considered. I also think it's about time you had a plan of action. An itinerary."

Donna nodded. "We didn't exactly have time to come up with one before. . . ."

"I know that. Like I said, you did very well. Now, it's time to plan. What's the specific goal of your plan?"

Roger grinned lamely. "To get Kevin Matthews off our backs."

"Okay, son. How do you plan to do that?"

Roger glanced down for a moment, then looked at his father again. "It's obvious that we can't go to the authorities. To convince them to deal with him, I'd have to show them what I can do. That could cause us all one hell of a lot of trouble. It probably *would* expose us to Kevin while the authorities dithered around. So whatever it is, we have to do it by ourselves.

"I see two ways to do it. One way is to persuade him we're strong enough that he can't afford to mess with us. The other way . . ." He fell silent.

"Go on, son."

Roger grimaced. "Kill him."

Donna was shocked. Elsie and C.J. didn't seem to be. Donna's words were heated: "Wait a second! We can't just kill somebody, Roger. Even killing characters out of a painting is bad enough. Killing Kevin is different."

Elsie shook her head no. "*I* don't think so. I think it's the same."

Donna couldn't argue with her, but turned back to C.J. and his son. "Roger, it's just wrong."

Roger nodded. "Yes, it is. But so is letting him kill us." He took a deep breath. "Donna, even though he's tried to kill us all — more than once with some of us — I'm going to give him a chance to back off. A chance he never gave us. If he doesn't take it, it means he'll never give up until we're dead. Right?" He fixed her with his stare.

She just sat, reluctant to answer. "I suppose so."

"And if he won't back down, if he won't give up, what are we supposed to do?"

Donna shifted, uncomfortable. "Run away."

"And hide for the rest of our lives. Do you think we'd be able to hide from him, with all his powers, forever? He can paint Sherlock Holmes, too. Track us down."

"We could catch him, put him in a prison."

"Like he did with us? We just can't assume that we'd be able to hold him. He's a dummy, but he has more experience at this than we do." He shook his head, his expression regretful. "Donna, I don't like this either. I never, *ever* wanted to think about deliberately taking a human life. But Kevin has backed me into a corner.

"If it were just me, I might risk running, hiding. But it isn't just me. I won't risk the rest of you. I think he'd catch us eventually.

"So, if he won't back off, I have to *make* myself be willing to kill him. I'll kill him before I'll give him another chance to hurt you. Or Elsie. Or Dad. I'll pull the trigger myself." He looked a little startled by his own determination, then continued, "Even now, all he has to do is cease hostilities. If he won't . . . well, we finish it like a war. *We don't have a choice.* Unless you can think of one."

She wanted to argue with him, to argue on the side of life. But she was scared of Kevin, of what he planned for her, what he could do to her. She gave up and sat back, still unhappy. "But we can't get to him. We don't know where he is."

C.J. shook his head. "We can get a message to him, and we know where he will be on at least one occasion." He flipped through his notebook. "You told me about a fellow named Berman, Arnold."

Roger nodded. "His PR man."

"He's in the phone book. I imagine he can get a message to Kevin. So that's one option.

"Another one — you talked about something your flying drone saw on his calendar. Something about a convention."

"MArtCon," Donna said. "Media Art Convention. We've gone several times. He's probably Guest of Honor this year; he's big enough."

"So you know where he'll be in about a month."

Roger shook his head. "These conventions announce their guest lists in advance. He has to assume that we know he'll be there. He'll paint a self-portrait and send it instead."

His father grimaced. "Okay . . . then we *don't* know where he'll be. Dammit." He made a note on his page.

Donna opened her mouth, closed it as her ethics fought with one another. *Tell them and it means Kevin might be killed. Don't tell them . . . maybe they'll die.* She told them. "Kevin won't send a duplicate. It'll be him."

Roger looked at her. "How do you know?"

"I don't *know*, but I'm pretty sure. He lives to have people suck up to him, Roger. You know that. That's why he does all those signings, even in podunk little stores. If he sent a duplicate to the convention, he wouldn't get to lord it over the fans and the convention staff. He has to go."

C.J. grinned, made another note. "Good. Back in business."

Elsie said, "There's another way to get to Kevin. He still has your paintings."

Donna shook her head. "He'll have set things up so that anything coming out of those paintings will be blown to pieces."

"Oh." The nymph sat back, looking defeated.

But C.J. flipped to another page. "About your paintings, Roger. You're still missing one. You called it 'Deceit of My Pants.' The painting of the satyr."

"Kevin got it."

"You saw it?"

"No, but no one else could have it." Roger thought about it. "No, you're right. I don't know for sure. When we have time, I'll look for it. Thanks to Kevin, we know how to do that without getting blown up.

"Okay, here's my plan. You can all run over it with cleats and tell me where it's stupid.

"I'm going to paint a self-portrait. Bring out a fake Roger Simons. A robot, a simulation. I don't want to put a real person" — he glanced at Elsie — "into danger.

"From a phone in town, I call Arnold Berman. Tell him that I want to have a parley with Kevin. Give him a place and time.

"Kevin and the fake Roger meet. Fake Roger tells Kevin to lay off or else. Fake Roger will be tough, so if Kevin tries something, it'll be obvious that I'm not kidding around.

"If Kevin goes for it, we stay on our toes for a while, and if he lives up to his agreement, we can relax. Otherwise . . . we work up Plan Two. Meet him at MArtCon. And deal with him." He looked uncomfortable. "I hate euphemisms. Kill him, I mean."

Donna kept her objections to herself. They talked

through Roger's plan a while longer, discussing details, but eventually agreed that it was the way they wanted to get their message across to Kevin Matthews.

"Hey."

Donna grinned into the phone receiver. "Dylan? It's your aunt Lucy, in L.A." She didn't disguise her voice. "I hope you're all packed."

"I'm packed."

"Good. I've made all your travel plans. Get someone to take you to the city airport tomorrow. Be there by two in the afternoon; your flight leaves at three. Your tickets will be waiting at the desk, just like you wanted."

They hadn't discussed anything of the sort, but Dylan played along. "Anything special I should bring?"

"No, just yourself. We'll see you tomorrow."

Donna hung up. Beside her, Roger smiled encouragement. Both of them took a good look around; the drivers passing along the adjacent street took no undue notice of her at the pay phone. She dialed another number and heard the line click a moment later.

"Berman residence."

"Arnold, this is Donna Matthews."

There was a brief silence, then, "Donna! It's been a while. How are you doing?"

"Pretty well. I sure am doing a lot of work lately. Listen, you may think this is strange, but I'm trying to get a message to Kevin. He moved and forgot to tell me his new number."

Another short silence. "Ummm, well, I have standing orders from Kevin. I can't give out his number to anyone. But if you want to give me your home number, I can get it to him."

"No, thanks. I'd appreciate it if you could just pass a message to him. Tell him Roger Simons wants to see him."

"Simons? The artist, right? I remember him. He used to be pretty good."

Donna grinned at Roger. Berman's use of the past tense would annoy the hell out him; she decided to keep it to herself. "That's the one. Tell Kevin that Roger's going to be on Old Denton Road, at the turnoff to the radio tower, tonight at 9:00 P.M. That's a few miles east of Kevin's townhouse. Roger would really like to see him."

Berman repeated the directions back to her as he wrote them down. "I'll pass that along. But that's sort of a strange place for a rendezvous, Donna. What's going on?"

"Kevin knows."

"Well, okay."

"Bye." Donna hung up. "It's set up."

Roger checked his new wristwatch. "We've got a few hours until dark . . . but I can use them to touch up the painting. Let's go home."

Donna walked into the bedroom that served them as an office, leaned over Roger where he worked, and draped her arms around his shoulders. He acknowledged her presence with a quick grin and continued to study the finished painting.

The work was a self-portrait by way of science fiction. It showed Roger Simons in his usual jeans and shirt, seated on a metal stool. Jacks plugged into the side of his head and fed information into a computer. Behind him, a diagram tacked on the wall was half-nude Roger Simons, half-humanoid robot.

She looked it over for a few moments. "All finished tinkering with it?"

"Just finished a few minutes ago."

"It's a good likeness. Looks just like you. Think it'll fool anybody?"

"It already has." The voice was Roger's, but the man she held hadn't said it. The voice came from behind her.

She let go of Roger and spun around. Another Roger Simons stood in the doorway, arms crossed as he leaned against the jamb.

Donna looked at him, then at the Roger behind her, and quickly moved away from both. She couldn't hide the shock and anger she felt. "What kind of sick joke is this?"

The Roger at the table shook his head sadly. "No joke, Donna. I just pulled the robot Roger out of the painting a minute ago."

The Roger at the door nodded agreement. "I didn't figure you'd walk in on my doppelganger. I wasn't really trying to trick you."

The Roger at the table just looked sad. "I'm sorry, Donna."

She peered between them. "Oh, God. Which one of you is real?"

The two Rogers looked at one another. They nodded nearly simultaneously, then each reached up to his neck, pinched some skin there.

It was like a high-technology version of "What's My Line." But only the Roger at the table continued the motion, tugging upward, pulling the mask of his face completely clear of his head, revealing a sinister metallic skull with clear yellow eyes faintly glowing.

Donna felt her knees go weak and she backed toward the Roger at the door. Then she looked suspiciously at him, too.

He shook his head. "No, I'm the real one. Pinch me."

She did. Hard. He cursed and swatted her hand from his thigh, and she finally recovered enough to laugh at him.

Donna's viewscreen was black, while the view on Roger's screen was of old, potholed highway stretching ahead; the camera view was from within a moving car, so the screen showed dashboard and windshield as well. The image was all in shades of green: light green stripes down the center of the road, dark green asphalt and sky. "The night-sight gear's doing just fine," he told Donna.

The car slowed down and pulled onto the shoulder of the road. The camera point of view turned and framed C.J., seated behind the wheel. C.J. glanced toward the camera and looked away just as quickly. "We're three miles from Old Denton Road," the old man said, his voice sounding gruff over the speakers. "Do you, uh, need anything?"

At his console, Roger quickly thumbed the button on his microphone. "Give him the speech."

A moment later, the robot Roger spoke; its voice was identical to Roger's. "Roger wants me to remind you that I'm not human. I can't feel anything. I can't be hurt. I don't care what happens to me."

C.J. held himself stiffly and wouldn't look into the camera — into the face of the robot Roger. "Yeah. Well, I just wish you didn't look quite so much like him." Even Elsie, at first glance, had been fooled by the robot. Roger's paintings were that much better than Kevin's and the self-portrait had been very good indeed.

The camera's point of view wavered up and down as the robot nodded, then the view shifted as it got out of the car. The simulacrum began jogging. In fifteen minutes, it would reach the gravel road that led to the radio tower.

Donna powered up her viewscreen, the camera showed shades-of-green details of the interior of a car's trunk. A moment later, the trunk lid opened; C.J. held it open and looked disapprovingly down into this camera. "He's gone," the old man said. "I mean, it's gone."

Donna took the controls of the new flying drone and had it rise slowly out of the trunk. She thumbed her own microphone. "We've already got it on the other screen. Thanks. Listen, you'd better get going. We're going to follow you with the drone for a couple of miles to make sure nothing else is after you."

C.J. slammed the trunk shut, nodded grumpily, and got back into the car, obviously not trusting himself to speak. Donna sent the drone into a fast climb, while Roger kept its camera trained on the old man's car.

"He's not happy," Donna said.

"I know. I have this feeling he's going to give me the 'Why couldn't you have been a photographer, like your old man?' speech when he gets home. The robot just gave him the creeps, is all." In Donna's viewscreen, C.J.'s car turned back the way it had come and sped away along the badly maintained road.

After several minutes, there was still no sign of pursuit; at Roger's request, Donna took the drone up so high that they had to switch to telescopic magnification even to see the car.

At last satisfied that nothing was following his father, Roger said, "Back to the tower."

Donna silently brought the drone around, sent it zooming toward the radio tower at high speed.

"You're awfully quiet. You still mad at me?"

She smiled gently to deny it. "I just want this to be done. I hope Kevin is willing to leave us alone."

"Me, too." But he doubted Kevin would be that smart.

The drone reached the unlit radio tower first and hovered above the spot where the gravel trail met Old Denton Road.

Over the speakers, they could hear the robot Roger's steady jogging footsteps. There was a roar as a car caught up to the robot, passed it; in the screen, they saw the woman in the passenger seat sparing it a curious glance.

Then the robot reached the gravel turnoff to the radio tower and stopped.

Roger glanced over at Donna's viewscreen, at the

view from the hovering drone. In it, the robot stood right at road's edge, stiffly waiting for the meeting with Kevin. Roger got back on the microphone, instructed his double to move in a few yards from the road, pace, kick small rocks, check its watch, do all the things a waiting human would do.

At 9:04, a black limousine glided up, turned onto the gravel road, and stopped. Its driver killed the lights.

The robot walked to the driver's window, which glided down. Through its eyes, Roger and Donna saw Kevin staring out at them.

The robot launched into his script. "Hi, Kevin."

Kevin's smile was tight, forced. "Get on with it, Roger. You've wasted enough of my time."

"I'm not wasting anyone's time. This could be the best investment of time you ever made." The real Roger wanted to cheer; his robotic double had taken one possible conversational hurdle without a problem. "I want you to leave us alone. I've already shown you I'm not easy to kill. If you keep after us, I'm going to mess you up bad. You'll wish you'd never *heard* of Roger Simons."

Kevin's expression became rueful. "I already do."

In Donna's screen, the car exploded into a huge, brilliant fireball that grew until it engulfed the drone; the drone's own screen went to static. Roger's screen was static from the moment of the explosion.

Donna's screen cleared a few moments later. Roger and Donna looked down at the crater where the car had been. The charred pit was yards deep and was broad enough to cover half the adjacent roadway. Flaming bits of metal and fabric from the car continued to rain down all over the area. Of the robot there was not one identifiable piece remaining.

Roger glared at the picture, then lifted the little hatch over the self-destruct device and pressed that button home. Donna's screen went to static, too. There was no chance *this* drone would be followed home; he'd create another one in the morning.

"That's our answer," he said, dispirited.

Donna said nothing. She just looked at the screen.

"Hey, what's wrong?"

"I was just trying to remember the Kevin I married. But I can't. He's just gone. I wonder if he ever existed."

Chapter Nine

The Canvas

Wearing a gray wool suit, his hair, mustache and beard a dignified silvery color, all of it pulled from a painting this morning, Roger looked like somebody's wealthy uncle — so Donna had told him. His mirror had told him he didn't look like Roger any more and that was the important thing.

He walked through the thick airport-lobby traffic — people streaming by, hauling luggage, hauling children, heading toward departure gates and taxi stands, not at all interested in a fugitive artist in a fake beard. Dylan sat in one of the uncomfortable black plastic lobby chairs, staring fretfully at the clock on the wall, and didn't notice Roger until he stood looming over the chair.

Dylan whipped around to stare at him. "Can I do something for —" Then his expression turned suspicious. "Hey. Roger?"

Roger's face fell. "So much for disguises."

"No, no, it's good," Dylan said, too hastily. "I'm a film student, remember? I'm used to looking at makeup and seeing makeup."

"Yeah, sure." Roger sighed. "Ready to go?"

Dylan stood and caught up his single bag, then followed Roger out the sliding glass exterior doors. Outside, Roger paused a moment to nod to someone — a scruffy-looking man in an aloha shirt and reflective sunglasses, sitting in a dark Plymouth Fury. Then Roger turned right and continued up the sidewalk.

Dylan followed. "Who was that?"

"An undercover cop from a TV show. His disguises are better than mine."

"Huh?"

"No, really. He's there to make sure we're not followed."

"Right." Dylan shook his head, obviously trying hard not to let on that he thought Roger had gone a little funny.

They were nearly at the end of the terminal sidewalk when the rear door opened on the last car in line — and Elsie stepped out. Dylan ran to grab her, kissed her; her smile shone up into his face. "I missed you," she said.

"You, too."

They held each other until Roger got into the driver's seat, closed the door, started the car, fiddled with the radio and air conditioner, and cleared his throat a couple of times. Finally, Elsie tossed Dylan's bag into the back seat, then dragged him in beside her. A moment later, the car was in motion, merging with traffic.

In the rearview mirror, Roger could see Dylan slide his arm across Elsie's shoulders and look out through the rear window. "So, was anybody following me?"

Roger shook his head. "Probably not. But Mr. Undercover Cop will tail us for a while to make sure nobody else is. Plus, you wouldn't believe what else we have pacing us." He looked up through the windshield. There was no way he could spot the new drone he'd pulled out of the painting this morning — it was too high; but he waved anyway for the benefit of Donna and C.J. who were at the console controls.

Dylan turned away, shaking his head at Roger's cryptic answers, and returned his attention to Elsie. "So, what now?"

"We go to school."

"School! Not for months. Get serious."

"I'm serious. School." She tucked herself more comfortably under his arm. "C.J. — that's Roger's dad — he's going to teach us all how to shoot. How to assemble and disassemble guns. How to use cameras, if we're interested. I'm going to show everybody how to move quietly in the underbrush and read tracks. I'm better at that than anybody else. Roger's learning more about what he does with his art, and he's trying to teach Donna to do the same things."

Dylan looked confused. "What is it Roger does?"

Elsie shook her head. "I can't tell you. You have to see it. Or you'll never believe it."

The car, flanked by defenders, cruised toward home.

Dylan's eyes opened wide when Roger pulled the tiny black-and-white dragon out of the drawing on the table. They stayed that way when Roger pushed the dragon back into the illustration. They got wider when Roger took him into a small painting of a mountain meadow, a place straight out of "Heidi." The two of them were suddenly *there*, breathing cold, thin air and kicking their way through the flowers.

"This isn't drugs?" Dylan asked, weakly, and plucked a flower.

"This isn't drugs." Roger grinned at him. "The reason we're hiding out is because there's another guy who can do this, and he wants to kill us. That's what you've gotten yourself into."

"He wants to kill Elsie, too?"

"He's already tried once."

Dylan lost his sick expression. "Just point him out to me. I'll tear the bastard's head off."

They popped back into the office. Roger leaned on the wall as the anticipated weariness hit him. Dylan handed his flower to Elsie. Donna, looking gleeful, shoved the stopwatch in Roger's face. "You're getting faster! Roughly two and three-quarters seconds from the time you started to the time you two disappeared.

You barely had your eyes closed before you went."

"Hot damn. I wish I could pull things *out* of paintings that fast."

"And something else, too." Her grin was conspiratorial. "You bumped up against Dylan just before you made the transition, instead of grabbing him or something."

"So?"

"You didn't feel it? He leaned away from you. *You weren't touching him when you went there.*"

He digested that information, thoughtful. "I think I need to practice some more," he decided. "Find out exactly what I can do, and how fast."

That evening, they told Dylan the whole story. He wanted not to believe it, but Roger had already proven it to him. It obviously didn't even occur to Dylan to be unnerved at Elsie's origin; painted or not, she was as real as ever. His first comment was, "That explains the pointed ears."

Elsie nodded apologetically, the flower he'd given her tucked above one of those pointed ears, and gave him a kiss.

His next comment was to Roger: "So, if you think this bastard has booby-trapped your paintings, why don't you send your drone through to make sure?"

Roger shook his head. "We'd lose control of the drone. I don't think that TV and radio waves will travel from a painting-world into the real world."

"Yeah, but this isn't real TV and radio. You told me Matthews said it's *magic.*"

Roger looked at him thoughtfully, and finally said, "Dylan, I think you just earned your first week's rent. We never thought of that."

Not long after, C.J., self-proclaimed chief cook and bottle-washer, started dinner. "By default," he told Dylan. "I'm the only one who can cook worth a damn."

Dylan shook his head. "I can cook. Simple stuff, anyway."

The old man grinned. "Buster, you just joined the staff of Simons University. You're the backup cooking crew. And when you want advanced training, you come to me."

"Deal."

At his art table, Roger altered his painting of the drone and control board, making small cosmetic changes. But as he painted, he reinterpreted the drone in his mind, imagining that its transmissions would cut through barriers of space and dimension to reach the control board. The next time he drew a drone out, it should, if he was right, be able to serve as an advance scout even into painted worlds.

"You have something else to do, you know," Donna reminded him and toyed with the hair at the nape of his neck.

"What's that?"

"Talk to Elsie. Dylan's here now. He has his own room, but . . ."

"He might want to share hers. And she might want that, too. Yeah." Roger sighed, then dipped his brush into a small tub of water and vigorously whisked it back and forth to clean it. "How'd you like to talk to her?"

"No way."

"I thought you'd say that."

After dinner, Roger asked Elsie to come back into the office, and sat her down beside him. He picked up the sketch he'd just started; for the first time in weeks, he worked on something he wouldn't be using in the war against Kevin. It was a picture of Donna, dressed casually, seated in the house's overstuffed easy chair, reading a book with her legs tucked up under her — a pretty, sentimental picture.

"I, uh, wanted to talk to you about something." He felt embarrassment creeping over him; having sex was one thing, talking about it was another. For some reason, one seemed so much easier than the other. He dealt with it as he was learning to deal with most problems: a headlong charge. "A few weeks back, you just discovered that there was such a thing as sex. You were going to do some, uh, reading up on it. Did you do that?"

Silently, she nodded. She kept her gaze on Roger's drawing.

"So you must have learned about some of the problems that can go with it. Sexually transmitted diseases."

She nodded again. "And getting pregnant."

"That's right. I don't want that happening to you."

He saw, in his peripheral vision, as her jaw set in a stubborn line. Her voice took on a trace of defiance: "You're telling me to keep away from Dylan."

"No, no, no, Elsie. If I were trying to keep you two apart, I'd never have let him come here." He breathed a long, weary sigh. "I just want you to be safe. I'd prefer that you not . . . get that involved with him. Not yet. You're still awfully young in a lot of ways. But if you do — well, I can't stop you. I'm not going to try.

"But I am going to insist that you be smart about it. Use condoms. You know about them?"

She nodded. Her expression was curious; she tried to read what was in Roger's eyes, but his attention was on the drawing.

"If you don't have any, I'll give you some. And I want you to use them. That's what I insist on. Will you?"

"I — yes, Roger." She was silent a moment. "Do you and Donna do that?"

His shoulders hunched a little as he thought through his answer. *Better tell the truth*, he decided. "The first time, that first night — no, we didn't. We didn't see it coming. Since then, definitely yes." Finally, he turned to look into Elsie's eyes. "We didn't see it coming, but I kind of think you and Dylan do."

She nodded again, slowly. "Maybe."

"If it does happen, you *can* tell me about it. I won't be mad."

"Okay." She dropped her eyes and was silent a long moment. "I heard what Kevin Matthews said."

"About what?"

"About how he can change his paintings. How he can put Penthesilia back in her painting and change the painting, so when she comes out again she'll be more like what he wants."

"Uh-huh. So?"

"Did you . . ." She paused, drew a breath. "Did you ever want to do that to me? When you were mad at me?"

Roger almost dropped his pencil; he set it and the drawing aside. He caught her gaze and held it, shook his head. "Elsie, when Kevin talked about that — well, it was interesting. It showed me some interesting things I could do to things like robots and drones. But to do it to you, to do it to a living thing . . . Well, that would be slavery, and the cruelest *kind* of slavery. I couldn't think of anything more awful to do to someone if I tried. And I'd never, ever do it to you. Do you understand?"

Mutely, she nodded. There were little tears at the corners of her eyes, not yet large enough to roll down her cheeks.

He leaned forward to wrap his arms around her and she settled against him. "Were you worried that I might do that?"

She nodded again. "I remembered how mad you used to get. How you wanted to tear things up when they didn't do exactly what you wanted. I thought how easy it would be for you to fix me the way you wanted me to be. . . ."

He pulled her tighter to him, stroked her hair. "It's been a long time since I was that mad," he told her. "I'm not exactly the Roger you met the day you were born. And you're not exactly the Elsie you were then. We both get to grow up, Elsie. Okay?"

"Okay." She sniffled into his shoulder, then said something that surprised him. "I think maybe that's why your troll didn't crumble into paint flakes."

"Huh?"

"Kevin paints things to serve him. He doesn't care about them. He changes them whenever they annoy him. You paint people. You give them personality and, what's the word, identity. *People* don't crumble into paint flakes when they die. I'm not going to. I know."

When she left him a few minutes later, he just sat thinking. Not about his rages of a few weeks before. He thought of Achilles and Penthesilia, of false Secret Service agents and Julia Dover, and what it must be like to live under Kevin Matthews' thumb, even to be altered and reshaped whenever they displeased him. Then the shudders hit him and it was a while before he could return to work.

The next morning, Donna was the last one into the office; she sat down at the drone's control seat and gave Roger a thumbs-up.

"This mission," Roger announced, "we're calling Dylan-One, since it was his idea."

Dylan, seated at the sensor board of the control panel, grinned. "Hey."

"We're going to try a couple of things," Roger continued. "As usual, Donna has a test for me. I forget which one this is; let's designate it Test One Million and Four —"

Donna gave him a scowl of mock ferocity. "Watch it, mister."

Roger grinned. "Anyway, we know I can move people without actually touching them. Now, we're going to find out if I can do it without going myself. You still game, Dad?"

C.J. nodded, adjusted his jacket and patted his pocket and the hard metallic object in it. "I'm armed and still ready. Try getting rid of me."

Roger nodded and moved to stand beside the wall several feet from the console. "Okay. Elsie, get the stopwatch ready." The nymph held it up, finger on the button. "Donna, power up."

Donna wiggled the controls and the newest flying probe rose into the air, then flew nearly silently to hover beside C.J.

Roger looked at each of them in turn, then nodded to his father. "Start." He closed his eyes.

C.J. took a step forward, then another, slowly. The drone paced him.

Six feet from Roger, C.J. and the drone vanished. There was no pop of displaced air, no show of lights; they were there, and then they just weren't.

Elsie clicked the stopwatch button, and then did it again. "Six and forty-seven one-hundredths seconds," she said.

Then Roger, eyes still closed, made one final adjustment. He felt the temperature of the air change; he heard wood creak beneath his feet where there had been carpet a moment before. He opened his eyes and looked around at a dark, wood-panelled hallway, at his father and the flying drone. "Looks like Test One Million and Four was a success," he said.

His father held up a warning finger and pointed down the hall, at the open door there. Roger could hear shuffling feet and rustling clothes from beyond it. A wave of tiredness hit him, but he locked his knees and ignored it as best he could.

Inside the room, a man spoke: "Elizabeth, there's something I must tell you." His voice was cultured, accented. "I'm not like other men."

A woman chuckled, her voice low and throaty. "What do you mean? Do you have horns, or something?" Then they heard her gasp. "My God, you do —"

Roger tiptoed to the door and reached over to silently pull the door closed. Then he tiptoed back.

"What's that all about?" C.J. whispered.

"Woman—meets satyr," Roger answered, also in whisper. "But the way the two of them were going at it when I painted it, she's not going to raise a fuss. We're here. This is 'Deceit of My Pants,' all right."

"Then you've got work to do." C.J. positioned himself to keep an eye on the door.

Roger closed his eyes. He still had the image of the painting up front in his mind. Now, he tried to see the painting as others would see it, wherever it might actually be. In moments, another image formed in his mind.

It was a living room. There was a bare minimum of furniture present; the floors were hardwood; everything was scrupulously clean. Bright morning light shone through the drapes half drawn across the windows. Roger could even hear, dimly, the sound of cars passing on the street outside. Then, mattress squeakings from beyond the door C.J. guarded drowned out that faint sound.

Holding the image still in his mind, Roger reached toward the drone, then dropped his hand. Might as well try the new trick again . . . so he reached out only with his mind, and the drone was gone.

Rather, it was no longer beside him. It now hovered in the middle of the living room in his mind, and Roger smiled in satisfaction.

It stayed there only a second, then turned under Donna's control and began moving around the room. A moment later, it found a side hallway beyond his mental peripheral vision and moved out of his sight.

He kept the image uppermost in his mind and waited. It was all he *could* do; it took a lot of concentration just to manage that. From time to time he cracked an eyelid to glance at his father, but C.J. was doing just fine, scowling at the door and the merry noises floating through it.

Within just a couple of minutes, Roger felt himself

growing tired. *C'mon, Donna, don't mess around.* But it wasn't much longer before the drone drifted back into view.

Small ports irised open on its body and its manipulative waldoes emerged. One of them shaped its hand into a thumb-and-forefinger "okay" sign. Roger reached out again with his mind. . . .

The drone hummed back into existence beside him. He stage-whispered, "Dad, time to go."

The old man nodded gruffly and moved to stand beside him.

Roger suddenly felt weak; it was the exhaustion he normally felt after a full day of using his power. He had to lean back against the wall, but kept concentrating: *Not yet, get home first. . . .*

Then the quality of air changed and his friends were cheering. His knees gave way; he fell backwards six inches, stopped by the wall of his own office, and opened his eyes. "Success!" he said weakly and slid to sit on the floor.

Donna hurried to kneel beside him. "Roger, are you all right?"

He waved at her, using his hand like a fan to blow her worry away. "Just tired. The usual. What did you get?"

She smiled. "Plenty. That wasn't another of Kevin's places. It was Red and Penny's house! 1104 West Warren. The zip code is the same as Kevin's town house, so it can't be too far from there. And we got their phone number off their phone." She turned to sit beside him. "We didn't even have to go outside. Found a pile of mail, mostly bills made out to Red and Penny Taylor. Taylor is Kevin's middle name. There were Greek weapons in the closet, your painting on the wall. . . ."

He grabbed her hand and squeezed it, grinning. "I believe you, I believe you. We have them. Red and Penny, anyway. Now, we have to figure out what to do with them." It was, in fact, pointless to eliminate the two of them; Kevin could pull new ones out of his original painting. It was time to think of a way to exploit their new opportunity.

A couple of hours later, gunshots cracked outside the house, but Roger ignored them. Elsewhere on the property, C.J. was giving Donna and Dylan their firearms lesson. Roger just sat at his table while Elsie laid out open books in front of him.

She immediately tapped at one open page. "That's why your gun didn't hurt him. In the Greek myths, Achilles has bulletproof skin. His mother was a goddess. She dunked him in a magic river and it made his skin hard."

"Right, I remember that story. But she had to hold onto him by his ankle or his heel, and that part wasn't bulletproof. That's what gets him killed, right?"

She tapped another page in another book. "That's right. During a big war, the Trojan War. A prince named Paris shot him in the heel with an arrow, maybe a poisoned arrow. I thought Paris was a city."

"It is now." He glanced across the myriad pages Elsie had opened before him. "Now, was Penthesilia bulletproof?"

The nymph shook her head. "She had normal skin. She was an Amazon. That's a woman who fights. Some people thought that the Amazons cut their breasts off so they could draw a bow better, and some didn't." She made a face of disgust. "Anyway, she came to Troy to fight the Greeks. She fought Achilles and he killed her. But he fell in love with her. Some books say that he raped her body when she was dead." Her expression became even more revolted. "Some of these stories are just awful."

"But Kevin has the two of them alive, together, working for him. And —" He remembered Achilles kneeling beside Penthesilia on her stretcher, risking

Kevin's anger to get her to safety in the painting. "And Achilles is obviously in love with her here, too."

"I think that's nice." Elsie's expression became a little dreamy.

"They helped Kevin try to kill us, Elsie. That's not so nice."

She glared at him. "Maybe they don't have a choice."

"Maybe not. So a guy named Paris killed him, huh? Tell me about that."

Over the next several days, Roger and Donna worked up three paintings and a set of technical diagrams.

The first painting showed a dark-haired hero, young and handsome but hard-eyed, standing on the summit of angled city walls made of stone. He wore an archaic-looking tunic, elaborately embroidered, and held a powerful bow in his hands; it was nocked, the arrow drawn, and he laughed as he aimed at some target far below. It was called "Paris on the Walls of Troy."

The second painting showed a man and a woman on the bow of a boat on a rolling sea. This was no modern vessel; it was a primitive galley, long and shallow, with rowers straining away on both sides. The man in the foreground was young, handsome, with a touch of weakness to his features. He wore only a kilt whose hem was horizontal across the back of his legs but descended to a sharp point in front.

The woman was young, blonde, and beautiful. She wore a green robe of classical Greek design. From the way she leaned against the man and held him, it was obvious that she adored him, but the intensity of her gaze on him was intimidating. The man was not looking at her but staring ahead. The painting's name was "The Argonauts Flee Colchis."

The third painting showed the interior of a columned, classical-era building; there was an open-air hearth in the middle of the floor; on either side were tables laden with pots, bins, boxes, cauldrons, grinding bowls, and other, less identifiable items. Incongruously, a modern doctor and nurse, both white-clad and female, stood waiting. This one was called "The Sorceress' Workshop."

The technical diagrams showed a variety of items: several sets of SWAT team-style body armor and helmets, numerous guns, sets of oversized binoculars with starlight capability, a parabolic microphone, stun guns, tasers, tear-gas grenades — enough gear to equip a squad of urban commandos. Another diagram showed a long, sinister stretch limousine.

Donna was pleased to learn that her technical precision made a difference. They found out that when Roger drew a handgun from only his imagination, it would work fine . . . but when it was empty, it was useless. Normal ammunition would not fit it. But a handgun from one of Donna's excruciatingly detailed technical diagrams accepted normal ammunition of the correct caliber, could be broken down and cleaned just like the real-world gun it was patterned after; after examining a couple of them, C.J. announced, "They may be magic, but they work just like the real thing. Nobody's going to look at them and wonder where they came from."

They didn't spend all their time drawing and painting. They joined in the classes of "Simons University," learning to shoot, to move more quietly in underbrush, to spot signs of concealed animals, traps and attackers. Elsie was phenomenally skilled in the wilderness and could follow a faint animal trail days after it was left. Though she could teach only a fraction of her skill to the others, that fraction greatly improved their own powers of perception.

Roger practiced his speed and skill at getting into and out of paintings. He shaved fractions of a second off all his times, which Elsie meticulously recorded. He learned to pop people into painting-worlds from farther and farther away. So long as he was next to his painting, it seemed that it didn't matter how far away were the people he was transporting, so long as he could see them; when he was away from his painting, he was still able to extend his range to twenty-five or thirty feet.

Then, Donna had her first success with art-magic. Her painting was of a simple, translucent blue marble. With Roger holding onto her, coaching her, she felt the surface of the painting, then finally felt *beyond* the surface and touched the glassy smoothness of the marble beneath. She tried unsuccessfully for an hour; then, finally, she pulled and gasped as she came up with a blue marble in her hands. The little painting left behind on the table was blank.

She was so exhausted that Roger put her in bed for the rest of the day, but she went to sleep happy, still clutching the marble to her.

Roger didn't sleep at all. It *was* possible for Donna to learn to manipulate this power. Had she always had the potential? Had Roger and Kevin become collaborators in college, and then Kevin and Donna become romantically involved later, because they all had the potential — did the power itself draw people together? Or did all artists have the power to greater or lesser degrees? He shook his head; that didn't sound likely. But answers to the questions eluded him.

When the paintings and diagrams were ready, Roger and the others hammered out the final details of their operation against Achilles and Penthesilia.

"She's the dangerous one," Roger said, tapping the woman on the "Argonauts" painting. "Medea. She was a witch and a poisoner. Some of Elsie's sources say she later killed her own children by Jason because he abandoned her. That's one reason I painted her early in her career, before she got old and bitter . . . and because it gives me an extra measure of control on her motivations. But while she's here, I want all of you to keep your eyes open."

C.J. and Dylan nodded, but Donna frowned and spoke. "Roger, I've given this a lot of thought . . . and I don't think you should do this at all. I think we need a different plan. This whole thing with Achilles is wrong, just wrong."

Roger stared at her, surprised. "Donna, we have to learn what he and Penthesilia know. It could mean the difference between life and death. For us."

"I know, but . . ." She stalled, scowling. "What you're saying is true. It doesn't mean that this isn't wrong. But if you're dead set on doing it, I want you to promise me something. If Penthesilia calls your bluff, I want you to cave in."

Elsie said, "I think so, too." Even Dylan nodded.

Roger looked between them and frowned. "Guys, it's taken me a lot of time to decide that I'm willing to kill to keep us alive. It really is us or them."

Donna shook her head. "I don't care. I know he's tried to kill you Roger, but we *can't* let him die that way. It would be horrible. Roger, I've given in on Kevin. I can't see any way to save him. But I want you to give in on Achilles."

He gave her a long look, then nodded. "All right." He was startled at the relief that flooded him — not even for Donna would he be forced to kill someone this way. "But when it comes down to the confrontation, don't let on you feel this way. I have to come across as the second most cold-hearted bastard in the world — Kevin being the first — and I can't do it if you're undermining me."

"All right." She bit her lip, then continued. "And I think you ought to send in another robot Roger for this."

Roger shook his head. "I can't give you that. We don't know what all Achilles and Penthesilia can do. If they have any way of knowing whether I'm the real

Roger or not, they have to understand it really is me. I
need them to realize that I'm confident enough to go
out myself, not relying on a duplicate. I think that will
spook them. Maybe it'll spook Kevin."

Donna looked resigned, then her expression became
stubborn. "Then I'm going, too." The rest chimed in
with similar words.

Roger grudgingly nodded. "I won't try to stop you.
But everybody's going to be armored and carrying
weapons. Each one of us has to be ready to protect
everyone else."

An hour later, they had their first interview with
Medea, the witch of Greek myth.

Her expression of joy and adoration vanished when
Roger pulled her from the painting. It gave way to the
most perfect poker face Roger had ever seen. Not one
iota of emotion showed on her beautiful features. She
did look around; she must have been curious about the
thousand modern objects to be seen in the office, but
for all Roger could tell she was simply evaluating the
decor. He took his time, kept his speech simple and
free of colloquialism, and explained her task to her.

"And why should I do this for you?" she asked. Her
tone was bored, and her words were thick with an
accent that sounded vaguely Russian to Roger's ears.

"Because if you don't, you stay here, or in the
workshop, forever." Roger tried to keep his voice cold,
and succeeded. "You never see Jason again."

There — was that the slightest crack in her armor of
emotionlessness? The faintest beginning of a pained
look? But it might have been nothing but a shadow; it
was gone almost before Roger could register it. Medea
didn't answer; she just stared at Roger with her
unsettling eyes. He steeled himself against her and
continued. "Like I said, it has to incapacitate him
immediately. But it can't kill him that fast. He has to
hang on for quite a while, the length of a long
conversation and longer. And if we administer the

antidote anytime during that period, he has to be able to make a full recovery." He wanted to add, "Can you do it?" but didn't. She *had* to be able to do it.

She might as well have been reading his mind. "I can do that," she said. "But I want something more than a return to Jason. I want gold, enough to fill an amphora. I fled Colchis without a fitting dowry."

Roger grinned before he could stop himself. Adding a jug filled with gold to his "Argonauts" painting would cost him, oh, a few cents and a few minutes of time. "Very well," he said. "If your poison and antidote work exactly as described."

"They will."

He stood and extended his hand for her, then led her to the painting of the empty workshop. "This is a painting of a spacious house on a deserted island," he told her. "I'm going to send you there just like I brought you here. You'll find servants and supplies, some modern healers who might be able to show you a thing or two, everything you need."

She just nodded, her expression still cool. Roger suppressed a shudder. Civil as she was, he knew she'd exact revenge on him if she had the chance. He promised himself he'd never give her one. Roger closed his eyes and a moment later Medea was gone. Roger wasn't the only one to breathe a sigh of relief.

Two days later Paris, Prince of Troy, glared at Roger, his friends and Medea. He echoed the sorceress' question, "And why should I do this for you?"

Roger tried to keep his voice cold. "You'll have a chance to shoot Achilles, greatest warrior of the Greeks, your enemy. I would have thought you'd do it just for your own glory. But if you don't, I won't do a thing to you. I certainly won't send you back home. To Helen."

"Helen." Paris didn't have Medea's control; he looked shattered. "Bring her to me, magician! Or I will not help you."

Roger thought about exerting his will against the legendary prince's, but decided to hold that option in reserve. "No. Help us, or stay here forever. You've seen enough to know that this world is too strange for you. You'd be killed or jailed in a week. Do what I ask, or that's what happens to you."

Paris' face twitched as he struggled to hide his capitulation. Roger pointed at Elsie and continued, "She'll help you get into position. All we need is one perfect shot, but we'll prepare half a dozen of your arrows."

"One is all I need." The Trojan prince regained some of his natural arrogance. He eyed Elsie. "My first wife was a nymph. Good at lovemaking and woodcraft both. I would wager you are the same."

She didn't give him satisfaction by getting angry or embarrassed. "You're right about the woodcraft. You'll never know about the rest."

Roger turned his attention to Medea. "And you know what you have to do."

The woman said calmly, "I have now practiced with your invasive device." She tapped the small case in her lap, the case containing hypodermic needles. "It will make my task much easier. I wish to take it with me when you send me home."

"Whatever. I mean, very well." Roger forced himself to remember that Medea thought of herself as a living woman with a past and a future; he couldn't afford to challenge that belief by treating her demands lightly.

Roger glanced around at the rest of them. "We've got a two-hour drive into the city. Time to get your gear on, folks. Let's pray that the limo's air conditioning works. And pray that they're home tonight. Otherwise, we'll be making a long trip for nothing."

A few minutes before 10 P.M., the black limousine glided to a halt on West Warren Street, two houses down from the home of Achilles and Penthesilia. Elsie, clad in the same cumbersome riot-police armor that her friends wore, emerged, followed by Paris, who still wore his Trojan garments. The two of them vanished into the shadows of a front yard.

In the driver's seat, C.J. didn't even have to use the special binoculars on the target house. "The lights are on inside. And . . . yep, that dumb red-headed buck is moving around. They're home."

Beside him, in the front passenger seat, Dylan set down the parabolic microphone he'd been readying and brought up his weapon instead. It was an Uzi submachine gun, compact and deadly.

Roger was in the oversized rear compartment; it had two passenger seats facing one another. He looked at Donna beside him, Medea opposite. Donna gave him a nervous look. "If you screw this up and get hurt, I'm going to kill you," she hissed. Medea just smiled coolly.

Roger waited another few minutes to give Elsie and Paris time to get into position, then said, "Pull 'er up, Dad."

C.J. drove up a few yards and pulled to a stop directly in front of the house. Roger got out and gave Donna a thumbs-up sign. She reached for the limo's cellular phone and dialed. Roger checked the rest of his gear: riot-police armor and helmet all in place, his pistol holstered at his side. He looked like a menacing figure from a movie about some totalitarian regime, and grinned at his own pretension.

He heard the phone ring inside Achilles' house, heard it stop. Nothing happened for a minute, but Donna would be talking to the Greek warrior, informing him that he had a visitor outside. Then Achilles banged his way out the front door, Penthesilia behind him, both dressed in modern clothes.

The Greek warrior's eyes were open wide. "I can't believe you came here," he said, his tone low. "I have to kill you, you know. I have been given orders." His hand came up, a short, sharp sword held in it.

Penthesilia's expression was more worried. "He's up to something," she whispered. "Don't go. Call Kevin."

But Roger didn't intend for the warrior to get smart. He pulled his handgun from his holster. "I hear you have bulletproof skin," he said cheerfully. The gun was a Colt .45 semiautomatic pistol with an extended barrel . . . and a suppressor screwed onto that barrel. He pointed it at the Greek hero. "Is it true?" He pulled the trigger three times and noises like three loud animal coughs echoed against the surrounding houses.

All three bullets hit, smacking through Achilles' shirt and into his chest. They did affect him; he looked pained and, with a short, deep growl of anger, he charged Roger.

Lord, he moved fast. He was most of the way across the yard before Roger had time to react.

But arrows move faster than runners. Paris' missile sliced out of the night sky, from the roof next door, to strike the running warrior. In the heel. The sudden injury threw off Achilles' pace, tripped him, and he crashed to the ground with an injured grunt only six feet from Roger.

He jumped up again instantly, his shoe leaking blood. But he was unimpaired, and Roger felt sudden fear — fear that Medea had failed or betrayed him, fear that Achilles would get to him and cut him open. . . .

But Achilles managed only one short hop forward. Then his eyes rolled up in his head. He reeled and fell backwards.

"Achilles!" The Amazon ran forward, a long, wicked knife in either hand.

But Roger brought his weapon up to cover her. She skidded to a halt yards from him. "Talk to me," Roger said icily. "And maybe I can save him. But if you attack me, or refuse me . . . he's a dead man." *Like hell. I promised. But let's just hope you don't call that bluff.*

Achilles writhed. Even in the little light afforded by

the moon, he already looked flushed. His arms and legs twitched as muscles contracted against his will; he moaned, unable to overcome the pain that gripped him.

Penthesilia glared at Roger, a hate-filled expression that would have picked him up and twisted him to pieces if there were justice in the world . . . but she dropped her knives, then ran to kneel at Achilles' head and take him into her lap. "I can't tell you anything. It's not my fault. Save him." Her last words were a plea, a wail of desperation.

Dammit. "The hell you can't. Time's wasting, Penny." He knocked on the car door behind him and Donna emerged. She managed to keep her face impartial as she looked at Achilles. Then she trotted up the walk and into the house.

Roger continued. "Where's Kevin, Penny? Where does he live?"

She just gripped Achilles to her tighter and shook her head. Tears began to roll down her cheeks, but she did not sob. *"I can't tell you! It is forbidden. I . . . physically . . . can't . . . tell you! Please* don't let him die!"

Roger stared down at the two of them and tried to remember his next question. He couldn't. His carefully prepared script just vanished from his memory.

Jesus Christ, I'm torturing him and it's killing her. With a flash of clarity he could see himself as Penthesilia saw him: another monster like Kevin, some cruel thing who created living beings and then used them up like fuel. And the vision shook him. He couldn't keep his sudden dismay from his face.

"Okay, Penny." His voice was a little softer. "You win. But we're going to talk." He rapped on the car door again and his blonde passenger emerged with her hypodermic case and first-aid kit. "Penthesilia, Amazon Queen, I'd like you to meet Medea, Princess of Colchis."

Penthesilia didn't answer. It was obvious she had heard of Medea. An expression of shock crossed her face. She shrank away from Medea, but still held on to Achilles as if she could protect him from this new monster.

Medea smiled at the Amazon, amused, then knelt beside Achilles. First, she drew the hypodermic from its case and injected its contents into his hip, where the muscle twitching was less pronounced. Then, with the blade in the first-aid kit, she cut away the shoe around Paris' arrow. She doused the blade with a modern antiseptic and began a quick, deft surgery to remove the arrow itself.

Donna emerged from the house with "Deceit of My Pants" in her hands. Her look asked a question of Roger, and he shook his head no: No, Penny hadn't talked.

But he wasn't done yet. He moved nearer to Penthesilia, crouched beside her. "This may not mean anything to you," he started, "but we couldn't really murder him. Not like this.

"But we got the best of you this time without any trouble. And we're going to meet again. Next time, we may have to kill you. You'll get to watch Achilles die, or he'll watch you die, and it'll be all over because of Kevin.

"If Kevin kills us, you'll never be free of him. But if we get to him first — you've got a chance. Do you understand?"

She nodded, but was watching Medea, who now pulled the arrow free from Achilles' foot and began cleaning the wound.

"So you need to tell me what you can. Can you tell me about Kevin's other houses, where he isn't living right now?"

"No. That's expressly forbidden." Her voice was dull.

Paris and Elsie emerged from the darkness, returned to the limousine's interior. Penthesilia's face showed no recognition when she glanced at Paris, and for a moment Roger was confused — they were contemporaries during the Trojan War, weren't they? Then he understood. She was Kevin's version of Penthesilia. He was Roger's version of Paris. There was no reason for them to recognize one another. He turned back to Penny.

"How about his personal security — what sort of magical gadgets he uses to protect his own person?"

"No."

"How about —"

"Wait. Yes."

"You can tell me about his personal security?"

She thought about it, her eyes moving across events of the past. "That was never . . . *expressly* forbidden. I can't tell anyone that he has such things. But you already know it. . . ."

"I do. And now you need to tell me what they are."

She started talking.

Dylan emerged from the car to help Penthesilia carry the semiconscious Achilles back into the house, into the bedroom. Roger and Penny continued their conversation inside. Five minutes later, they were nearly done.

Roger moved to the doorway and looked down at the notes he'd taken. "So the little paintings in his wallet are his main offense. And the thing he had surgically implanted in him —"

"The little shield."

"The shield. It keeps harm from reaching him."

"It's as though he has an invisible suit of armor on. A bullet will flatten and fall off half an inch before reaching him. A blade will stop short and be blunted. Before he had it implanted . . . I had to test it for him." She shuddered at the memory. "It can stop anything. It can stop a modern explosive missile. I know."

Roger sighed. "And there are no flaws in it. No —"

He almost said "Achilles heel." "No gaps in the coverage."

She shook her head. "No. But it makes him tired. He gets tired fast if it is stopping a lot of damage."

"Come again?"

"After a few tests, he would get tired. Just as when he pulls people from paintings. When he was too tired, it would not protect him any longer. It was just to stop the one assassin's bullet, the one killer's knife. To give him time to get away or give us time to deal with the assassin."

Roger added a note. "That makes a big difference." He looked at her, at the feverish, unconscious Achilles. "And that's all you know about."

"Yes. Except I know he has more than he told me. Reserve weapons, reserve defenses. He doesn't tell anyone everything he has prepared."

"Is there any way to tell one of Kevin's people . . ." He stopped himself from saying "from a real person." "From someone who isn't?"

"Just by looking?" She thought about it. "We are all his slaves, Roger. Every one of us wears something." She pulled the scarf away from her neck, revealing jewelry — a ring of heavy gold, like an ancient Celtic torc. Except this item had no gap in it, could not be pulled free. "They are special. Magical. We use these to bring our weapons and armor to us when we need them. But they also remind us . . . that Kevin owns us."

Roger could see a similar gold band on Achilles' neck. "Julia doesn't have anything like that."

"On her wrists. Her bracelets do not come off. The agents have rings. Every one of us bears Kevin's mark in some way."

Soberly, Roger flipped the notebook closed. "I don't think you want to mention this visit to Kevin."

She shook her head. "But this house is watched. All his safe houses are watched."

"Will the watcher still be here, or has it already flown off to tell Kevin?"

"It will be here. It will follow you, to your home."

"I don't think so. What is it?"

"A halcyon."

"A what?"

"A kingfisher. A sea bird with a crest on its head. Many colors."

He nodded. It took him a long moment to manage his next statement. "I'm sorry we hurt Achilles like that. We're enemies, but . . . I didn't know."

She didn't answer. She just stroked Achilles' brow. The warrior still sweated heavily and occasionally shook with the poison's aftereffects. Not knowing what else to say, Roger left.

As they drove homeward, Dylan, Elsie, and C.J. were exuberant. Medea looked completely at ease.

Paris, voice haughty, said, "I have done my task, magician. It is time for you to send me home. Now."

Roger glared. Next time, he'd choose an agent who wasn't a brat at heart. "Paris, you get home as soon as the rest of us do. Take a nap or something. Wait a moment; how'd you like to shoot a bird?"

The Trojan prince's eyes glittered. "I made my one perfect shot. I will do no more."

"That's your right, I suppose." Roger addressed the others. "Who's the best shot here?"

C.J., Donna, and Dylan all chimed in together: "Elsie." The nymph blushed and hid her face in her hands.

"Figures. Elsie, we're being followed by a halcyon. Do you know what that is?"

"A bird. Very colorful. Some eat insects, some eat fish —"

"Never mind. This one is Kevin Matthews'. Like the raven."

The nymph wasted no time; she drew her own pistol, a long-barrelled revolver, and flipped the cylinder out to see if it were loaded, just as C.J. taught her.

C.J. pulled the car to the side of the road and Dylan hit the button to open the limousine's sun roof. As soon as the car was at rest, Elsie stood up through the sun roof, took a look around, aimed for a long moment and fired. The crack of the shot made Paris jump . . . and thirty yards away, an artificial kingfisher exploded in a mass of bloody, multicolored feathers.

She sat down again. "No more halcyon."

C.J. shook his head. "Wish we'd had her in the big war." He put the limousine in gear.

It was four hours before everything was settled for the night. Half of that time was spent getting back to the house. Then Roger put Paris back into his painting, transferred Medea back into hers, added the Greek-style jug full of gold on the deck of the famous *Argo* . . . and finally put his paints away.

He thought about the night's events, thought about what had to be done. He thought until his jangled nerves were settled. Then he went to his room.

His bed was empty, so he rapped lightly on Donna's door and entered at her quiet invitation. In a moment, he was between the sheets with her, soaking up her embrace as if it were sunlight on his skin.

"Everything done?" she asked.

"Everything done."

"You did good tonight."

"Tonight never should have happened." He thought about Penthesilia's face as Achilles lay dying. "You were right. The poison was a really bad idea. I'm turning into Kevin. Don't let me turn into Kevin." There was desperation in his voice.

Donna took his face in her hands and kissed him. "You'll never turn into Kevin. When I knew that you'd given in and brought Medea out to fix him . . . I figured out why. I was so proud of you. And then you got what you wanted to know anyway. . . ."

"I felt like shit." He sighed.

"Well, you should've. If you hadn't . . . then, yeah, maybe you'd be turning into Kevin. But you did."

He didn't answer, just nuzzled her, and she changed the subject. "Did you put Medea to bed?" Her voice was teasing. "Did you think she was good-looking?"

He grinned. "You know she is. Apollonius of Rhodes thought she was a major babe, so I had to follow suit. But she's not *that* good-looking."

"No?"

"I was thinking about painting my dream girl. I've finally settled on a set of features that are perfection." He felt her breath catch from the sudden injury to her self-confidence. "But what good is it to paint her? I can't drag her into the real world."

She managed to keep most of the hurt from her voice. "Why not?"

"Because she's already here, silly. In bed. With me." He kissed her.

When, a breathless while later, they broke for air, she swatted his backside for teasing. "That wasn't nice."

"But it's true." He pulled himself a few inches up so she could make a pillow of his chest. "I spent all that time chasing this image, a set of features, that was my dream girl. I figured that if I could find someone who matched this mental image, well, she would be everything *else* I imagined my dream girl to be. She'd love art; she'd have a thing about guys who refused to work a nine-to-five . . . It never happened, and that image kept changing over the years. I guess Elsie was closest to the last version, physically.

"And then you walked up and hit me when I wasn't looking. And helped me figure it out. There's just one woman I want for my dream girl. And my friend, and my collaborator, and my lover. I can see these perfect features: long brown hair . . ." He thumbed Donna's nose. "Just short of too many freckles . . ."

"Roger?"

"Yes?"

"Shut up and kiss me."

He did.

This time she kept her eyes open, and he could see happiness in them, happiness he'd helped bring to life.

Chapter Ten

The Art Show

Roger sat in the chair by the window and stared down eight stories into the front parking lot of the Stafford Hotel. Nerves were eating him. His leg fidgeted; he tapped out a nervous rhythm on the air conditioning unit. From the corner of his eye, he could see Donna and Elsie trying not to be annoyed with him. That made it worse.

He looked at Donna where she lounged on one of the beds. She was either calm or concealing her nervousness far better than he was. "What if he comes in a side door?" he asked.

"He'll come in the front way. I'm sure." With studied casualness, she flipped another page in her magazine. "I even asked some of the convention people. They're aware of his ego. They really do have a representative waiting at the front door to make him feel like Mr. Big Shot when he shows up. He won't miss that."

"Yeah." He turned back to the window. Then it was Elsie's turn; he pinned her with his gaze. "Supercop's in position, right?"

From her chair, she gave him a little smile, held up her walkie-talkie. "He says so. He's really anxious for this 'bust to go down.' How are you going to tell him Kevin's not a drug dealer? He'll be disappointed."

"I'll figure something out." He returned to tapping out his stuttering rhythm, then cursed. "There are so many ways this can go wrong. All they have to do is figure out that our cop's a painting —"

Donna shook her head. "They won't. We've had enough practice with this to know. Elsie can tell Kevin's painted people at a glance because they're sloppy, Roger. She can't usually tell yours. They're real people."

"Not hollow," Elsie added.

Roger glanced out the window again, then looked over the battery of new paintings set up on easels throughout the room. Each was as polished as he and Donna could make it — and as accurate as possible, given the information they had assembled in the last two weeks. C.J.'s photographs were tucked away in a file folder, now that every possible bit of information had been learned from them.

A key rattled in the door lock, and C.J. and Dylan came in. They were barely recognizable; C.J. affected glasses and a fisherman's cap filled with lures, while Dylan sported a two-week beard and mustache, his hair temporarily dyed black, to Elsie's dislike.

Roger asked, "Any changes downstairs?"

C.J. shook his head, then grinned at Donna. "Is he still driving you crazy?"

She nodded, then smiled in Roger's direction. "Not too bad. I've got butterflies myself."

Dylan moved to the window. "Take a break. I'll take over." Roger nodded reluctantly, moved over to lie down beside Donna.

Roger was silent for a minute, then said "One last time," and the other four groaned. "No, really, one last time. When I go downstairs, you don't have to come down with me. You can stay here."

But each one shook his head one last time.

"We know you can do it," Donna whispered. "It all depends on you being better than Kevin. And you are. In spades. He will *not* smell a rat. But we're going to be there, to help you if you need it. To see it end. We deserve that."

"Yeah. You do." He leaned over to settle his face

against her neck. Then: "What if he comes in by a side door?"

"Roger, just shut up."

Dylan spoke calmly, as if he were announcing that it were time for a TV show, "They're here."

Roger thumped into the wall next to the window and looked down into the parking lot. Dylan was right; two large limos were discharging a load of passengers. Kevin Matthews, in a three-piece suit so blue it was nearly black, carrying a glossy black briefcase, was one of the many.

He was flanked by a half-dozen men in suits and sunglasses — his standard contingent of agents, according to Penthesilia. Julia Dover was there, decked out in something red and shimmery; it looked like it was made of glittering fringe, and her shoes were the same color. Even from this distance, Roger and Dylan could see the gleaming white of her teeth.

Two more suits-and-sunglasses emerged from Kevin's limo, but they were a little different from the others. The first was tall and redheaded. The second was female. "Achilles and Penthesilia," Donna noted. "That seems to be everybody except the limo drivers. Elsie?"

"Right, right." She squeezed the button on her walkie-talkie. "Dali-Two, this is Dali-One. He's in sight. He's coming up the big lane straight out from the front doors. You ready to distract him?"

The speaker-distorted voice came back immediately, "Baby, I was born ready. Out."

Outside, the mass of suits including Kevin Matthews flowed closer and closer, until the foremost of them reached the lane that circled the hotel itself. And Roger said, "It's time."

Kevin Matthews and entourage waited for one last car to pass. But as they stepped into the lane in front of the hotel, a car motor revved, brakes screeched, and agents spun to deal with the threat.

An oncoming Plymouth Fury screeched to an abrupt halt just short of two of the agents. Six agents reached under their jackets for sidearms, but stopped before they drew; the car hadn't hit them and both the driver's hands were in sight on the wheel.

And, for the briefest second, Kevin felt disoriented. He wavered a moment, then looked suspiciously in all directions.

The Fury's driver, a lean, scruffy man wearing a flower-print shirt, his sunglasses just like the agents', held up his hands. His expression was alarmed. "Hey, sorry! Stand out in the middle of the street, why don't ya!"

Red waved downward, signalling the agents to stand down. "This is no threat," he told them. Then he gestured for the Plymouth driver to pass. Mr. Flower Print turned the wheel, goosed the gas, and sped by. As he did, he stuck his hand out the window and made a gesture of his own.

Kevin would normally have memorized the car's license plate — so that he could ruin the idiot's life for rudeness to Kevin Matthews. This time he didn't bother. "Did you feel that?" he asked no one in particular.

Julia shook her head. "Feel what?"

"I don't know." Out in the open air, he suddenly felt vulnerable. "Maybe good ol' Rog has some sort of invisible weapon and gave me a dose. Not that it would do me any harm. But if he's here, I want you to find him. Let's get inside." He smoothed down his hair and continued across the lane, his retinue smoothly keeping pace all around him.

Before they got there, the doors into the lobby opened and a woman emerged: small, officious, in her late twenties. She was dark-haired and good-looking, and her glasses enhanced rather than diminished her looks; her face would lack character without them. She walked straight through the line of agents, held out her hand. "Mr. Matthews? Patrice Anderson. I'm your personal liaison with MArtCon XIII. You need anything, you ask me. I'm so glad to meet you at last. I've seen so much of your work." From her purse, she extracted a large, shiny gold badge embossed with the words:

KEVIN MATTHEWS
GUEST OF HONOR
MARTCON XIII

"I'm glad to meet you, too." Kevin let the woman pin his badge on him, and indulgently tried to catch a glimpse down her blouse as she did so. "I have eight guests of my own."

She smiled, not taken aback by the sudden demand for extra convention memberships, not disconcerted at the prospect of an artist who surrounded himself with bodyguards. She dug around in her purse and came up with a handful of plastic badges. "As many guest memberships as you need. Come on inside. Do you want to see the art show first? Take a tour of the place? See the convention suite?"

"Whatever. The tour, I guess." He let her take him by the arm; he kept his attention on her chest as they walked. *You need anything, you ask me.* He was certain he'd need something from her before the convention was done. He was equally sure she'd supply it. He'd make sure of it. He always did.

Life was good to Kevin Matthews, and he smiled in simple appreciation of the fact. He relaxed as his paranoia of a moment ago faded away.

They walked through the hotel lobby, where a few guests checking in noticed Matthews and murmured among themselves. Then they passed through a hallway that led to the function-room area of the ground floor. Ms. Anderson kept talking. "I know we're a small convention, compared to what you're used to these days, but we're going to do our best to give you a con you'll never forget.

"On your left are the hotel ballrooms; they're our function rooms. The panels you'll be giving are scheduled for the Crystal Ballroom; that's the largest one."

Matthews glanced indifferently at the bank of oversized doors and nodded.

"On your right, the dealers' room. We have a hundred and fifty tables set up. Your PR man — Berman? — has your prints set up at your own table."

Kevin looked in briefly as they passed. Though it was early afternoon on the first day of the convention, the dealers' room was already thick with buyers and most of the dealers' tables were already set up. He saw tables piled high with art prints, movie posters, notebooks filled with prints from movies, videotaped movies, books, T-shirts, knickknacks, too many things to catalogue with his quick look.

"And just ahead on your right, the art room. Your people already delivered your art for display. Are you selling any originals at the convention?" Her voice was bright, hopeful.

He shook his head. "I don't sell my originals anymore. Of course, I sometimes part with one . . . for special people, on special occasions." He let that statement hang between them as they swept into the art room. He knew Julia would be fuming and the thought made him smile.

The art gallery was a large room filled with standing, cloth-draped panels lined end to end. On each panel was hung a variety of paintings, hand-colored prints, and black-and-white line drawings.

Kevin beamed as he moved along the rows of art. His face was cheerful and serene as he evaluated each artist in turn. *Crap. Crap. Extra-bad crap. Loser. Has-been. What's he still doing here? Oh, this one's not bad.* He stopped and took an especially close look at a pair of paintings. One showed dragons in flight, the other showed dragons mating in midair. The colors were dramatic, the detail was crisp and clean. They were perfect for book covers.

He noted the artist's name. *Andrea Ericson. Too bad, Andrea. You shouldn't have left these around where I could see them. Your career just went down the toilet, and you don't even know it yet.* His grin got wider. Life was good.

A few steps away, Penthesilia stopped, looking at the people moving among the paintings, and frowned.

Kevin leaned in to whisper in her ear. "What is it?"

"Something smells wrong. A rotting odor. It's very faint."

He sniffed, too, but smelled nothing. Not surprising; her sense of smell was much keener than his. "Rotting meat from room service, maybe?"

"Maybe." She didn't look convinced.

After Kevin had spent some time maliciously maneuvering through tight aisles so his agents would have to work extra hard to keep him safe, something occurred to him. He turned to Patrice. "Where are my paintings?"

"Oh." She gestured to their left. "You have the entire south wall, of course." Then she looked where she'd pointed. Her second "Oh" was much louder.

The wall was blank. Not one painting or print hung there.

Kevin gave her a stiff glare. "Just what's going on here?"

"Uh . . ." She looked around, alarmed. "I'm sure they just haven't been set up yet. I can't imagine why. I'll ask Mike."

Kevin kept the stern expression on his face, but inwardly was delighted. *Typical snafu. Happens all the time. But she'll be so apologetic. So anxious to make it up to me.*

Patrice caught the eye of the bright-looking man at the security desk. "Mike, where are Mr. Matthews' paintings?"

He waved at the blank wall. "Over there." Then he looked. "Shit. They *were* there! Where the hell did they go?"

"I have them. Just returning the favor."

The voice came from behind them. Kevin recognized it and stiffened, then turned.

Roger Simons stood at the north wall, leaning against a spot where no paintings hung, his arms crossed over his chest. He wore crisp new jeans, a black MArtCon XIII T-Shirt, and a big grin. "Big Kev! How are you doing?"

Kevin pulled his face-the-world grin across his face, but he wasn't happy. He was confused. Still, he turned to Julia, pointed his thumb at Roger. "Can you believe the balls on this guy?" He didn't wait for her answer; he turned back to Roger. "Big Rog! Look, let's keep this civilized. Some of my boys will take us both outside. We can talk." Kevin reached out with his mind, touched the simple minds of two of his agents, set them into motion. Both stepped forward toward Roger.

"Oh, I'm through being civilized." Roger uncrossed his arms and the smile left his face. He held a rectangular object in his hand — a small painting. "I'm here to finish this. Kevin, you're dead." He closed his eyes in what was barely a blink and snapped his fingers.

The wall beside him shattered inward, destroying paintings and throwing them from the wall. Then something massive stepped into the room.

It was shaped like an old-fashioned diving suit, but twice as tall, silver-gray in color, bristling with gun barrels. Its hands, its wrists, its chest, its faceplate were all thick with the cylindrical arrays of Vulcan machine guns — horrible, modern Gatling guns that could fire thousands of rounds a minute.

Patrice Anderson shrieked. Kevin was shocked into stillness for an instant; then he grabbed Julia and hit the floor, automatically landing atop her and cushioning his fall with her body.

His agents weren't smart, but they knew how to do their job. Two jumped atop Kevin to shield him. Two went left and two more went right. All six drew their firearms. Achilles leaped into Patrice, skidding with her underneath a table beside the wall, while Penthesilia went down and rolled to the side, out of the line of fire.

Then the gun cylinders began to rotate and it sounded like someone had substituted sticks of dynamite for firecrackers on the Fourth of July.

Streams of bullets roared out of the barrels and streams of ejected brass fired off at different angles.

Kevin's people were no longer in the way; the projectiles hit convention-goers and panels of art. A dozen convention-goers melted under the streams of Vulcan rounds as if they were confectioner's sugar hit by water from a high-pressure hose. But sugar didn't disintegrate into gruesome sprays of blood and bits of flesh. These people did. Kevin stared wide-eyed at the carnage, at the red chunks and gobbets that had been people just a moment ago. He heaved, nearly throwing up on the polished wooden floor.

Achilles, unmoved, screamed an order to the agents, but they couldn't hear him over the deafening roar from the guns. It didn't matter; they were already acting. As the streams of bullets began to traverse the room, threatening to sweep across them, the agents ejected clips from their guns, slapped in new clips from belt pouches, and opened fire.

These weren't real-world bullets; they were much better. Each exploded when it hit the robot, shearing away shards of metal, exposing some of the robot's interior to further deadly fire. The robot jerked and wavered as it was hit, its Vulcans spraying fire all over the art room . . . and then, finally, one of its legs literally torn to pieces by the agents' fire, it collapsed on its side. A moment later it rolled onto its back and was still; the Vulcans all over its body seized up and stopped.

In the sudden silence, Kevin resumed control of the situation. "Get off me," he told one agent, then had to reinforce the order with his mental touch — the agent was nearly deaf. Kevin would be, too, if not for his special protection.

He got up and took quick stock of his surroundings. The robot was down. Roger Simons was nowhere to be seen. More than a dozen convention guests were sprayed all over the room, but none of his own people had been hit. Panels and art were perforated trash. The floor was indescribable.

Achilles squeezed out from beneath the table. Patrice Anderson, eyes wide but unseeing, stayed where she was. "What now?" Achilles shouted, assuming that Kevin was as deaf as he was.

Kevin spoke in a normal tone, enhancing his words with his mental touch. "You and Penthesilia, stay close. You agents, spread out. Find Simons. Kill him." The agents rushed out of the room.

He looked around the gruesome mess of the art room and shook his head admiringly. *Roger, I never thought you had it in you. Too bad you didn't wise up sooner.*

Julia, pale, shaking, stood and rubbed her bruised hip. "He brought that robot out so fast. How did he do that?"

"I don't know. It doesn't matter. We'll figure it out after he's dead. Get moving." He handed Julia his briefcase, then gestured to Achilles and Penthesilia. Achilles fell into step just ahead of him, Penthesilia just behind.

The hall outside was thick with onlookers who stood in the doorway and peered in at the carnage. Most paled, puked, or shouted. Achilles shoved them out of the way and led Kevin down the hall back the way they'd come. More convention-goers, ghoulish, were hurrying to join the others at the art room door. Oddly, it wasn't quite the crush of people Kevin had expected.

Kevin reached into his jacket pocket for his wallet. *So, you want to play, Roger. I'll show you what playing is all about.*

But his pocket was empty.

Kevin groped around for a few seconds, then swore. He could really use the miniature paintings the wallet held. Somehow, when he was getting away from the chaingun fire, he'd lost it. He'd look for it later. Good thing he thought ahead.

He reached instead into a vest pocket and pulled out his antique-looking pocket watch, then popped it open. With a deft twist, he pulled out the microscopically thin, working clock mechanism. This he tossed on the ground.

Left in the watch case were paintings — tiny, delicate, meticulously crafted paintings. Each was painted on a thin surface of metal, each metal disk joined to the next by a tiny hinge, and he could pull the whole chain of paintings out as a belt of metal links. He rapidly scanned the sequence of paintings. *Antitank missiles? Not yet. Army of skeletons? No, more armor first, troops second. Ah, yes. The Cyclops.*

Then Donna spoke to him. Her voice came across the hotel public address system, mocking him: "Mr. Kevin Matthews, please meet your party in the dealers' room. Paging Kevin Matthews, your party is in the dealers' room."

Kevin stopped, staring offended at the speaker in the ceiling. *The bitch is making fun of me. She thinks they're playing with me. Oh, she's not going to laugh when I get my hands on her again. . . .*

But he was only a few steps from the dealers' room door and, lacking a better idea of what to do, he decided to "meet his party." He moved to within ten feet of the door, then closed his eyes.

His agents responded to his mental touch. *Find the convention office,* he told two of them. *Donna is there. Bring her to me.*

Hotel officials passed by, en route to the art show room, shrieking for calm and order, announcing that the police had been called. Then they reached the door to that room and their shrieks became inarticulate.

At Kevin's gesture, Julia held up the briefcase. He popped the latches, tossed most of the promotional material inside on the floor, and lifted the false bottom, revealing the gun beneath. It looked like a large-framed semiautomatic, but he smiled at it, remembering the modifications his magic had made to it. Like a pistol from a bad western movie, it would never run out of the ammunition that could pierce an inch of steel. He took it in his right hand and closed his left on the little painting of the Cyclops.

He closed his eyes and concentrated. Long seconds later, he pulled, and heard a gratifying chorus of gasps from the convention-goers in his vicinity; he opened his eyes. Before him, kneeling on the hall carpet, was the Cyclops — a twelve-foot-tall statue of the one-eyed monster from myth. People all around him shrank away. He ignored them; if Roger really intended to fight this out, they'd all probably be dead in a few minutes.

The Cyclops' back was to him, as he wanted it. He issued a mental command and a hinged door of stone swung open in its back. He stepped up into the coffin-sized chamber behind the door.

"What about me?" Julia demanded, suddenly frightened as she was abandoned.

"Don't get killed," he said absently. "But don't worry. If you are, I'll just pull out a new you." Then the door swung shut, locking him into safety. Here, he was protected from all harm and was automatically joined to the Cyclops, seeing with its eye, shielded by its skin. He was safe.

At his command, the Cyclops rose to its feet, its upper body smashing into the ceiling to a chorus of cries from the onlookers. Kevin put the Cyclops' legs into motion, shoving it forward, digging a trench in the ceiling, then turning to smash through the wall as it forced its way into the dealers' room.

The ceiling here was much higher; his Cyclops was unencumbered and he had a good view of the entire area. There were still a lot of people in the dealers' room; obviously, not everyone had run toward the sound of the gunfire. Far too many were still standing at dealers' tables. Amazed, they now stared at the giant stone Cyclops entering the room.

Except for one of them. Not fifty feet from the Cyclops, standing behind a table full of paperback books as though he were a dealer, was Roger Simons. Roger was flipping through a book, apparently unconcerned with the noise of the Cyclops' arrival.

For a moment, Kevin simply didn't know what to do. *How can he ignore me? Hasn't he figured out that he's dead?* Then, infuriated, he began walking toward Roger.

Roger did catch sight of the approaching Cyclops. He looked up — and waved cheerfully. The other people in the dealers' room were not so happy; they began circling around behind tables, moving closer and closer toward the exits from the room. Achilles and Penthesilia shoved their way in through the crowd and took a quick look around.

Kevin's Cyclops charged through a row of dealers' tables, heedless of the men and women it kicked aside, and stomped its way up to stand over Roger. Kevin had to bend the Cyclops over just a bit to look at the other artist. He spoke through the Cyclops' booming voice: "Roger, are you just crazy?"

Roger shook his head. "Nope. I'm just safe. Kevin, I've learned so much. Thanks for pushing me into this. I know so many things now that you don't."

"Like hell."

"For example, I can pull things out of other peoples'

art now. Hell, out of prints. Off paperback books."

"Bullshit. That's impossible."

Roger shook his head as if saddened by Kevin's stupidity. "For instance —"

Roger wasn't holding onto an original painting; there was a paperback book in his hand, a book with a gigantic tarantula as the centerpiece of its cover art. Then Roger blinked — and the Cyclops shook as something huge and heavy landed upon it from above.

Kevin twisted the Cyclops' body around to look at his attacker.

It was a spider, a great hairy tarantula whose legs would have spanned thirty feet if stretched out. They weren't stretched now; they gripped the Cyclops from behind. The spider spread wide its mandibles and bit, arched its midsection and stung. Its attacks chewed away pieces of the Cyclops' back, leaving rough gouges drenched with saliva and poison.

Kevin lashed out at Achilles with his mind: *Where did this come from? Did Roger bring it out of midair?*

He felt Achilles' mind flinch from the contact, and part of him was pleased at the way he could always make lesser minds wilt. The warrior's reply came back: *We didn't see it before it fell from the ceiling. Do you want us to attack it?* Kevin saw Roger take the opportunity to scramble out from under a table and run for the far wall.

No, you moron, get Roger. Kevin cursed. If Roger really was able to pull in minions from other peoples' book covers, to pop them into reality yards away from himself, Kevin needed him dead. Immediately. Kevin mentally put the Cyclops "on autopilot," turning the fight over to the instincts he'd built into it. Then he shut his eyes and turned his mind to pulling more gear out of his disk paintings. What next? Oh, yes, the sword: the soul sucker . . . A moment later, he held the heavy, uncomfortably warm hilt in his hand, and felt the long-familiar weariness from the use of his powers tug at him. While resting, he divided his perceptions between the Cyclops' and Achilles' actions.

The Cyclops reached back and got one hand on a tarantula arm. The Cyclops yanked and strained, and the tarantula came free; the Cyclops threw it to the floor, then raised a leg and stomped hard on the spider's back. The room trembled from the blow, with books and tapes and prints jumping off tabletops; the sound of the spider's thorax being crushed was stomach-wrenching. But the enormous arachnid wasn't dead; its mandibles clamped down on the Cyclops' other foot and dug in.

Yards away, Achilles and Penthesilia went into action. They shed their jackets and ties, then popped shirt buttons to grab the golden torcs around their throats.

One moment, they stood in ripped suits and ties. The next, their modern garments were gone, replaced by Greek hoplite armor; Achilles held a round shield and a short spear, while Penthesilia gripped her wicked-looking curved bow. They immediately went into motion, charging down the aisles of tables, circling around the Cyclops-spider fight, heading toward Roger Simons.

Achilles, the faster runner, crossed half the distance between himself and his prey in a few short moments. But there was an amplified "pop" from overhead, then Donna Matthews' voice came over the public address system: "Roger, Achilles in motion." Kevin could tell that the Greek warrior actually heard it; Achilles' hearing was returning.

Roger didn't break stride. He just grabbed a book at random from the next table he passed, looked at it, and blinked. He kept running.

The table he'd passed heaved and was tossed aside as something rose from beneath it; Achilles skidded to a halt a dozen feet short of the new menace.

It was a bear, a white bear, and even when it bent

over double to roar at the Greek warrior, it was taller
than he was. Achilles, eyes widening, brought his
shield up and evaluated the polar bear. Kevin could
feel the warrior smile thinly; here was a new and
powerful enemy, another opponent to slay to add to
Achilles' personal glory.

Penthesilia circled wide; her gaze, on Achilles, was
worried, but her orders were explicit, and she was not
being directly interfered with as Achilles was. She
drew back her arrow, sighted in on Roger, and
released; her yard-long shaft rocketed across the room
and hit Roger between the shoulder blades.

And bounced off. It didn't even slow his run. Kevin
swore, and switched his attention to Penthesilia's mind:
*Stupid bitch. You're useless. Okay, help Achilles; I'll
take Roger myself.* He felt her nock another arrow as
the polar bear lunged for Achilles. The Greek warrior
brought his spear in line. When the bear moved within
range, it struck out at him with a lightning-quick
paw . . . and Achilles leaned back, a spare inch out of
the path of the blow, then lunged forward to bury his
spearhead in the beast's neck. Penthesilia opened fire
on it.

The Cyclops brought its foot down viciously on the
head of the spider. Kevin felt immense satisfaction as
the head pulped beneath the blow, as the spider
spasmed in death. Kevin took personal control again;
the Cyclops reached down, picked up the hairy carcass,
and heaved it at Roger's retreating back.

And then there was Donna's voice from overhead,
interrupting again, intruding again: "Roger, get down!"

Roger Simons dove for the ground. It didn't really
matter; Kevin's throw was too high. The spider corpse
flew well over Roger's head and crashed into a crowd
of fleeing convention-goers, killing some of them
instantly, sending a tremor through the floor.

Kevin cursed. *Okay, okay. So he took the hotel over
in spite of my precautions. No need to freak out. He's in*

the open; let the agents take him down. He reached out for the minds of the agents.

First, the ones already looking for Donna. *Hurry up and find her, you idiots!*

The reply came, emotionless: *We're at the office. The public address is secured. None of the bodies is Donna Matthews.*

Kevin rolled his eyes. *They must have set up their real office somewhere else. Get back here.*

Yes, sir. I — danger. Old man in the doorway. He threw something. Then the agent's thoughts became incoherent as burning pain and shock hit him. Kevin switched to monitor the mind of the other agent, felt pain and confusion there, too.

The agents didn't die. They went blind, choked, coughed, suffered; Kevin could feel it all before he broke contact. He ground his teeth. *Tear gas. An old man? Roger's dad, probably. One old man wipes out two of my agents!*

Kevin's temper finally snapped. He bellowed in anger and frustration, kicking and punching at the Cyclops' interior. *Roger's not going to get away with this. He can't make me look bad. He's going to suffer while he dies. . . .* Raging, Kevin felt around for the minds of the other agents.

There they were, four in a group, nearby; he could feel that they'd just entered the dealers' room.

Then four became three. One of the minds winked out of existence. And suddenly another of the three flared up in incredible agony.

Kevin swivelled the Cyclops body to look back toward the entrance. One agent was on the ground in a pool of his own blood, already beginning to dissolve into paint flakes; three agents still stood. One was twitching in pain; the massive shock he was feeling paralyzed him. His gun was on the ground, his severed hand still holding it.

The other two agents faced another of Roger's

black-clad ninjas. This was no crude black-and-white; it was fully human, stylishly black-clad. The agents swivelled to aim their firearms, but were slow, too slow. The killer whipped his *no-daichi* sword around, driving it into the third agent's chest at the sternum. The blade came out just below the right shoulder blade. The third agent started a slow-motion collapse as his knees gave way, and his mind faded out of Kevin's perceptions.

The fourth agent, unhurt, fired three times in quick succession.

He still had explosive bullets in the gun. Before the gun's slide locked back in the "empty" position, three tiny missiles struck the ninja and detonated, literally blowing the assassin's body into pieces. Blood, meat and fabric rained down on the agent.

The agent couldn't see, as Kevin could, the second ninja emerging from beneath a nearby table. Kevin swore again, then reached out his mind to lash at Penthesilia's. *Achilles can handle the teddy bear. Get the ninja!* He seized control of her body for a moment, wrenched it around, then let go when she was faced in the right direction. He would normally have grinned as he felt her disorientation, her anger at the violent invasion of her mind, her blind hatred of Kevin . . . but he was too busy.

Penthesilia, face pale, sighted on the new enemy and fired.

The second ninja sprang up beside the unhurt agent, so fast that the agent wouldn't have a chance to fire.

But the ninja didn't get to strike. Penthesilia's shaft slammed into his ribcage, shearing through his heart, dropping him instantly. The agent automatically changed clips as he watched the ninja die, then he gave Penthesilia a cool nod. The injured agent regained control of himself; still jerking with pain, he reached down, pried his severed hand from the butt of his gun, and picked up the pistol in his left hand. Penthesilia turned back to her lover and the polar bear. Kevin returned his attention to Roger.

It wasn't easy to spot him using the Cyclops' single eye, with all the pathetic convention-goers running around, futilely trying to get out of harm's way — but, no, there he was, headed for the far wall of the dealers' room. Kevin grinned. There were no doors on that wall. Roger had no exits. He lurched forward.

Then he felt Achilles' mind wink down to unconsciousness. He spared that fight a glance. The Greek warrior was down; the bear, half-covered with its own blood, was gnawing at the man's impenetrable skin. Bones would be breaking under that skin, Kevin knew. Penthesilia fired arrow after arrow into its back . . . and then a man, a good-looking young man with black hair, scrambled out from underneath a table and pressed something to the bare flesh above the greaves that protected her lower legs. She jerked and shook . . . and Kevin felt *her* mind, too, spiral down into unconsciousness as she fell, victim to what had to be a stun-gun.

Kevin felt anger swelling within him, and his mind clamped down on those of his surviving agents: *Kill the bear and that asshole. Then join me.* Roger was going to pay for all the trouble he'd caused.

The Cyclops crashed through a rectangular arrangement of dealer's tables, casually crushing people who weren't fast enough to get out of the way. In moments, at the far wall, he stood over Roger again. Roger held no painting; he didn't even have a paperback. He was trapped. He was doomed.

But he was smiling, still smiling.

For a moment, fear crawled across Kevin's heart. *What the hell is he up to? How is he doing what he's doing? He's not afraid. He's tricking me. He's better than me. He's —*

And Roger blinked.

A man burst up from beneath the table beside him.

The new arrival was tall, built like a muscleman, handsome, with an old-fashioned square-jawed face reeking of integrity. The man wore a silvery body stocking, black boots, and a long-sleeved black tunic that lay loose on his body except where the belt constrained it.

Roger said, "Kevin, I'd like you to meet Captain Steele, the Man of Living Metal. Steele, this is a miscreant. Kick his ass."

Captain Steele's eyes narrowed. "You bet, Roger."

Kevin rolled the Cyclops' eye in exasperation. Then he swung a pile-driving fist down at the costumed figure before him.

The blow drove Steele down into the floor up to his knees. But the superhero just smiled. Smiled, and launched himself out of the floor and crashed into the Cyclops' chest, knocking Kevin's fighting machine over on its back, smashing into pulp the dealer displays and dealers still standing there.

Steele's impact compressed the Cyclops' chest, slamming Kevin himself. It would have jarred every bone of his body but for his personal defenses . . . and though the defenses held, they cost Kevin. Maintaining his shield, pulling out defenders and weapons in quick succession, were taking a toll on his vitality. He lost sight for a moment as his concentration wavered; then he gritted his teeth and focused again through the Cyclops' eye.

Captain Steele sat atop him, straddling the Cyclops' chest. He was winding up for another blow. But Kevin brought up the Cyclops' own fist to slam into the painted hero's side. Steele flew a dozen yards from the impact and crashed into the room's back wall.

Kevin had a moment to assess the situation. He ordered the Cyclops to rise and advance, then tapped into his agents' minds. The uninjured one opened fire on the bear, getting off three quick rounds before the dying mass of hair, blood, teeth and hate leaped upon him, tore at his throat, and collapsed upon him, kicking in death.

The injured agent drew a careful bead on the black-headed young man, who was dragging Penthesilia off toward one wall. Then Kevin heard the crack of a bullet — not from the agent's handgun. It came from another wall of the dealers' room, the wall to the right of the entryway. Kevin felt the agent's brief agony as the bullet tore through his brain . . . and the last agent was gone.

Kevin didn't have time even to react. Captain Steele literally flew from where he'd hit the wall. He crashed into the Cyclops as it was rising to its feet. He didn't hit its chest; he flew around behind in a fast, deadly arc and slammed into its back. It toppled forward this time, and Kevin could feel his attacker push on the monolith's back, holding it to the floor. Captain Steele struck the Cyclops' back again and again, shearing away pieces of impossibly hard stone with every blow, furiously beating his way through Kevin's vehicle.

Kevin felt every blow, shuddering under the impact. His shield was still holding, keeping him safe from harm, but he began to sweat as it drained at his vitality. He tried to rise, but Steele's greater strength kept the Cyclops pinned. Kevin knew that Steele would be on him in a moment.

It didn't matter. He had his gun, his sword, his personal defenses. He'd rest for a moment; when he had to leave, he could meet Captain Steele blow for blow.

But it ate at him: *How did Roger bring out something like Captain Steele? So much power in a single slave? Roger can't be that much better than I am. He can't be better at all.* Even in his own mind, his words were desperate, frightened.

The Cyclops' body shook and pebbles dislodged from the interior of its back rained down on Kevin. Then a little stream of light broke through where

Steele's fist made a hole. The hole grew larger as Kevin lay, marshalling his strength.

Finally, Steele's silver-clad hands reached through the manhole-sized opening and grabbed Kevin's lapels. The hero's voice was triumphant and harsh: "All right, murderer, time for you to meet your judge —"

Kevin stabbed him. He brought up the short sword with the wavy black blade and shoved it into Steele's chest with all his strength. And it penetrated. He'd painted a weapon for a greater evil, something for the devil himself to use, and it pierced Steele's chest as though the hero were the Man of Living Butter.

Steele's eyes widened. In agony, he pushed away, sliding off the unholy blade as Kevin held onto the hilt. No blood spilled from the wound, but the hero could not speak. He staggered back, folded around his injury. Kevin, his smile triumphant, pushed his way out of the hole in the Cyclops' back and followed.

And Roger Simons, out of line of sight until Kevin emerged, reached around from the Cyclops' side and snatched the belt of painting-links from Kevin's hand.

Kevin swore and swung the black sword at Roger, but he was no swordsman. Roger backpedalled out of his reach. Off-balance from the swing, Kevin stumbled over the lip of the wound in the Cyclops' back and tumbled to the floor, cursing again.

The impact didn't slow him a bit; he stood immediately. But his momentary distraction gave Captain Steele time to recover. The black-and-silver hero, moving painfully, lunged forward and struck Kevin's jaw, snapping his head back with a sharp crack, knocking him off his feet again.

The blow hurt. Kevin felt a wave of exhaustion wash over him. It was followed by panic: *My shield is fading! So tired. . . .* He brought the sword up again, positioning it between himself and Captain Steele, but the man of living metal brushed it aside as he dived on top of Kevin.

The hero struck again, pounding Kevin's gut. Kevin screamed from the pain and felt his invisible shield tear and finally fall away.

He managed to stretch his arm to full extension, angled the black blade point toward Captain Steele, and drove it home into the superhero's neck. Steele screamed; the noise was like a steam whistle going off.

Steele slumped and slid off Kevin's chest, hitting the floor with a sound of metal on wood.

Kevin tried to pull the sword free but couldn't; he didn't have the strength. Maintaining his shield against Steele's blows had taken every ounce of energy he had. Now the shield was gone. But so was Captain Steele.

Kevin looked around. Only six yards away, leaning against the wall, was Roger Simons. Roger held the links of Kevin's paintings with one hand. He panted and looked as tired as Kevin was. The effort of controlling the bear, Captain Steele, and all the rest must have drained him completely.

As if reading his thoughts, Roger looked down at the belt of disk-paintings in his hand. This he tossed into the middle of the room, where the fight had left trash and broken bodies everywhere. It would take time to find the belt there.

"That doesn't matter," Kevin said. He pulled his special handgun from his pocket and pointed it at Roger. His hand shook with exhaustion, but he was sure he could still kill his enemy at this range. "Fight's over, Roger. Your people are down. My people are down. No power left for our little shields. The difference is, I have the gun." He managed a shadow of his usual smile. There was still a sniper out there, he knew, but he was now shielded from that side of the dealers' room by the bulk of the fallen Cyclops.

Roger just glared at him.

Kevin pulled himself upright; the pain in his gut didn't make it easy. After another few breaths, he glared, too. "God damn, Roger," he said. "You really did it. You really cost me." His throat was dry. In a minute, when he had the strength, he'd reach out for Julia's weak little mind and force her to get him a drink. If she made it all the way to him alive, he'd have reason to believe the sniper had fled. "I might actually have to disappear. Change my identity. Start over. Thank God you're about to be dead. Otherwise this wouldn't be worth it.

. "I'm not going to give you time enough to recover," he said. "But I'm going to ask you a question. I'd really appreciate it if you'd answer me. After all you've cost me, you sort of owe it to me. You have to agree with that."

Roger's breathing didn't slow. He licked his dry lips and gave Kevin a weary look. "What?"

"How did you bring this Captain Steele guy into the real world? I'd have sworn he was too powerful."

"I didn't."

Kevin frowned. "Don't be like that, Roger. Try another one. How did you pull all of those guys out in quick succession?"

"I didn't."

"You're pissing me off, Rog. I might have to shoot you in the balls and let you suffer a while before you die. One more try. How did you bring out things from other peoples' art? From printed covers, for God's sake?"

"I didn't." Roger finally smiled, a dark little smile. "Don't you get it, Kevin? I didn't do any of that. This isn't the real world. You're in my painting."

Something in Kevin's mind closed down, like a wall between him and the place where he did his thinking. Roger had to be lying.

Roger continued. "The guy who nearly hit you with his car outside, he's a painting. And while you were distracted by him, I popped you into another painting, and there was the guy again. That's called continuity. Otherwise even *you* would figure out something was wrong.

"Patrice Anderson is a painting. She's not an art fan. She's a master thief. She stole your wallet for me, and all the little paintings you had in it.

"This room, it's a painting. I stashed all those minions under tables and told them to wait. There are more of them out there that I haven't brought into play yet. I didn't use any energy pulling them out, Kev, they were already here. I'm fresh.

"All those people the two of us killed? They were already dead, Kev. A painting of the living dead. Nobody real died here, Kev. Nobody until now."

Kevin stared at Roger as a cold trickle of fear stirred inside him. "You're lying."

Roger shook his head. "We had to tire you out until your shield failed you. But we couldn't scare you badly enough that you'd run for it. You had to stick around, sure that you'd win, until you had nothing left to protect you." His tone was honestly regretful. "You should have backed off when you had the chance." Roger straightened, brushed his hair back. Suddenly he didn't look tired at all.

Kevin pulled the trigger. His high-powered bullet hit Roger just over the nose. No, it stopped half an inch short. It flattened on Roger's invisible shield and fell into his lap. "Told you so," Roger said quietly.

All over the dealers' room, the crushed, mangled bodies of the slain convention-goers shifted and began to rise. Kevin caught the motion in his peripheral vision and turned to look. The undead victims turned toward him, staggered forward, began to run. . . .

Kevin Matthews didn't bother to open fire. He squeezed his eyes shut. He thought of a painting, a French villa, safe and secure and far, far away. Then he knew he just didn't have time, and the scream that erupted from his throat was one of pure fear and hatred.

The walking dead grabbed him, clawed him, bit him. There were a few moments of pain. Then there was nothing.

❖   ❖   ❖

Roger stood and grimaced as he watched the pack of feasting zombies.

A section of the back wall, thick with armor, rumbled and slid aside. Beyond was a control room filled with contoured chairs, computerized controls, wall-mounted closed-circuit cameras. Donna stepped out and looked around, then moved to stand with Roger. She stared down at the body of Captain Steele with sorrow in her expression.

Moments later, Dylan wandered over from the far side of the room, tucking his stun gun away into a belt pouch.

A smaller door in the wall slid aside and Elsie, carrying a sniper rifle, emerged. She spared a quick look at Dylan to make sure he hadn't been hurt by the agent she'd slain for him. Then, solemn and upset, she set the rifle aside and ran to his arms.

The last of them, C.J., came in through the main entrance, snapping shut the pouch of potato-masher grenades he carried, shoving the protesting Julia Dover ahead of him. He counted the living but he did not smile.

The five of them stared across the yards of carnage, at the tragedy of destruction. Not one of them could speak.

Subdued, the five reappeared in their room in the real Stafford Hotel.

The paintings were where they'd been left. One showed the hotel exterior. Another was the art show. There was a hidden chamber holding a diving-suit robot loaded with chainguns, a giant spider clinging to a dark patch of ceiling, a shadowy corner where ninjas dwelt. The lights and controls in Donna's control room gleamed. Elsie's hidden sniper station was crowded with ammunition. One painting was a simple portrait, without a background, of Kevin Matthews. There were others.

The biggest and most complicated painting showed the dealers' room they had just left — but pristine, no damage, no blood. In the painting, the unblinking eeriness of the undead convention-goers was evident, and here and there one could see the still forms of superheroes, polar bears and other allies hidden beneath tables.

Then Roger exerted himself and the living Julia Dover appeared. Miraculously, she had not been injured or even stained. Roger found that fitting.

She launched herself at Roger, screaming, tearing at his clothes with her fingernails. "You killed Kevin! You —"

In spite of the tiredness he felt, he caught her wrists with his hands, shook his head. "Shut up. Kevin's just fine. Better than ever." The who-do-you-trust, me-or-your-eyes nature of his statement and his calm confidence caught her off-guard. She just stared at him.

"Here, I'll show you." He furrowed his brow, touched the portrait of Matthews, and Kevin appeared: unhurt, in his best gray suit, his expression bland but friendly. "Kevin, tell her you're all right."

Kevin Matthews smiled. "I'm just fine, Julia. Really. Are you ready to see the convention?"

She couldn't make any reply for a moment. She looked at Roger, who nodded as if to say, "Believe it, it's real." Then she turned to Kevin and nodded in turn. The last fear and shock left her features; she gave Kevin a radiant, simplistic smile.

Kevin took her by the arm and led her to the door. "Julia, I've been a real bastard for the last year. I'm sorry about that. I'll see what I can do to make it up to you. Roger, Donna, everybody — a pleasure, as always. We'll see you later." He steered Julia out and shut the door behind him.

Donna shivered. "How can she believe that was Kevin? She knows he had to have . . . died."

Roger smiled grimly. "Her understanding of what's

real and what isn't always depended on Kevin anyway. If he tells her the sky is pink, she'll believe it. If he says he didn't die, she'll believe it. But this is a much better Kevin. I think she'll be happier."

She looked at him. "I don't object, but . . . why do you care? Roger, you always hated her."

"Yep. But that wasn't her fault, was it? She was what Kevin made her. With this new, improved Kevin, maybe she'll turn into something we can like. A real human being." He shrugged. "And this Kevin will paint just about as well as the original, for what that's worth. His fans won't have anything to miss."

He just stood for a minute, collecting himself, then closed his eyes again and brushed his fingers across the dealers' room painting. Achilles and Penthesilia appeared, awake and alert . . . but without their armor or weapons. Achilles' chest was taped; bandages held his broken ribs tight. The Greek warrior tried to step forward — the movement obviously pained him, and the man's ribs ground audibly — but Roger grimly shook his head. Penthesilia dragged him back.

"Don't try anything, Red." Roger sat down on the corner of the bed to face the two legendary warriors. "I'd just have to wipe you out. I can."

Achilles nodded, slowly, reluctantly. "Yes. It's over. We have lost. Are you going to kill us now?"

"That depends." Roger shrugged. "Do you want me to kill you, or do you want to get the hell out of my life?"

The warrior looked surprised, but didn't spend any time thinking about it. "We want to get the hell out of your life."

"Then promise me that you'll never again come against me or my friends. That's all I want, your word on it. Do that, and you can go. Live up to what you promise, and we'll never have to face one another again."

Confusion and hope crossed the warrior's face. "I

swear on my honor that I shall never again oppose you."

Penthesilia repeated the words. Roger nodded. "That's it. You're free. Free of Kevin, free of any obligation to come after me."

Penthesilia blinked. "As simple as that?" She looked at her enemies and obviously felt no danger from them. She and Achilles took cautious steps toward the door.

Roger nodded. "That simple. Scram. Go on and find something useful to do with your lives.

"And don't worry about sneaking out. At a convention like this, you'll just blend in with the crowd."

Epilogue

Signature

The big house was echoingly empty.

Roger paused at the open door of Elsie's room. Most of her clothes were still in the closet, most of her personal items were scattered around the room, but she was gone. Gone with Dylan, gone to California, gone to see if she wanted to stay with him while he began college. Roger knew what her decision would be, knew that he'd lost his . . . child. That hurt.

C.J.'s room was bare. Roger checked his watch. His father would be somewhere over the mid-Atlantic now, and in a few hours would be reminiscing about World War II experiences with a handful of old men who'd shared them with him. The vacation trip, his first in fifteen years, would take C.J. all over Europe and then back by way of the Bahamas.

A little depressed, Roger padded into the room he now shared with Donna, acknowledged her smile with one of his own, and slid into bed beside her. "Everything locked up?" she asked.

He nodded. "Do you think we ought to buy this place? We can."

Donna shrugged. "Roger, we don't have to hide out any more. That means we shouldn't be using any funny money."

"I'm not talking about funny money. I had a good, long talk with my old buddy Kevin Matthews today. Nonesuch Books is going to pay me too much money for book covers over the next few years. You, too, if you want a contract."

Her expression became half amazement, half disgust at his duplicity. "That's, that's cheating. . . ."

"It's just desserts, that's what it is. It's also a way to earn an honest living and stop spending funny money."

"Okay, then." She needed only a little persuasion. "But do we earn enough to pay the government back for what we made?"

Roger shook his head. "We'll figure out some other way to do that. We'll do things. Make things better. That'll be worth more money than we ever created."

She snuggled against him and smiled, changed the subject. "And what about us?" she asked. "We have to straighten out our lives. When we go back home, we'll have landlords sitting on my house and your apartment, all our stuff impounded, friends wanting to know what happened. . . ."

"That's simple." He kissed her. "Here's what happened. Two stressed-out, unemployed artists bump into each other at Escape Velocity Books. They decide to take off together and figure out how to turn their careers around . . . and while they're at it, they fall in love. By the time they get home, they have new contracts to fulfill and new money to pay off old debts."

She beamed at him. "Why, Roger, I'm ashamed of you. That's just the truth."

"Yeah. Truth. I thought I'd experiment with it for a while. See if I can make anything out of it. Here's another one. I love you."

She slid her arms around his neck and kissed him. "I love *you*. But that doesn't let you off the hook. You have to keep proving it to me."

"That won't be hard. You're still with me; you must not be *too* bright." He yelped as she bit him.

Donna glanced at the walls. There, recovered from Kevin's country home by Kevin "himself," hung several of Roger's paintings. "So what're you going to paint first?"

Roger looked over at the old painting of Tricia Davis. She was seated on her tree log, wearing her sarong, staring up at the moon, waiting for a dream lover to come to her. Roger imagined another figure on the log with her, a younger version of the real Tricia's husband, and he smiled. "Happy endings," he said.

THE END

There Are Elves Out There

An excerpt from

Mercedes Lackey
Larry Dixon

The main bay was eerily quiet. There were no
screams of grinders, no buzz of technical talk or
rapping of wrenches. There was no whine of test
engines on dynos coming through the walls.
Instead, there was a dull-bladed tension amid all
the machinery, generated by the humans and the
Sidhe gathered there.

Tannim laid the envelope on the rear deck of
the only fully-operated GTP car that Fairgrove had
built to date, the one that Donal had spent his
waking hours building, and Conal had spent track-
testing. He'd designed it for beauty and power in
equal measure, and had given its key to Conal, its
elected driver, in the same brother's-gift ceremony
used to present an elvensteed. Conal now sat on

its sculpted door, and absently traced a slender finger along an air intake, glowering at the envelope.

Tannim finished his magical tests, and asked for a knife. An even dozen were offered, but Dottie's Leatherman was accepted. Keighvin stood a little apart from the group, hand on his short knife. His eyes glittered with suppressed anger, and he appeared less human than usual, Tannim noticed. Something was bound to break soon.

Tannim folded out the knifeblade, slit the envelope open, and then unfolded the Leatherman's pliers. With them he withdrew six Polaroids of Tania and two others, unconscious, each bound at the wrists and neck. Their silver chains were held by some-*things* from the Realm of the Unseleighe—inside a limo. And, out of focus through the limo's windows, was a stretch of flat tarmac, and large buildings—

Tannim dropped the Leatherman, his fingers gone numb. It clattered twice before wedging into the cockpit's fresh-air vent. Keighvin took one startled step forward, then halted as the magical alarms at Fairgrove's perimeter flared around them all. Tannim's hand went into a jacket pocket, and he threw down the letter from the P.I. He saw Conal pick up the photographs, blanch, then snatch the letter up.

Tannim had already turned by then, and was sprinting for the office door, and the parking lot beyond.

Behind him, he could hear startled questions directed at him, but all he could answer before disappearing into the offices was "Airport!" His bad leg was slowing him down, and screamed at him like a sharp rock grinding into his bones. There was some kind of attack beginning, but he had no time for that.

Have to get to the airport, have to save Tania

from Vidal Dhu, the bastard, the son of a bitch, the—

Tannim rounded a corner and banged his left knee into a file cabinet. He went down hard, hands instinctively clutching at his over-damaged leg. His eyes swam with a private galaxy of red stars, and he struggled while his eyes refocused.

Son of a bitch son of a bitch son of a bitch. . . .

Behind him he heard the sounds of a war-party, and above it all, the banshee wail of a high-performance engine. He pulled himself up, holding the bleeding knee, and limp-ran towards the parking lot, to the Mustang, and Thunder Road.

Vidal Dhu stood in full armor before the gates of Fairgrove, laughing, lashing out with levin-bolts to set off its alarms. It was easy for Vidal to imagine what must be going on inside—easy to picture that smug, orphaned witling Keighvin Silverhair barking orders to weak mortals, marshaling them to fight. Let him rally them, Vidal thought—it will do him no good. None at all. He may have won before, but ultimately, the mortals will have damned him.

It has been so many centuries, Silverhair. I swore I'd kill your entire lineage, and I shall. I shall!

Vidal prepared to open the gate to Underhill. Through that gate all the Court would watch as Keighvin was destroyed—Aurilia's plan be hanged! Vidal's blood sang with triumph—he had driven Silverhair into a winless position at last! And when he accepted the Challenge, before the whole Court, none of his human-world tricks would benefit him—theirs would be a purely magical combat, one Sidhe to another.

To the death.

*   *   *

Keighvin Silverhair recognized the scent of the magic at Fairgrove's gates—he had smelled it for centuries. It reeked of obsession and fear, hatred and lust. It was born of pain inflicted without consideration of repercussions. It was the magic of one who had stalked innocents and stolen their last breaths.

He recognized, too, the rhythm that was being beaten against the walls of Fairgrove.

So be it, murderer. I will suffer your stench no more.

"They will expect us to dither and delay; the sooner we act, the more likely it is that we will catch them unprepared. They do not know how well we work together."

Around him, the humans and Sidhe of his home sprang into action, taking up arms with such speed he'd have thought them possessed. Conal had thrown down the letter after reading it, and barked, "Hangar 2A at Savannah Regional; they've got children as hostages!" The doors of the bay began rolling open, and outside, elvensteeds stamped and reared, eyes glowing, anxious for battle. Conal looked to him, then, for orders.

Keighvin met his eyes for one long moment, and said, "Go, Conal. I shall deal with our attacker for the last time. If naught else, the barrier at the gates can act as a trap to hold him until we can deal with him as he deserves." He did not add what he was thinking—that he only hoped it would hold Vidal. The Unseleighe was a strong mage; he might escape even a trap laid with death metal, if he were clever enough. Then, with the swiftness of a falcon, he was astride his elvensteed Rosaleen Dhu, headed for the perimeter of Fairgrove.

He was out there, all right, and had begun laying a spell outside the fences, like a snare. Perhaps in his sickening arrogance he'd forgotten that Keighvin could see such things. Perhaps in his insanity, he no longer cared.

Rosaleen tore across the grounds as fast as a stroke of lightning, and cleared the fence in a soaring leap. She landed a few yards from the laughing, mad Vidal Dhu, on the roadside, with him between Keighvin and the gates. He stopped lashing his mocking bolts at the gates of Fairgrove and turned to face Keighvin.

"So, you've come to face me alone, at last? No walls or mortals to hide behind, as usual, coward? So sad that you've chosen *now* to change, within minutes of your death, traitor."

"Vidal Dhu," Keighvin said, trying to sound unimpressed despite the heat of his blood, "if you wish to duel me, I shall accept. But before I accept, you must release the children you hold."

The Unseleighe laughed bitterly. "It's your concern for these mortals that raised you that have *made* you a traitor, boy. Those children do not matter." Vidal lifted his lip in a sneer as Keighvin struggled to maintain his composure. "Oh, I will do more than duel you, Silverhair. I wish to Challenge you before the Court, and kill you as they watch."

That was what Keighvin had noted—it was the initial layout of a Gate to the High Court Underhill. Vidal was serious about this Challenge—already the Court would be assembling to judge the battle. Keighvin sat atop Rosaleen, who snorted and stamped, enraged by the other's tauntings. Vidal's pitted face twisted in a maniacal smirk.

"How long must I wait for you to show courage, witling?"

Keighvin's mind swam for a moment, before he remembered the full protocols of a formal Challenge. It had been so long since he'd even seen one. . . .

Once accepted, the Gate activates, and all the Court watches as the two battle with blade and magic. Only one leaves the field; the Court is bound to slay anyone who runs. So it had always been. Vidal would not Challenge unless he were confident of winning, and Keighvin was still tired from the last battle—which Vidal had not even been at. . . .

But Vidal must die. That much Keighvin knew.

From Born to Run *by Mercedes Lackey & Larry Dixon.*

*   *   *

Watch for more from the SERRAted Edge:
Wheels of Fire by Mercedes Lackey & Mark Shepherd

When the Bough Breaks by Mercedes Lackey & Holly Lisle

MAGIC AND COMPUTERS DON'T MIX!

RICK COOK

Or . . . do they? That's what Walter "Wiz" Zumwalt is wondering. Just a short time ago, he was a master hacker in a
Silicon Valley office, a very ordinary fellow in a very mundane
world. But magic spells, it seems, are a lot like computer
programs: they're both formulas, recipes for getting things
done. Unfortunately, just like those computer programs, they
can be full of bugs. Now, thanks to a *particularly* buggy spell,
Wiz has been transported to a world of magic—and incredible peril. The wizard who summoned him is dead, Wiz has
fallen for a red-headed witch who despises him, and no
one—not the elves, not the dwarves, not even the dragons—
can figure out why he's here, or what to do with him. Worse:
the sorcerers of the deadly Black League, rulers of an entire
continent, want Wiz dead—and he doesn't even know why!
Wiz had better figure out the rules of this strange new
world—and fast—or he's not going to live to see Silicon
Valley again.

Here's a refreshing tale from an exciting new writer. It's also a
rarity: a well-drawn fantasy told with all the rigorous logic of
hard science fiction.

69803-6 • 320 pages • $4.99